T0000013

Murder
in
Masquerade

MARY WINTERS

BERKLEY PRIME CRIME

NEW YORK

BERKLEY PRIME CRIME
Published by Berkley
An imprint of Penguin Random House LLC
penguinrandomhouse.com

Copyright © 2024 by Mary Honerman
Penguin Random House supports copyright. Copyright fuels creativity, encourages diverse voices, promotes free speech, and creates a vibrant culture. Thank you for buying an authorized edition of this book and for complying with copyright laws by not reproducing, scanning, or distributing any part of it in any form without permission. You are supporting writers and allowing Penguin Random House to continue to publish books for every reader.

BERKLEY and the BERKLEY & B colophon are registered trademarks and BERKLEY PRIME CRIME is a trademark of Penguin Random House LLC.

Library of Congress Cataloging-in-Publication Data

Names: Winters, Mary, author.
Title: Murder in masquerade / Mary Winters.
Description: First edition. | New York: Berkley Prime Crime, 2024. |
  Series: A lady of letters mystery
Identifiers: LCCN 2023022544 (print) | LCCN 2023022545 (ebook) |
ISBN 9780593548783 (trade paperback) | ISBN 9780593548790 (ebook)
Subjects: LCSH: Murder—Investigation—Fiction. | London
  (England)—History—19th century—Fiction. |
  LCGFT: Detective and mystery fiction. | Novels.
Classification: LCC PS3601.N5535 M86 2024 (print) |
LCC PS3601.N5535 (ebook) | DDC 813/.6—dc23/eng/20230512
LC record available at https://lccn.loc.gov/2023022544
LC ebook record available at https://lccn.loc.gov/2023022545

First Edition: February 2024

Printed in the United States of America
1st Printing

Book design by George Towne
Interior art: quill © veronchick_84/Shutterstock Images

For my sister Penny, who was there when I needed her most

Murder in Masquerade

Chapter 1

Dear Lady Agony,

I'm very much in love with a man my father will never consent to. His opinions on marriage are quite strict, for ours is an important family. But my heart is mine alone to give. I will not marry a man I do not love. Therefore, we must depart for Gretna Green at once. I see no other alternative. Do you?

Devotedly,
Going to Gretna Green

. . . .

Dear Going to Gretna Green,

The words Gretna Green evoke an image of a clandestine excursion through verdant fields ending in eternal happiness. But I daresay it is a false image and one that has ruined many girls' chances for a good life. Running away never solves problems; it only creates more. You state that the man you love *is undesirable to your family. Have you asked yourself why they resist the match? Sometimes those closest to us see that which we cannot. In your case, you must try to discover the reasons, for departing to Gretna Green would be disastrous. The journey is perilous, and even if you make it, a three-week waiting period must pass before the ceremony is allowed. By then your reputation will be in tatters. My stringent advice is do not go.*

Yours in Secret,
Lady Agony

Amelia reread her advice to Marielle, Simon Bainbridge's sister, which Amelia had sent to the magazine under the guise of Lady Agony. The response had been printed. All that was to be done was wait and see if the advice would be taken.

Amelia leaned back in her well-used desk chair. The library was alight with cheery afternoon sun, and if she focused on the miniature rainbows it reflected off the cordial glasses on the corner table, she could almost pretend a girl's future didn't hang in the balance. *Not just any girl's,* she reminded herself. *Simon's sister.*

For the past week, Simon had circled her house like a shark waiting for food. She was his keeper and her advice his meal. He was adamant that his sister not run away with their onetime stable manager George Davies, who, according to him, was a no-good gambler and social climber. Unfortunately, fervor rarely guaranteed success. Sometimes it ensured the opposite. Now that the letter was printed, Simon's attention had turned to Marielle, whom he was observing for any signs of departure. Tonight, for instance, Mr. Davies had invited Marielle to attend the opera with him in the box of the esteemed Lord and Lady

Burton, so of course, Amelia and Simon were attending also. Simon had informed her of their plans no less than twenty-four hours ago. His exact words were, "We'll be attending *Rigoletto* tomorrow. Don't wear black."

Amelia glanced at her light-colored dress, lingering over the dusky rose color, and smiled. She cared not a whit for fashion, but wearing colors again *was* nice. It felt like an age since she'd worn mourning, yet it'd been only a month. For over two years, she'd kept to black and gray out of respect for her deceased husband, Edgar, Earl of Amesbury, to whom she'd been married for just two months when he passed. But in those two months, they were closer than any patient and nurse could have been. His degenerative disease moved quickly, making him reliant on her for his care and everything else, and she learned more about life in those few precious, daunting months than in her previous years combined. Although she was only five and twenty, she was more mature than her age belied, having seen a lifetime pass before her eyes.

Edgar was gone, but she wasn't alone. In his absence, he'd entrusted her to the sizable Amesbury fortune, his dear niece Winifred, and his formidable Aunt Tabitha. Of the three, only the last gave her trouble.

Amelia's eyes turned upward to the second floor of the library, where the punctuated sounds of Tabitha's cane went *tap, tap, tap*. Leatherbound histories of the Norman Conquest vibrated gently in the cherrywood bookshelves. Someone had made a blunder, and for once it wasn't Amelia. Her lips twisted into a smile as she imagined the misstep of the butler or perhaps Tabitha's cherished lady's maid, Patty Addington. No. Tabitha and Mrs. Addington were of one mind. They rarely disagreed.

The smile dropped from Amelia's lips as she heard the cane

thumping down the steps: one, two, three. *Drat*. Maybe she *had* done something wrong, but what? As the stomps grew closer, she understood she was about to find out. She shut the paper and stood from her desk. No one—especially not Tabitha Amesbury—could find out about her secret pseudonym. Only Simon; her best friend, Kitty Hamsted; and her editor, Grady Armstrong, knew of her clandestine occupation, and she must keep it that way.

With cheap paper and low postage, the magazine was becoming ever more popular, and the advice of Lady Agony was in high demand. Grady said the magazine's circulation was nearing 500,000, and Amelia believed it. She answered letters every day just to keep up with the weekly print, forgoing some letters for others. Costumes, manners, relationships—they covered the bulk of inquiries. But increasingly, readers asked about *her* life. Who was she, and why was a lady (a countess, if they knew her real identity) answering letters in a penny weekly? God willing, no one would ever find out.

With a hard push, the door flew open, and Tabitha stood like Nike, the goddess of victory, but instead of holding a crown for victory, she brandished a cane. She wore stiff gray, out of respect for her dearly departed nephew, Edgar. On her, however, the color appeared lavender, perhaps because of her crystal blue eyes, for which the Amesburys were known. Her high cheekbones, another familial attribute, were flushed with exertion or irritation. Amelia was about to find out which.

"Something is afoot," declared Tabitha.

"The three best words in the English language." With a smile, Amelia met her in the middle of the room.

Tabitha dipped her head ever so slightly, but her height was untrimmed. She towered several inches over Amelia. "No, Amelia, they are not the three best words in the English language. Winifred is keeping something from me, and I want to know what."

Amelia gestured to the green leather couch.

Tabitha took the striped chair.

"Winifred doesn't keep secrets." Amelia heard the edge in her own words. Although there was no blood relation, she thought of Winifred as her own daughter, and her ire rose like a mother hen's at the accusation.

Tabitha crossed her hands over her cane. Whatever weakness her arthritis caused was compensated by a strong upper body and perfect posture. "Correction. Winifred did not use to keep secrets. Winifred is almost eleven. Children change."

Amelia *had* noticed some changes of late. Winifred was spending less time in the nursery and taking more interest in the opposite sex. Which was to say, tittering whenever she passed the neighbor boy in the street. "Continue," said Amelia, sliding back into the plush leather cushions of the couch.

Now that Tabitha had her ear, she leaned into her cane. "Several times I've come across Winifred, and she stops whatever it is she's doing. Hiding something. I cannot make it out."

"Maybe it's *private*." Amelia stressed the word, knowing Tabitha understood no boundaries when it came to family. She was the eldest and most Amesbury of the Amesburys. She took the job quite seriously.

Tabitha's crystal blue eyes turned to frost. "She is a child. Nothing is private."

"But you said times are changing."

"I said *children* change—and I don't approve of this change." Her cane punctuated the words *I don't approve*. "As her mother, you must see to it."

Despite Tabitha's irritation, Amelia basked in the comment. Even Tabitha recognized her as Winifred's surrogate parent. That meant she was doing something right. Truth be told, neither she nor Tabitha had parenting experience. Tabitha hadn't married, and the closest Amelia had come to child-rearing was telling her younger sister, Margaret, what to do. Yet Tabitha was obviously struggling with Winifred's age more than she was. "I can't turn back time, Aunt, and even if I could, I wouldn't. I'm looking forward to seeing Winifred grow into a young woman."

Tabitha pursed her lips, and the delicate skin above them creased.

"However, I'll look into the matter. I'll make certain nothing untoward is going on."

The promise placated Tabitha. Or at least she leaned back into her chair. "Now, about tonight's business with Simon Bainbridge. I'm not sure you should attend the opera unchaperoned."

"Blazes!" Amelia sat upright. "Why would you say such a thing? I'm a *widow*, for goodness' sake."

Tabitha pointed her cane at her. "To the Amesbury fortune. And do not curse like a sailor."

I'm not even close to a sailor, Amelia thought. But she had grown up at the Feathered Nest, a busy inn tucked into the outskirts of Mells, a frequent stop of travelers on their way to London. Nights could and did grow rowdy when sleep-deprived guests indulged in good wine, food, and entertainment, and her family wasn't above joining in on the fun. Father would push back the tables, her sister Sarah would take up the pianoforte, and Amelia and her other sisters, Penelope and Margaret, would sing songs.

But now Amelia was the Countess of Amesbury and all that title implied. Her responsibilities didn't include physical labor.

Sometimes she wished they did, for she was used to work. If it weren't for her column at the magazine, she might have lost her mind by now. "I am not a girl, Aunt Tabitha. I will not be followed around like a debutante. Simon is a family friend."

"In whom you've taken a great interest."

"I have not!"

Tabitha raised silvery eyebrows, and three soft wrinkles appeared on her forehead. "Vying for his attention will prove fruitless, Amelia. He has many admirers yet none whose ardor he returns. It would do our family little credit to have you throw yourself at him."

"I'm not vying for his attention," Amelia countered. "We're friends."

"Men and women cannot be friends."

Amelia understood its truth from her time at the magazine. Attraction got in the way of most male-female relationships she wrote about. Friends, employees, employers. Despite best intentions, curiosity abounded when it came to the opposite sex. But she and Grady were friends, dear friends. Aunt Tabitha would say their friendship was the rare example. "Regardless, Simon's sister, Lady Marielle, will be there tonight, and we're basically . . . mostly . . . acting as her chaperone." *Yes, that's right.* "How could a chaperone be in need of a chaperone? It would not make sense."

Tabitha's pursed lips slackened, and Amelia knew she'd won. Widows—especially widows of a considerable fortune—were allowed exceptions. Edgar had left her independent and wealthy, the two best ways a widow could be in 1860. Amelia wasn't going to do something foolish to risk her autonomy. And neither would Simon.

"I didn't realize you were escorting Lady Marielle." Tabitha rested her cane on the arm of the chair, indicating the battle was finished. Although she had many beautiful canes, this wasn't one of them. A curved black raven, worn at the wings from Tabitha's strong grip, perched atop a long ebony stick. Amelia didn't subscribe to magic, but she did believe the bird could peck someone's eyes out if Tabitha willed it.

"Lady Marielle is much sought after, this being her first season out," continued Tabitha. "Her debut at the Smythe ball is still being discussed in many circles. Has Simon mentioned any particular suitors?"

Every. Single. Day.

According to Simon, George Davies was a gambler, a rogue, and a cheat. Was it all true, or brotherly protection? If anyone had insider knowledge, it was Tabitha. She was held in high esteem by all of London. Amelia decided to ask. "He has mentioned one person, a Mr. George Davies. He was once stable manager for the Bainbridge family before he became a trainer to some of the fastest horses at the Derby, including theirs, and his fortune changed. His advice is requested often, I've heard."

Tabitha sniffed. "Mr. Davies? That cannot be. Simon cannot allow it."

"Simon's not excited about Lady Marielle's interest, either. He compares it to a schoolgirl infatuation with a teacher. As it so happens, Mr. Davies taught her to ride. That was years before he began training her father's racehorses."

"Simon's right," said Tabitha. "It would be best for him to remove Mr. Davies from the picture altogether. Being seen with such a man will draw unwanted attention."

Amelia wrinkled her nose. London society could be positively archaic when it came to whom one could and could not see. Outside of the city, rules were not as stringent; why must they be so here, in a city of diverse multitudes? Amelia didn't want to see Marielle escape with a ruffian, either, but confronted with this attitude, she also understood why the girl felt she had no other choice but to flee. "What do you mean by 'remove Mr. Davies from the picture'? I don't understand."

Tabitha grasped her cane to stand. Amelia reached out, but Tabitha swatted her hand away, opting instead for the raven's long beak.

"What I mean is to let the man know he's not welcome in the Bainbridge family." Tabitha straightened her gown. "Rebuff him."

"Is that what you would have done to me if Edgar hadn't married me straightaway?" Amelia couldn't hide her incredulity. "Rebuff me?" Hers was a respected family in the country, but here, her name meant nothing. Under the protection of Edgar's wealth and title, however, she was welcomed in every plush drawing room in London.

"Don't be incensed. It's the way the world is."

Amelia tipped her chin, meeting Tabitha's eyes. "Maybe it shouldn't be."

Tabitha strode toward the door. She paused with her hand on the knob, turning around and pointing the cane at her. "You're going to be a terrible chaperone, Amelia."

"I've been called worse things."

Then Amelia was alone, the punctuation of Tabitha's cane sounding all the way down the hall.

Chapter 2

Dear Lady Agony,

My husband insists we only attend the opera, for it is the fashionable place to be seen. The theatre, he proclaims, entices the low and tawdry, and he won't deign to go. But I enjoy plays, and my friends attend. Shouldn't I be allowed the entertainment as well? I don't want to create friction in our marriage.

Devotedly,
Fan of Fun

. . . .

Dear Fan of Fun,

I, myself, am a fan of fun, which your husband seems to have little concept of. If I take your letter correctly, he attends the opera for one reason only: to be seen. It's my assumption, then, that the only performance he cares for is his own. Therefore, I

*say leave him at home with his own good company and attend
the theatre with your friends. Friction causes fire but also
warmth. Maybe your husband could use some of the latter.*

*Yours in Secret,
Lady Agony*

"You're staring, Lady Amesbury."

Amelia jerked her gaze to Simon. *This from a man peering
through his spyglasses before the performance begins.* "I'm not staring.
I'm observing."

"Then observe something else," Simon murmured.

"You said I was to keep an eye on your sister, and that is what
I am doing."

Simon lowered his binoculars. His face was almost Grecian:
broad forehead, slim nose, chiseled jawline. His eyes, however,
were brilliant green and full of mischief. They told a story not of
art but of work, with enough lines to convey his experience in
Her Majesty's Royal Navy, where he and her late husband, Edgar, had served side by side. "And the whole world knows it."

Amelia pointed. "*You're* observing her."

Simon covered her outstretched hand, placing it on her lap.
His eyes lingered on her fuchsia gown, made of rich satin with
black ruffles at the neck and sleeves. "Incorrect. I'm observing
him, and that frock is stunning."

The touch of his fingers zinged all the way through her glove
and up her arm. After she'd been a wife to a sick man for two
months and a widow for two years, a brush from Simon always
gave her quivers. "Do you really believe Mr. Davies is as bad as
you think?"

"Worse."

"Because he's without title or fortune?" she challenged, her mind on her and Tabitha's earlier conversation.

His eyes snapped to her face. "Because he's a scoundrel, Amelia. You know that. He tried to coerce my sister into going to Gretna Green to marry him. What kind of a man does that?"

The desperate kind, she thought, but said nothing. "How am I supposed to watch out for her without looking at her?"

"Be less obvious. And be aware of the eyes on *you*."

Amelia glanced left and right of the Bainbridge box. No less than ten pairs of gawking eyes returned the look. The purpose of attending the opera was to see and be seen. The production itself hardly mattered. As long as it was opening night, high society would be out in droves. She sank back in her chair, into the shadows of the velvet curtain, where her actions were cloaked by the dense material.

It was hard to hide her enthusiasm for their task, even though it had nothing to do with her or Simon personally. She was delighted to be at the opera with a man with whom she could be herself, including her secret self, Lady Agony. They shared a burgeoning friendship, open and forthright and, at times, bellicose, when something or someone they cared about was at stake. Currently, that someone was Lady Marielle.

Amelia smoothed the place on her dress where his hand had been, affecting nonchalance. It was not easy to be discreet in a place such as the Drury Lane Theatre, a landmark she'd wanted to visit since first coming to London. She'd been eager to leave Mells for the adventure of the city, yet how little she'd seen of it after Edgar passed. It was thrilling to be out and feel alive again. Still, she made a conscious effort to quell her ardor, lifting her eyes to the box of the esteemed baron and his wife, Lord and

Lady Burton, which was shared by Lady Marielle, Mr. Davies, and several friends.

George Davies appeared to be enjoying his invitation, which, according to Simon, had been extended by Lord Burton after Mr. Davies trained his horse to win the Cheltenham Gold Cup. The baroness seemed to be enjoying it less, cutting Mr. Davies a look when he laughed a little too loudly at a friend's joke. George's cheeks flushed, competing with the color of his auburn side whiskers, and he pressed his lips tight to prevent further laughter. His evening coat was well tailored, but carelessly left open, and he buttoned the garment as quickly as he'd buttoned his amusement. Marielle's blush-colored dress, on the other hand, was carefully done, with a modest neckline of cream ruffles. No greater care or expense could have been taken with the garment, and the contrast between the pair was noteworthy. Except when Marielle threw back her head with laughter. Then the difference all but disappeared.

Marielle was definitely her brother's sister. Same ebony hair, same emerald eyes, same dash of danger. The girl was brave, no doubt about it. This was the letter writer who would flee if forced.

We must not force her, then. Amelia sneaked a glance at Simon, who released a breath of steamy air. But how to convince the dragon sitting beside her . . .

A motion caught her eye, and she refocused on the group. A new man entered the box. That in and of itself wasn't surprising. Since most people attended the opera to be seen, mingling with one another before, during, and after the performance, tonight's play was a full thirty minutes delayed because of attendees' enthusiasm—for one another. What surprised her was the way the visitor cuffed George's arm in a not-so-friendly embrace. Although George shrugged it off with a laugh, the conversation in the box stilled. Simon reached back for his armrests, ready to join the group.

Amelia tried distracting him. "Who's that?"

"How the devil would I know? Most likely some fellow Mr. Davies picked up at the racetrack."

A discussion ensued between George Davies and the stranger, and George tensed. Through her binoculars, Amelia noted the strain of his neck muscles. He was shorter, unmatched in size and height. Whereas George was good-natured, the man was brisk and unpleasant, crowding George's personal space. Someone stumbled backward, and at first, Amelia thought it was George, but she quickly discovered it was Marielle.

Without warning, Simon stood and peered out from their ostentatious seat, making himself known to king and country. His broad frame, like a closed theatre curtain, blocked all light. If he were the leading actor in the performance, he wouldn't have been more noticeable.

"So much for discretion," muttered Amelia. But the implied threat worked. Spotting Simon, the man donned a more cordial manner and bid his company goodbye, inching backward out of the crowded box. Marielle's look, on the other hand, was decidedly not cordial. *Infuriated* better described it.

She fisted her hands on her hips, glaring at Simon.

Simon waved.

One box over, someone waved back. Amelia returned to her lorgnettes for a better look. A smiling Kitty Hamsted greeted her warmly. Accompanying her was her husband, Oliver, and his parents, the influential viscount and viscountess.

Amelia returned the wave enthusiastically. "It's Kitty."

"I didn't know the Hamsteds were attending tonight's production." Assured of his sister's safety, Simon returned to his seat.

Amelia dropped the lorgnettes. "Lady Hamsted always attends the opera, and it's Oliver's birthday. They told Kitty they have a surprise for him."

"I imagine Oliver's only birthday wish is to be left alone in the library. Hopefully he can do just that after the performance."

Amelia sniffed and leaned back in her chair, preparing for the start of the show. Oliver would live under a pile of books if he could, but Kitty was a social being with gracious manners and impeccable style. Tonight, she wore an emerald gown with a plunging neckline and a teardrop diamond necklace that accentuated the cut of her dress. In her golden locks was a diamond-and-emerald-studded comb, shaped like the wing of a bird, which made her profile even more striking.

If Amelia wore such a comb, it would become tangled in her mass of auburn hair the moment she stepped outside, or it would droop like the broken wing of a dove under its weight. Her fashion sense was more practical than vogue. Comfortable walking boots and her reliable parasol were her two must-haves, not combs or clips. Tonight, however, she wore delicate pink slippers that weren't meant for more than a few dozen steps. They were studded with silver rosettes and matched her necklace, ear baubles, and cape.

The music started, and Amelia forgot about shoes, slippers, and practically everything else. Instead, she focused on a single jester who gave way to the gold gowns and gilded masks of dancers who filled the stage. It was a party scene, and a duke arrived in splendor, commanding the notice of everyone on and off the stage.

The duke mingled with guests, enjoying their attention. His attention, however, landed on only one person: a young married woman. He selected her as his dancing partner, much to the chagrin of her husband, and whisked her in circles. A step, a turn, a shuffle. They disappeared from the stage.

Amelia didn't have to watch to know what happened next. She and her family had performed—adapted, really, for none of them sang opera—*Rigoletto* four years ago during the Summer Festival in Mells. Though the dancer's husband was helpless against the powerful duke, her father was not, and he courageously called out the duke for seducing his daughter. The jester, as a jester might, mocked the father, only to be cursed by him. The jester ran home with the curse on his mind, only to find his own daughter abducted by the duke later that night. The worst part? It was done with the help of the jester's own hand.

The lights returned, and Amelia realized how entranced she'd been by the performance. The first act had flown by without her even knowing it.

Simon didn't suffer the same problem and was on his feet for intermission. "What imbecile would put a ladder up to his own garden wall? I know he's a jester, but he helped them abduct his own daughter."

"A blindfolded one," she explained. "Part of the father's curse, I suppose, which compounds the jester's guilt that much more."

"I, for one, wouldn't be caught donning a blindfold after being cursed, thank you very much. Champagne?"

"Yes, please." She paused while he obtained the refreshment. "And isn't that what the Greeks called a *willing suspension of disbelief*?"

"I have a hard time suspending anything, Lady Amesbury, especially my wits."

A true lover of the arts, she thought, but remained silent as he led the way to the Burtons' box. They would be able to mingle with his sister and her friends for at least fifteen minutes, and Amelia was excited to meet the woman behind the letter to Lady Agony.

Even in a crowd, Marielle was easy to spot, for she commanded the same attention her brother did, not with her attire, exactly, but with her demeanor. It's what made half the men in the auditorium turn their heads when she lifted a gloved hand to sweep back a shock of raven hair. She was engaging and assertive, two rare qualities in women her age. She did not feign interest. She was either interested or not. And she wasn't afraid to express which. Amelia liked her immediately.

"I thought I spotted you." Simon's deep voice cut through all conversation in the Burtons' box. "How are you enjoying the performance?"

"Spotted me?" Marielle lifted her chin. "Spied on me is more like it."

The siblings locked eyes, and George Davies smiled at the exchange. Perhaps he was acquainted with their familial sparring.

Amelia didn't wait to see which one blinked first. She introduced herself to Lady Marielle and Mr. Davies.

Marielle remembered her manners, her stubborn chin dropping, and smiled. "Lady Amesbury. How nice to meet an acquaintance of my brother's. They are few and far between."

Amelia understood why men were besotted with her. Her smile made one feel like the only person in the room. Her sole focus was the person in front of her, and Amelia knew men would fight for her consideration this season. She was titled and wealthy, yes, but lacked pretension. A most refreshing quality, a quality Amelia recognized in Simon. She admired the trait a great deal.

"Lady Amesbury—of the Amesbury fortune?" George Davies cut in.

Never had Amelia's wealth been indicated so publicly. Though she might have been incensed, she bit her lip to keep from chuckling. It was what people were thinking when they met her. It was amusing to finally hear it said aloud.

Simon extended his hand. "Mr. Davies. You've always been one for surprises. I was stunned to see you here—and with my sister, no less. How have you been?"

George grasped his hand enthusiastically. "Lord Bainbridge. I couldn't be better. Thanks for asking."

"I surmise the horse business is treating you well?"

"Very well." George's tone was eager. "I trained the baron's horse to take the gold cup at Cheltenham. I imagine you heard. It's the fifth race I've won this year."

Amelia detected pride in his voice but also strain. Mr. Davies might be reciting his credentials instead of greeting a friend. It took strength and talent, not to mention ambition, to persevere on the racetrack. Amelia wondered how many races he must win to be accepted by men like those in the Burtons' box. Or by Simon himself.

Simon glanced at Lord Burton, but he and his wife were engaged in conversation with another couple who'd entered the box. "Congratulations."

"Thank you." George's eyes flickered at the compliment, sparkling blue and gray like a fish underwater.

"Yes, congratulations," Amelia added. "Do you race horses as well?"

"No," answered George. "I'm too old for that now."

He didn't look old, in Amelia's opinion. His build was athletic, like a jockey's, although his evening coat was snug at the waist. His shoulders bore the evidence of working with horses day in and day out. Even his skin, rosy from the sun, was a reflection of his time outdoors.

Marielle placed a hand on his arm. "You mean you're too popular. You're the best rider in London." She zeroed in on Simon. "Perhaps all of England." Her eyes flicked back to Amelia. "His training program is second to none."

"Last month I traveled to Scotland, where I trained a gelding that was to be a gift for a young prince." George preened a little, catching the eye of a woman passing by. The young lady twittered at his unconventional good looks, and he flashed her a smile. "A gorgeous creature."

The gesture was not lost on Simon, who sucked in a deep breath. Amelia quickly went into action before his hot air turned into words. She glanced at George's empty glass of champagne. He seemed like the kind of man who would indulge if the opportunity presented itself, perhaps to dull his nerves. She finished her champagne in one large gulp. "I wonder, Mr. Davies, if you might find us another glass of champagne. It's stifling in here."

George bowed deeply. "Certainly, my lady."

The second he was gone, Simon pointed a finger at Marielle. "You will no longer see Mr. Davies, Ellie, and that's final."

Marielle glanced at his outstretched finger. "Haven't you heard, Simon? It's impolite to point."

"And Mr. Davies is the height of politeness? Did you hear what he said to Lady Amesbury?"

Marielle turned to Amelia. "I apologize for my brother's behavior. He can be positively barbaric at times. I presume it comes from his time on a ship. At one point, I thought he'd never return from America, and then poof! He's here with all his brotherly wisdom. Aren't I the lucky one?"

"I don't have brothers, but I do have three sisters, and their advice can be . . . *insistent* at times." Amelia gave Marielle a quick smile. "If you know what I mean."

Marielle chuckled.

"This is no laughing matter." Simon leaned in, his voice dangerously quiet. "If Mr. Davies appears too friendly, people will talk. People will *assume*."

Marielle jerked her chin, all giggles gone. Like Simon's, her stubborn streak was fierce and immediate. "When have you cared a whit about what people say?"

Simon was silent. He had no retort.

"Never," Marielle answered. "That's when. And neither do I. I *will* see him, Simon. This is *my* season. I don't care what you or father or anyone else says."

Simon's jaw twitched. "Then you leave me no choice."

"Is that a threat?" Marielle asked, unable to disguise her disgust.

"Don't you see, Ellie? He's a confidence man. He's using you to get to your wealth and title. Trust me." Simon's voice was pleading, and Amelia wondered if he was thinking of his own troubled past. He'd once been the target of a woman who cared more for his title than his feelings. Amelia couldn't decipher where his history ended and Marielle's future began.

"Oh, how fickle your loyalties." Marielle's voice was full with gritty truth. "He grew up in our own household, Simon, in our mews. Or have you forgotten?"

"I wish I could forget," he spat back. "I wish I could take back every single ride you ever took with the man, for they were the imprints of his later designs. Twisting and turning and conniving even back then. Setting his sights on you—on this very moment."

Marielle frowned, real sadness stealing over her face. His insinuation had obviously stung a tender part of her childhood. Their mother had passed unexpectedly in a train accident. Amelia could only imagine how important Marielle's mentors might have been at that young age. George Davies must have been one of those individuals.

Amelia attempted to assuage the damage of Simon's words. "Your brother is concerned for your well-being. That's what he's trying to say." She cut him a look. "He's just saying it badly." She returned to Marielle. "He loves you and wants you to be happy. He doesn't want anyone, including Mr. Davies, to jeopardize that."

Marielle blinked, and for a moment, Amelia thought she would cry. But she sniffed and straightened her shoulders. "How ever did a nice woman like you end up at the opera with an obnoxious man like him?"

"Box seats?"

Marielle laughed her warm laugh, and a little of the tension melted. Amelia thought it a good thing, too, for a gentleman was approaching, and both siblings seemed to recognize him.

"Hooper," Simon called. "Don't be shy. How are you?"

With the mention of his name, the man stepped forward. He was lanky, all arms and elbows, and his shoulders appeared in the box before his feet. "Lord Bainbridge." He bowed politely. "Lady Marielle."

"Mr. Hooper!" Marielle greeted him warmly. "I didn't know you were a devotee of the opera."

Simon slapped his back. "Is anyone really a devotee of the opera?"

Mr. Hooper's demeanor relaxed with the joke, and Simon continued with introductions.

"Mr. Hooper is our neighbor," explained Simon. "His father is Captain Hooper. You might have heard of his famous capture of a pirate ship. A regular hero."

Amelia frowned, trying to recall Captain Hooper's service.

"It was over thirty years ago, Lady Amesbury." Mr. Hooper smiled, and the action lit up his plain face. "No one outside Her Majesty's Royal Navy would know of the incident."

"That explains why the name escapes me." Amelia appreciated Mr. Hooper's modesty. It was probably why he and the Bainbridge siblings seemed to be on friendly terms. Some men would boast of their or their father's war stories for hours if one let them, but not Mr. Hooper. He'd gone out of his way to make an excuse for her lack of knowledge.

"I didn't mean to interrupt," continued Mr. Hooper. "I only wanted to say good evening."

"You're never interrupting." Marielle's welcoming smile showed off her straight white teeth. "Goodness, we've known each other forever. How many missing ingredients have our cooks borrowed from each other's kitchens?"

"Plenty, to be sure."

Marielle's attention was drawn from the conversation, and Mr. Hooper followed her eyes, which settled on someone in the distance.

Amelia followed them, too. *Mr. Davies.*

"Why don't you join us?" Simon asked. "We'd love to have you sit with us, wouldn't we, Marielle?"

"Of course," Marielle put in, but she was watching Mr. Davies and his friends, who were headed their way.

Amelia wasn't sure whether Simon meant the Bainbridge

box or the Burton box, but it didn't matter anyway. Mr. Hooper was already making his excuses.

"Another time, perhaps." He nodded courteously, too well-mannered to push his presence. "Have a good evening, and enjoy the rest of the performance."

Marielle rejoined the conversation. "You as well."

Simon frowned, and Amelia understood his reaction.

With the touch of his hat, Mr. Hooper was gone—along with Simon's chances of distracting his sister from George Davies.

Chapter 3

Dear Lady Agony,

Siblings are the dickens to deal with! My sisters steal my clothes, and my brother frightens my friends. It's my first season out, yet they still treat me as a child. Just the other day, I had to sneak past the garden gate to talk to a gentleman. How will I ever make a successful match if this keeps up?

Devotedly,
Disheartened Debutante

. . . .

Dear Disheartened Debutante,

Siblings are the dickens to deal with, but they are also family, and I'm afraid the old adage is true. Blood is thicker—and in this case, stickier—than water. They are making things difficult for you now, but one day (and I'm still waiting for this day myself), you will look back on the difficulties and smile. If you *secure a successful match, that is. If you don't, you will blame them for all eternity.*

Yours in Secret,
Lady Agony

George returned with the champagne and three friends, two men and a woman. The woman was fair and willowy, her shoulders curving forward to trim her stature. She allowed the tallest man, who had a slim nose and small, watchful eyes, to guide her. The other man wore a dashing red opera cape, perhaps not wanting to leave it in the cloakroom. As they came closer, Amelia heard the gentlemen discussing horses, and George was in his element now, charming and polite. Nothing remained of his anxious chatter. It was Simon, Amelia decided, who'd brought it on. George might be trying to impress him or Marielle. The Bainbridge siblings were not an easy pair to be around.

They were strikingly handsome—not to mention wealthy and titled. But more than that, they were decisive, in look and action. They traded wits as others traded bits about the weather, and watching their banter, Amelia understood Simon's sister was every bit as smart, stubborn, and unconventional as her brother. *No wonder he's worried.* This girl would do whatever she liked, including run away with a man her brother disliked. If Simon thought rationalizing with her would work, he was mistaken.

Marielle introduced Simon and Amelia to her friends. The man with the handsome slim nose was Lord Cumberland, and the other man was Mr. Wells. The woman, Lady Jane Marsh, was recognizable by name. The Marsh family was well-known in London, even by Amelia, who'd lived in London just over two years.

"I'm enjoying the performance very much. And the theatre." Marielle lifted her hand briefly to indicate the crystal chandelier. "What a difference since the reconstruction. Don't you agree?"

Lady Jane frowned at her dessert. "The renovations are beautiful, but the ice cream"—she wrinkled her nose—"needs work." The strawberry-milk mixture slid off her spoon and into the cup, and the friends shared a laugh.

"I heard an interesting tale about the reconstruction." Simon's deep voice squelched their giggles. "I heard that when the builders tore down a wall, they found a skeleton, dressed in gray rags, with a knife—right through the chest." The last words were aimed at the men in the group, who bobbed their heads, delighting in the detail.

"That's dreadful!" Lady Jane exclaimed, rubbing her bare arms. Like her skin, the dress was pale in color, but it had a bright heather sash that matched the bow in her hair. The color emphasized her youth. Or perhaps it was the switch of topics that had her quivering like a schoolgirl.

Marielle crossed her arms. They were *not* quivering. "That's my brother for you—dreadful."

"I'm quite serious," added Simon.

"Why was he killed? Was it discovered?" George was clearly intrigued with the story.

"One account claims he was a scoundrel, playing with young girls' hearts." Simon shrugged. "I suppose he eventually chose the wrong girl, and her family retaliated."

George leaned back with a whistle.

Amelia had heard about the skeleton, too, but no mention was made of young girls or their family members committing the dastardly deed. Obviously, Simon hoped George would comprehend the veiled threat, but the connection seemed lost on him. It was not lost on Marielle, however. Her black ringlets quaked with anger.

"By the by, who was that man who stopped by the box earlier?" continued Simon. "He appeared distressed."

"'Distressed' is the word." Mr. Wells's voice was bright, like his fashionable red cape, and a bit tinny. One could tell he enjoyed adding to the conversation—and liked attention. "His manners were incorrigible."

"Thaddeus King," said Lord Cumberland.

"Thaddeus King," Simon repeated. "How do I know that name?"

"He's known by most men, if not by name, then reputation," Mr. Wells supplied. "He's a bookmaker at the new jockey club. You might recognize him from the Derby and Ascot. I know your father participated many times."

Recognition covered Simon's face. "Of course. That's where I heard his name."

"They say he shot a man for making a joke about his filly on Rotten Row." Mr. Wells had thin lips, and they curled with mischief as he leaned in, revealing the detail. "He's not to be irritated at any cost."

Lady Jane let out a little exclamation of surprise. She was either quite timid or wished to appear so in front of the men. She leaned toward Lord Cumberland, who reacted quickly to her feminine sensibilities, clearing his throat to indicate a change of subject.

Simon ignored the indication. "I presume your paths crossed at the Derby last month, Mr. Davies?"

George was distracted by the young woman who had passed by them earlier and pulled his attention back to the group. The mirth in his eyes made it seem as if he were always smiling, and not even when the discussion turned to Thaddeus King did he seem upset. "Yes, they did. Mr. King's path is hard to avoid on such a day. A lot of men bet on that race."

"With any luck, Dancer will win next year's race." Mr. Wells gave George a pointed look.

Mr. Davies's face clouded, but only for a moment. Then he returned Mr. Wells's stare with bright confidence. "He has a fine chance. I can make sure of it. With a little extra training, he'll be ready. It's a shame what happened this year."

Marielle leaned closer to Amelia to explain. "Mr. Wells's horse Dancer suffered an injury before the race."

Amelia recognized the scent of afternoon rain in the girl's hair. She guessed Marielle spent a lot of time outdoors. If Simon smelled of the ocean, she smelled of grass, rich and earthy. No wonder she was enamored with Mr. Davies, whose profession must have been fascinating to her.

"What of your father, Lord Bainbridge?" asked Mr. Wells. "Will he enter one of his Thoroughbreds next year?"

"I'm afraid not." Simon flicked away the question like an unwelcome gnat. "The duke ran his last race this spring. We have more important business to attend to now."

Simon's eyes landed on Marielle, and Amelia assumed he meant their focus was her first season, the unwanted affection of George Davies, or both.

"Most unfortunate for the sport," said Lord Cumberland. "I always enjoyed his wins."

"Myself most of all." A furrow crept over George's brow, revealing disappointment and perhaps a hint of real hurt. "We took the Derby, the Ascot. I'm not sure why he'd choose to stop now."

"Indeed." Though it wasn't a question, Simon's voice turned up enough to let George know he thought him an imbecile for not recognizing the reason. The duke must have cut all ties with the man once he realized George and his daughter had affection for each other. Yet George and everyone else seemed unaware of the coincidence.

"Better to go out on top," Mr. Wells concluded. "That's what my father used to say. I think it's wise advice." A smile entered his voice. "And it gives the rest of us a better chance at winning."

The men laughed.

Chimes indicated the show was resuming, and Amelia and Simon quickly said their goodbyes. When they were out of earshot, Simon revealed his displeasure with George's involvement with Thaddeus King. "You heard Mr. Wells. King is a dangerous man, and my sister was footsteps from him tonight."

"I understand, but she was unharmed." Amelia sidestepped a couple. "That's what's important."

Simon cleared a path with a wave of his hand. "They'll meet again. I'm certain of it. Mr. Davies wagers on races big and small. It's how he's come this far."

"A man has to make a living somehow."

He stopped. "That's *gambling*, Amelia." A shock of black hair fell over one brow as he emphasized the word.

"I'm familiar with the concept." Though, to be honest, she wasn't thinking about gambling at all. She was focused on the shadow over his eyes and their subsequent color change. His green eyes were now blue-green, the color of juniper perhaps, or myrtle. It was understandable why Aphrodite revered the plant. If this was its color, it had the power to mesmerize even the strongest hearts.

Simon blinked, and the spell was broken.

"Isn't gambling what many men do when they play cards at the club?" asked Amelia. "Including yourself?"

"That's different." Simon continued walking.

"How?" When he didn't elaborate, she did. "Besides, I fail to see how gambling makes one inherently bad or dangerous. Running away to Gretna Green, however, is another matter, one that is bad *and* dangerous."

"And must be stopped," Simon added.

They walked the rest of the way in silence. The crush of people prevented private conversation, as did several acquaintances of Simon's, who waylaid him on the path to their seats. A few of his friends hadn't seen him since he returned from America. Now that the season was in full swing and Marielle was out, they would be seeing more of him. There was no avoiding society or the beautiful Felicity Farnsworth, his once bride-to-be.

Amelia scanned the audience, frowning when she spotted her in a nearby box. The Farnsworth family was an important one, and Felicity was still held in high regard even after duping Simon. *No one knows she duped him, though*. Simon, a true gentleman, never revealed the difficulty, allowing her to beg off the engagement. Any suspicion was assuaged by her large dowry, which included an equestrian estate much sought-after. If the *ton* was right, and they usually were, she would be married this season. By the looks of the men swarming around her, any one might be a suitor.

Amelia settled into her seat, glad for the return of music and actors. Felicity might have admirers, but Amelia had a genuine love of theatre. From the time she was a young girl, she and her sisters performed skits for guests at the Feathered Nest. It was nothing like the opera, or even professional theatre, but in Mells, it was a close second.

If she closed her eyes, she could still see her father pushing back chairs, her sister Sarah settling in at the pianoforte, and her younger sister, Margaret—the best singer of them all—belting out arias. A smile spread across her face at the memory. She and Grady were usually animals or villains or extras, playing mostly insignificant parts. But they were fun parts, important to the light atmosphere the inn provided, allowing tired travelers to rest for a while and forget their troubles.

Fortunately, George Davies's troubles had disappeared, too. Amelia didn't see any more unexpected guests drop by their box, and for a while, she forgot about him altogether, focusing on the final act and the continued bad luck of the cursed jester. After unknowingly helping his daughter's abductees, the jester promised the other father they would be avenged when the next person through the door, whom they believed to be the duke, was shot. Unfortunately, all was ruined when his own daughter took the bullet, and the duke was heard singing in the distance.

Amelia sighed as the curtain came down. "Tragic."

Simon helped her into her cape. "Despite the glib advice you dole out in the magazine, you're a romantic at heart."

"A young girl took a bullet." She clasped the single button. "Of course I'm sad."

"You know she's not really dead, don't you?"

Amelia swatted him with her reticule. He stiffened, and for a moment, she thought she'd hurt him. Then she realized he was glaring at something: the half-empty box of Lord Burton. George Davies and his friends were missing.

"I have a feeling their absence has something to do with that man, Mr. King." Simon tossed his scarf over his shoulder. "Wait here. I'll be back."

"What? Where are you going? Why can't I come?"

"Stay here," he said over his shoulder, then darted out.

"I am *not* staying here," Amelia mumbled to the empty seat.

"At the very least, I'm seeing Kitty." The Hamsteds were leaving their box as well, and if Amelia hurried, she might meet them near the Grand Circle.

Audience members crowded the hallways and slowed her progress. Tapping her foot, she wished she'd brought her trusty parasol to assist her. It was good at nudging things and people out of the way. But Tabitha had convinced her to leave it at home. Her exact words were, "It belongs nowhere near that dress." But without it, Amelia felt invisible.

She glanced up at the broad man's shoulders in front of her. *Not invisible, exactly. Mostly short.* Her fuchsia gown was wide enough to provide her clearance. The turn of the decade had seen dresses reach a ridiculous span, in her opinion. But it was impossible to see anything beyond the man's black tailcoat. When she approached the top of the staircase, she could finally scan the crowd.

"Kitty!" Her friend was easy to spot. Kitty took great care in finding original dresses, and this one hovered between olive and emerald, made of a green tarlatan, with intricate black leaves, and trimmed in black velvet.

As if the color wasn't striking enough, her diamond necklace radiated in the light of the chandelier as she glanced up, meeting Amelia's smile with one of her own. Kitty's mother-in-law, Lady Hamsted, also wore diamonds—one diamond, actually, the size of an apricot. She, however, did not smile. She frowned, probably at Amelia's use of Kitty's first name.

I can't take it back now, Amelia thought as she descended the stairs. Like most words, it flew out of her mouth when she became excited or flustered, and if one person flustered her, it was Lady Hamsted. The viscountess, like Kitty, was a society favorite, but that's where their similarities ended. Lady Hamsted wanted the best for her son, Oliver, and her wish was granted with her daughter-in-law. No one was more beautiful or gracious than Kitty. But Kitty didn't just look good. She *was* good. The first one to befriend Amelia when she moved to Mayfair, Kitty made her feel welcome in the affluent and sometimes haughty neighborhood. Since then, they'd shared many good times, including several escapades surrounding Amelia's letters. Kitty was her trusted advisor in all things.

"Good evening, Ki—Mrs. Hamsted, Mr. Hamsted. Happy birthday." Amelia grasped Kitty's hand. She turned to Kitty's mother-in-law. "It's nice to see you again, Lady Hamsted."

Lady Hamsted dipped her chin, briefly closing her pale blue eyes. "Lady Amesbury."

"Where's Bainbridge?" asked Oliver, whose evening attire couldn't conceal his bookishness. Although he wore the obligatory black and white, his cravat sagged in the front, as if his chin had sat there a long time while reading a book. His glasses, which were wire-rimmed and too large for his face, had a smudge on one lens. He wouldn't have taken the time to clean them if he was in the middle of a good read.

"He had to check on something." Amelia scanned the area. No Simon in sight. "I was to wait in our box."

"Which explains why you're here," Oliver Hamsted said wryly.

Amelia smiled. She and Oliver didn't always get along, but they both adored Kitty. Amelia could only wish for a match like the couple's one day.

Kitty squeezed her hand. "It feels like an age since we've spoken."

"By age, you mean two days." Oliver grinned.

"You're keeping track," said Amelia. "How nice."

Kitty flashed pretty periwinkle eyes at him. "He's the best, isn't he?"

Oliver's grin melted into a lopsided smile.

Amelia refrained from rolling her eyes. Oliver looked the part of the wide-eyed schoolboy whenever Kitty turned that face on him.

"I should have known you'd find the Hamsteds." Simon's voice came from behind her. It turned buttery as he addressed Oliver's parents. "Good evening."

Lady Hamsted checked back in to the conversation. "Good evening, my lord." She touched her diamond as if to make certain it was still there, which it was, in the hollow of her thin neck.

"Bainbridge!" Oliver greeted him with a handshake.

"Happy birthday," said Simon. "Mrs. Hamsted, how are you?"

"Well," Kitty answered. "Thank you, my lord."

"I must say, your sister is a vision in pink." The viscountess's voice held a rare note of appreciation. "You might have your work cut out for you this season."

Simon followed the viscountess's gaze toward the double doors below, where Marielle was saying goodbye to Lady Burton. His look changed to one of brotherly relief at finding her. "I might indeed. In fact, I hear that work calling now." He dipped his chin. "Excuse us."

Amelia rushed her goodbyes and followed him.

When they reached her, Marielle met them with an unexpected question. "Where is he?"

"I assume you mean Mr. Davies." Simon's eyes perused the entry. "I was wondering the same thing."

"He's not one of your shipmates, Simon," Marielle spat. "You cannot throw him overboard if I don't obey your commands."

"I've never thrown one of my men overboard," Simon said through clenched teeth. "Although if he were on my ship, I'd be tempted, by God. You do not desert a lady."

"He didn't desert me."

"Then where is he?" Simon asked.

After noting a few stray glances, Amelia encouraged them to keep walking. "Maybe we should continue the conversation outside. If we find Mr. Davies, we can all ride home together."

Simon navigated them through the foot traffic. "Wait here," he instructed as they reached the door. "I'll find the carriage."

"It's hot," Marielle shot back. "I'm waiting outside."

"It *is* rather warm." Amelia attempted to broker a compromise. "Fresh air might be nice."

He said nothing more, so they followed him outside, where all of London's finery was on display. Beaded capes, lace handkerchiefs, cashmere gloves. Not to mention the regal coachmen, footmen, and horses. A distinguished line of hansom cabs and carriages snaked around the building.

Simon crossed his arms. "One guess where our dear Olsen is."

"At the end of the line?" answered Marielle, a brief smile tickling her lips.

The tension between them disappeared for a moment, and Amelia understood that while their relationship was tense now, it wasn't always.

Simon turned to Amelia. "Olsen is old and enjoys everything else that is old, including conversation with other old men. He's habitually late."

Amelia shrugged. "Rather than wait for him to come to us, why don't we go to him?"

"A fine idea," agreed Marielle. "We've been sitting too long as it is. I could use a walk."

Simon guided them down Russell Street toward Drury Lane, the elegant evening wear fading with each forward footstep. Street sellers appeared like phantoms, materializing from blind alleys and passages. The group huddled closer together, acknowledging the change.

Without warning, a door opened, and a man was tossed out of a gin house. Marielle squeaked, and Amelia grasped her hand. A thirsty fellow stepped over the man and wandered in, the rush of alcohol fumes enough to offend even the staunchest stomachs, including Amelia's.

She ignored the smell and focused on the dense fog, trying to ferret out any upcoming danger. Under a gas lamp, a woman was selling flowers. Though smudged with soil, her face was as bright as the flower in her buttonhole, her eyes betraying weariness and perhaps hunger.

Marielle must have recognized the look, too, for she stopped abruptly. "Yes, I'll take a bunch."

"I will also," added Amelia. "Violets are my favorite."

"Much obliged," said the woman, taking two bunches from her basket.

Simon begrudged them the coins. "Let's keep moving. I see Olsen at the corner."

"Mind your step," warned the woman. "And avoid the alleyway."

Simon pulled Marielle along, but, perplexed by the woman's words, Amelia threw a backward glance over her shoulder. What did she mean?

"That's Olsen, all right." Marielle let out a puff of laughter. "See the coachman fretting over the footman's hat, gone askew?" she asked Amelia. "He's incredibly fussy."

"I've known him to insist upon returning home after a

quarter hour's drive because of a soiled glove—watch out!" Simon skidded to a halt, jerking Marielle back with him.

Amelia, still distracted by the flower seller, kept right on walking—stumbling over an outstretched limb from the alley, catching herself only when she ran smack into an oyster cart.

Chapter 4

Dear Lady Agony,

My loved one is ill, and I am afraid. I don't know what I shall do when he is gone. Can you tell me how to prepare?

Devotedly,
How to Say Goodbye

. . . .

Dear How to Say Goodbye,

From what I know of goodbyes, preparation is impossible. Although you know the end is near, your heart does not. The organ will take time to repair itself, and even then, the fissure will be a scar you stumble over. Do not be too hard on yourself when you do. Take care, dearest reader, and know I am here for you.

Yours in Secret,
Lady Agony

The oyster seller grinned, revealing a missing tooth. "Penny a lot, misses."

"No, thank you." Amelia dislodged herself from his cart, straightened her cape, and turned around to see Simon bent over a fallen man in the alley. Was the man inebriated? Had he passed out from drink? They were close to the gin house, so close that Amelia could hear the carnival-like music pouring out the window. He might have spent too much time there.

And yet.

Marielle had her gloved hands at her mouth, possibly to keep from screaming. Her face was as pale as the moonlight, and she looked as if she might faint. The sight was ghostly.

Something was very wrong.

In another step, Amelia saw what. It wasn't any man. It was George Davies. And he wasn't drunk. He was dead. A knife pierced his chest, blood staining his white shirt red.

Amelia blinked, not believing her eyes. George had been so full of life. It seemed impossible he could be motionless. His blue eyes, his healthy complexion, his auburn side whiskers—all dull.

Amelia had seen death up close, what a body looked like after the soul flew away. How impossibly small it was. So, too, was the case here. The knowledge brought with it memories of her own experiences, and she swallowed a choke. This was not the time to think of herself. Marielle needed her.

Now.

She went to Marielle, bracing her up with an arm. Marielle sank into her shoulder, gasping a ragged breath. Amelia thought she might get sick and tried leading her to the Bainbridge carriage, but when Amelia took a step in that direction, Marielle held firm.

"Simon, you must help him," pleaded Marielle. "Take that . . . take it out of him."

Simon met Amelia's gaze instead of Marielle's. "Go at once. Please, Amelia. I'll take care of this."

Amelia nodded, understanding she had to get his sister away from here. The murderer might be nearby, on this very street or alley. The killer might attack her next. Gently, Amelia pushed Marielle forward.

"No!" Marielle exclaimed. "I'm not leaving until you help him."

"I can't help him, Ellie." Simon's voice was quiet but insistent. "I'm sorry. He's gone, and I must not tamper with evidence. It may be helpful to the constable."

Marielle looked to Amelia for confirmation, and Amelia nodded. Sobs racked Marielle's shoulders, and Amelia held her firmly to keep the girl from shaking to pieces. The position gave Amelia the ability to shield Marielle from further distress while observing Simon inspecting the body. However ill-timed the observation, she wouldn't be this close to a crime scene again, and it *was* a crime—one in which she had a special interest. She squinted into the inky night, forcing herself to take in as many details as possible.

Even from a distance, she could see the knife was large, noticeably so. It pierced the lower chest. George Davies had faced his killer. But who that killer might be was anyone's guess.

Simon's hand roved over George's clothing and his fallen top hat, looking for discrepancies. It paused over the expanded left coat pocket, and Amelia's eyes flicked there. Simon reached inside and fanned a small stack of notes.

She checked her reaction, making sure Marielle did not sense her surprise. What was George Davies doing with that amount of money on his personage? Even if he was well-to-do, he wouldn't carry it. The wealthy relied heavily on credit, and Amelia, one of the wealthiest women in London, rarely had a shilling on her. Further still, how had the money gone undetected in this neighborhood, where sellers and beggars battled for farthings? Yet here remained a large amount of money, untouched.

Mr. Davies bet on horse races. Perhaps money was a motive for his murder. But if that was the case, the killer would have taken the money with him. Unless the killer had been interrupted. On the busy street, he might have been.

Simon returned the money to George's coat, scanning the remaining pockets. Coming up empty, he took one last glance at the body, stopping when something small and shiny caught his eye. It was on the ground near George's wrist. Amelia squinted. A man's cuff link? A woman's ear bauble? It was no use; she couldn't see past the darkness. When Simon stood, she assumed it was nothing—until she no longer saw the sparkle next to the body. Her breath caught in her throat. *He's taken it!*

Marielle noted the reaction and unburied herself from Amelia's embrace. Turning around, she wiped her tears with her hand. "This is your fault, Simon."

"Keep your voice down," Simon cautioned. "You don't know what you're saying."

When Amelia tried to soothe her, Marielle shook off her hand. "Oh yes I do. You didn't want us to be together. You said so tonight. And now." She gestured toward George. "He has a knife in his chest—just like the man you described at intermission."

It was an unfortunate coincidence, Amelia knew, nothing more.

"Wait a minute, Marielle." Simon inhaled a shaky breath, and Amelia noted the desperation creeping into his voice. "That has nothing to do with anything. I might not have wanted him to court you, but I didn't wish him harm. I swear it."

Marielle looked unconvinced.

"My lord," interrupted a young man, slightly winded. It was the footman from the Bainbridge carriage.

"Thank God," said Simon. "Please escort Lady Marielle and Lady Amesbury home. There's been an accident."

The young man stared at the knife in George's chest.

"Right away, if you please," prompted Simon.

The young man flinched. "Yes, my lord." He held out his arm to Marielle.

"I can't leave him alone," Marielle insisted. "It wouldn't be right."

Amelia put a hand on her elbow. "I think it's best. There's nothing we can do here, and you don't feel well. You're shaking."

"Please, Ellie—"

Not acknowledging Simon, Marielle took the footman's out-stretched arm and let him lead her across the street.

Amelia hung back a moment. "She's upset. She's not thinking clearly."

"You don't know Marielle." He shook his head. "She doesn't say things she doesn't mean."

"I'll talk to her," Amelia said. "I'll make sure she understands this isn't your fault."

Simon surveyed the gathering onlookers. An officer was coming down the street, stopping to talk to a vagrant in his way. Simon lowered his voice. "I know my sister. Only one thing will convince her that I'm on her side."

Amelia leaned in.

"We must catch the killer."

With his words, the mood changed. The idea of solving a mystery with him again made her pulse jump to her throat. Questions, theories, accusations. She loved this city, even its crimes, and investigating George Davies's murder would be an opportunity to right a wrong. They weren't helpless against villainy. They could bring the murderer to justice.

Together.

She met his eyes. "And so we shall."

Chapter 5

Dear Lady Agony,

I detest the country, but with the arrival of the latest round of invites for house parties, I feel pressured to accept. The rural smell of the countryside bothers me, not to mention the perpetual dust that clings to one's clothes. And the tedium! There is nothing to do, except yard games, and how many of those can one play before ruining one's boots? But how to get out of going? That is the real question. Maybe you know the answer.

Devotedly,
City Girl

. . . .

Dear City Girl,

I sympathize with your predicament, for the country has lost its flavor for me as well. The season is short, and I wouldn't like to miss a second of it wandering the grounds of an ancient house.

But how to get out of going? That is easily done by declining the invitations. Women make so much of saying no. Trust me. The more one says it, the easier it is to repeat.

Yours in Secret,
Lady Agony

The next morning, Amelia opted for her usual brisk walk in Hyde Park. Walking always ignited her brain, making her feel as if she could take on the world. With a new murder to solve, that's what she needed to do. *Or if not the world, at least George Davies's killer.*

Thankfully, the initial shock of George's death wore off in the carriage ride home, and Marielle regretted her undue harshness toward Simon. That didn't mean she wasn't upset with him for keeping her and George apart, however. Over and over, she said she wished they had more time together. Now there would be no more chances.

The sister and brother obviously cared for each other a great deal. Marielle told Amelia that after their mother passed, she and Simon weathered the tragedy together, depending on each other for solace. Their father, the duke, had been largely absent. When Simon enlisted in the Royal Navy, she felt abandoned. She couldn't bear the memories in the house alone and spent most of her time outside, with the horses. That's where George Davies entered the picture. He was a friend when she needed one most, and now he was gone, too.

That revelation had induced another bout of tears, and Amelia promised herself that she would do everything in her power to not only solve the murder but mend their bond. Neither sibling seemed to have a strong relationship with their father, and if the familial tie was broken, they would have no one to turn to in times of trouble. She couldn't allow that to happen.

She picked up a badly placed rock and tossed it off the walking path. Someone would thank her for not twisting an ankle, maybe a member of the *ton*, who would later crowd infamous Rotten Row, a place where they showed off their fashions, riding skills, and horseflesh.

But it was still early, and the morning rain, though gone, clung to the trees and grass, making them glisten green. She paused, listening to the city come alive. It was quiet enough that she could enjoy the stray chirp of a bird, the splash of a swan on the water. And yet, there was the call of a costermonger on Oxford Street!

The city was waking to the news of George Davies's death. A man had lost his life to a seemingly random act of violence, but Amelia knew it wasn't random. In the carriage, Marielle revealed that Mr. King interrupted their evening to inquire about their seats. King implied they were an extravagance George couldn't afford. But select seats were select for a reason; they were secured for an entire season. Even if Mr. Davies had wanted to, he couldn't have purchased them. Most likely, they'd been owned by the Burtons for years. Still, the connection was implicit. If George had that kind of money, it should have gone to King, and now King was number one on Amelia's suspect list.

A list I intend on adding to today.

She passed through the gate of Hyde Park to return home.

Home. Never in her life had she thought she'd call Mayfair home. And despite its ostentatious affluence, it *was* home. It was where she'd nursed Edgar through his final days on earth. It was where Aunt Tabitha and sweet Winifred resided. It was where she had met her best friend, Kitty. Thinking of these blessings, she picked up her pace.

She was almost to the brick abode, a towering three-story that spanned the entire block, when she saw Winifred dart through the carefully crafted front hedge. Amelia smiled at the white ruffles and blue sash disappearing into the green. Winifred didn't dart much anymore. She talked more often than she played.

Tabitha's words rang reminders in her ears. Amelia doubted anything was amiss, but as Winifred's mother, she needed to make sure. Winifred was a curious and active girl. She was mature beyond her years because of the tragedy she'd weathered at a very young age. Her parents and grandparents were on the same boat that capsized, leaving her in Edgar's care and then Amelia's after Edgar passed. Though Edgar hadn't desired children, not wanting to pass on his degenerative disease, Amelia couldn't have asked for a better daughter.

But that didn't mean she didn't need checking up on now and again.

Amelia used her parasol to poke through the hedge.

Winifred yelped in surprise. A plain girl with a freckled face and fringed bangs laughed. It was a raucous sound that betrayed her age, maybe two years older than Winifred.

"I'm sorry," Amelia apologized. "I spotted you on the way back from my walk. I didn't realize you had a friend over."

"Amelia—you scared me." Winifred scooted something under her seat. "This is Beatrice."

"Glad to meet you, Beatrice." Amelia reached out her hand.

"You can call me Bee." Beatrice popped a chocolate in her mouth before clasping her hand.

"All right, Bee." The girl's palm was sticky from the sweet, and her mouth was crooked, as if unsure whether to laugh or chew. "It's a little early for candy. Is that what you ladies are doing outside? Sneaking chocolates?"

"No," Winifred was quick to answer.

"Then what are you doing out here?"

Beatrice swallowed the chocolate in one big gulp. "Talking."

The girls shared a giggle, and, instantly annoyed, Amelia felt the singular stress motherhood brought. She reminded herself it was a beautiful summer day in the finest square of Mayfair. If she were a dozen years younger and could get away with it, she would be eating chocolates and giggling, too. "Come in for breakfast when you're done. You need more than candy to sustain you."

They agreed to join her shortly, and Amelia continued inside to the breakfast room, where the sideboard was set with all the foods Amelia enjoyed after a walk: tea, bread, jam, cheese, meat, eggs, and fruit. Cook had poached the eggs perfectly, and Amelia was selecting a second egg when a noise stopped her. As a mother, she was always subconsciously listening for signs of distress. She looked over her shoulder, and her intuition was rewarded with the arrival of Kitty in the doorway.

But Kitty didn't look like Kitty. Her blonde curls had toppled to one side, and her dress, a drab gray, was trimmed in dew—and was that a smudge of dirt on the skirt? The second egg slid off the serving utensil in Amelia's hand and onto the floor. "Kitty! What's the matter?"

A footman appeared like a fairy godmother—or father—cleaning up the spilt food before Amelia could. Bailey was an imposing young man with broad shoulders, a narrow waist, and intelligent brown eyes. Like most footmen, he was pleasant to look at, his job to be seen as much as to see to, but his quick action was known to all in the house. Often, he was the first person sought when a problem arose.

Kitty tossed her reticule on the table. "The worst thing has happened."

Amelia left her plate on the sideboard, going to her friend. She grasped her hands. "Whatever it is, we'll get through it together."

Tears filled Kitty's blue eyes. "That's just it. We can't get through this problem together." She shook her head, and another clump of curls fell out of their pins. "I'm leaving London!"

"What? What are you talking about? You love London."

Kitty's only answer was a loud cry, and Amelia hugged her to her chest, waiting patiently for an explanation.

"Mrs. Hamsted." Tabitha tapped her cane three times at the doorway. "That explains the sobbing."

Kitty sniffed, and Amelia released her.

Tabitha called to Bailey. "Tea and toast, please." She selected a chair. "In my day, women did not sob uncontrollably in each other's breakfast rooms, especially before noon." She scanned Kitty from head to foot. "Certainly not without their hair done."

Kitty fell into the chair across from Tabitha. "I'm sorry, but I have terrible news. Just dreadful."

Tabitha held up a hand to stop further explanation. "My tea."

Amelia gathered her plate and selected a chair next to Kitty, giving her a sympathetic look while they waited patiently for Bailey to bring Tabitha's meal.

When he did, Tabitha thanked and dismissed him. Then she turned to Kitty. "Now what's the news that has toppled your fashion sense, Mrs. Hamsted? It must be of gargantuan proportion."

"It's huge and horrible." Kitty was uncharacteristically un-composed. "For Oliver's birthday, the viscount and viscountess gave us their country estate—in Norfolk! They want us to take possession of it immediately." Kitty dropped her head into folded arms. "What am I going to do?" Her voice was muffled by the tablecloth.

"Norfolk?" Amelia repeated. Norfolk was an agricultural county north of London, an area which in no way suited Kitty.

"Blazes," muttered Tabitha.

Amelia jerked her head. *Did she just say—*

Tabitha took a sip of tea before speaking again. "You're going to start by not crying. Tears won't win Lady Hamsted's heart."

Kitty gathered a lace-trimmed hankie from her reticule, dab-bing her eyes. "But I hate the country. I don't want to grow cows."

Grow cows? Goodness, Kitty wouldn't survive rural life, and Amelia wouldn't survive without her best friend. Not to mention the loss to her column. Amelia would miss Kitty's assistance and input. They were a team when it came to ferreting out London's injustices. She couldn't lose her coconspirator. "What does Oli-ver say?"

"He thinks it's a splendid idea, especially after the business with George Davies last evening. We were a hairsbreadth from the violence, according to him. A move would keep me safe from the perils of London—and give him more quiet time for reading and writing." A new sob shook Kitty's shoulders.

Amelia put a hand over hers. "Oh, Kitty."

"Nonsense," declared Tabitha. She was one of the least sym-pathetic women Amelia knew, but sometimes her toughness, like now, was reassuring. The problem could be solved. It was just a matter of figuring out how.

"That man has plenty of quiet time already," Tabitha continued. "And can you imagine him fraternizing with tenants?" She waited a beat. "No, you cannot. The consequences would be dastardly. They would despise you for your pretty clothes and him for his pretty words."

Amelia cringed. Sometimes the older woman could be *too* tough. Amelia turned to Kitty. "Why don't you tell Oliver you don't want to leave? He's always been sensitive to your needs."

Kitty blew her nose. "Oliver's an only son, and it's his birthday gift. It's not exactly something one can give back."

Tabitha narrowed her eyes on Kitty's hankie. It was unlike Kitty to use it in the breakfast room. "Come now. Get ahold of yourself."

"Sorry." Kitty tucked her hankie away.

"What do you suggest she do, Aunt?" prodded Amelia.

"Convince Lady Hamsted she's not the woman for the job. It won't be hard."

Amelia tapped her chin, warming to the idea. "We could convince her a move to Norfolk would be disastrous." Amelia considered all the ways Oliver and Kitty would make a mess of rural life. A handful sprung up immediately. "By the time we're finished, she'll be begging you to stay in London."

"How?" asked Kitty.

"We'll show her all the ways you'd fail at managing the estate." Amelia's stomach rumbled, and she cut into the perfectly poached egg, dipping her toast. She took a bite. *Heaven*. Now for the bacon.

"And there are so many ways . . ." added Tabitha under her breath.

"How can you eat at a time like this, Amelia?"

"She can eat anytime," explained Tabitha. "I've seen her engulf two eggs, sausage, and a Danish in half the time we've been sitting here."

"That's an exaggeration." Amelia scowled in Tabitha's direction. "Breakfast is the most important meal of the day. You should really try to eat something yourself, Kitty."

"I'd rather eat my hat," Kitty said. "That's how upset my stomach is."

Tabitha lifted her teacup. "Cook's porridge is comparable."

"Think of it this way. If we can't convince the Hamsteds, we can surely convince Oliver." Amelia's voice was stronger, more assured. Food, like walking, always bolstered her mood. "He's quite susceptible to your charms."

"That's true," Kitty admitted.

"See where rational thinking can get you?" put in Tabitha. "Now dry your tears, and do as Amelia says. Make a plan, and make it a good one."

"And if it doesn't work?"

Tabitha chewed her toast thoughtfully. "Trade in your hats for sunbonnets?"

Kitty crossed her arms in protest. "Never! You know how much my hats mean to me."

They did indeed. Amelia had known Kitty to spend the better part of an hour deciding between lace or flower trim at the milliner. Kitty's clothing, like her parties, was an extension of her creativity. Silk, muslin, taffeta. So many fabrics and colors went into her dress choices, and each was a beauty to behold. It was more than fashion sense; it was art.

Amelia glanced at her own blue morning frock. She enjoyed the color, which contrasted nicely with her olive skin tone, and its length, which was amiable for walking. Those two facts pleased her a good deal. The fashionable could keep their overly full skirts and tight-laced corsets. The most important aspect of her dress was function, and she planned to keep it that way.

A rush of footsteps drew her attention to the hallway. "Winifred?" Amelia called. "Have you met Winifred's new friend?" Amelia directed her question at Tabitha. "I met her this morning when I came in from my walk. Beatrice—Bee, for short."

Tabitha placed her teacup in the saucer, a close-lipped smile widening her narrow face.

Amelia recognized that smug look. It was the one that taunted her like a child teasing another child. *I know more than you do.* But what did she know, and when would Amelia know it? Those were the questions to be answered, and Tabitha would decide when.

"Did you call me?" Winifred poked her head into the breakfast room.

Amelia motioned her in. It was good to see a fresh young face in the midst of Kitty's trouble. Her peachy skin, blue eyes, and fair hair brightened the room tenfold. Although approaching that precarious age between child and young adult, she was still little enough that Amelia wanted to pull her onto her lap every time she entered a room. "Yes, I did. I was just telling Aunt Tabitha about your new friend Beatrice."

Beatrice entered the room behind Winifred. "Hallo."

"Oh yes, I've met *Lady* Beatrice." Tabitha turned a sly eye on Amelia. "I believe you know her father, Lady Amesbury. Lord *Grey*?"

Chapter 6

Dear Lady Agony,

I read the column for its unique point of view, but your rivals think it scandalous. They claim readers who follow your advice will undoubtedly disgrace themselves or perish from good society altogether. Do you think there is merit to their beliefs? Do you believe anyone has perished from reading your column?

Devotedly,
Intrepid Reader

....

Dear Intrepid Reader,

If anyone has perished from reading, it would be a first. Reading is one of the safest—and greatest—occupations I've found to date. I admit that following my advice might be less safe. However, my readers know the alternative. The known *path is known for a reason. The unknown path is rockier but leads to undiscovered spaces. I think you know where This Author and her readers prefer to spend their time.*

Yours in Secret,
Lady Agony

Lord Grey? Amelia absolutely knew Beatrice's father. She despised the man. She could still picture him standing in her foyer, clothed in an impeccably tailored dress coat, a stiff collar, and a severe cravat tied at his pompous chin. They'd argued at dinner about child labor laws, and she'd refused to yield her position. He'd claimed, as a member of the weaker sex, she was *confused* about the impact the laws would have on the country. With the case of Martha Appleton—a girl of thirteen who fainted and lost all the fingers on her left hand in an unattended machine in a textile mill—fresh in her mind, she'd retorted she was the only one of them thinking clearly. He'd left immediately, making excuses, but she knew him to be a coward who didn't have the courage to face the facts. Children didn't belong in textile mills.

Amelia put away the incident and forced a smile. "Of course, Lord Grey. I thought you looked familiar."

Bee's mustard-colored dress swung back and forth as she rocked on her heels. A smirk flicked over her round face. "I don't resemble my father at all, Lady Amesbury, but it's kind of you to say so. He's very fashionable."

"Indeed." Amelia forced out the word. The girl was right about her appearance. She was the opposite of her father in every way, as careless as he was careful. The twitch on her lips looked as if it held back a laugh or comment. Amelia could only imagine what the girl was saying inside her head.

Bee surprised her by adding, "But his opinions are quite old-fashioned."

Had Lord Grey told Bee about their disagreement? Amelia couldn't imagine what purpose it would serve except to caution the girl. *Infuriating!* She would be the bigger person and not disparage him in her response. "I'm afraid a good deal of daughters must feel the same way."

Beatrice lifted her bushy eyebrows, which looked as if they'd be better placed on an old man or a Scottish terrier.

Winifred took advantage of the pause in conversation to rush over and kiss Amelia on the cheek. "Bye!"

"Wait, where are you going? What about practice?"

"Didn't you hear? Miss Walters is in bed with the flu." Winifred clasped Bee's hand. "I have the day off!" And with the explanation, they skipped down the hallway and out of sight.

The hasty departure was not like Winifred. Music meant everything to her. She didn't miss practice. Amelia stabbed a sausage. If *Bee* did anything to negatively influence her dear Winifred, she would send her packing, just as she had her father. Amelia sawed the sausage in half. Beatrice wouldn't sway Winifred as her father had swayed Amelia's dinner party guests.

"You don't like the girl," whispered Kitty.

"I never said that," Amelia whispered back.

Tabitha squinted at her from over her teacup. "You didn't have to. Your breakfast meat says it all."

Amelia considered the sausage, diced into several small pieces. Suddenly she'd lost her appetite. She placed her napkin on her plate and changed topics. "When should we commence the plan with Lady Hamsted?"

"What about tomorrow?" Kitty asked. "At the croquet tournament."

"The croquet tournament," Amelia repeated. "A sporting idea, Kitty. I'd almost forgotten. After last year's win, how could I? Do you remember, Aunt?"

"I'd have to be senile to forget." Tabitha tipped her chin.

"It was one for the annals, to be certain," muttered Kitty.

"You're not still sore about it, are you?" Amelia asked. When it came to games, Amelia and Tabitha could be competitive to a fault. Especially when the viscountess offered such praiseworthy prizes. Last year, she'd offered winners a dozen bottles of vintage wine she'd brought back from a trip to Bordeaux, France. When Amelia spotted them, she determined then and there to win the game. Tabitha, always one to disprove her age, didn't need encouragement.

The viscountess's mother, Katherine Collins, was in attendance, and she and Tabitha had once been rivals. According to Tabitha, Katherine Collins stole the only beau she'd ever cared about. Amelia asked why there hadn't been others, for even now, Tabitha was a striking woman with unforgettable blue eyes and lovely cheekbones. Tabitha explained she was a quick learner. It was the only lesson she needed to understand man's fickleness. Instead, she devoted herself to her brother's family, who ended up needing her a great deal.

But that didn't mean she didn't hold a grudge, which worked in her favor during the last round of play. Tabitha knocked Katherine's ball clear into a hedge, a move that put Katherine out of the game and Amelia and Tabitha in the winner's circle. They'd waited until they were home to gloat—over a glass of fine wine—but the result was the same. They gained a reputation for being boastful players, too confident for their own good.

"Of course not." Kitty blinked demurely. "Why would I be sore? You only knocked Oliver's grandmother's ball halfway to kingdom come."

Tabitha dabbed her lips, carefully replacing the napkin on the table. Then she leaned back and smoothed the cuff of her lace sleeve. "I've never known my own strength. It's one of my few faults."

Amelia bit back a smile. "I'm certain you'll be able to make it up to her this year, Aunt."

"In fact, you won't." Kitty lifted a blonde eyebrow. "She isn't coming. Something about a headache plaguing her for the past two weeks."

"A headache," Tabitha said dismissively, standing from the table. "Pish. A little warm brandy and water always cures mine. Let her know."

Kitty stood, too. "I will pass it along."

"We'll see you tomorrow, Kitty." Amelia walked with her to the foyer. "Lady Hamsted will be convinced one way or the other. I promise."

"I'm looking forward to it—I think."

Amelia waved her on. "You overestimate our abilities."

"Be good," Kitty warned, crooking a finger at her, and slipped out the door.

We'll be good, all right. Good enough to win.

Bailey entered with a parcel.

Today's post!

"I'll take that, Bailey. Thank you." Amelia retrieved the package sent from Grady Armstrong, her editor and friend, and brought it straight to the library, shutting the door. Her heart rate increased on the way to her desk. This was her secret employment, her secret self. How thrilling it was to have work to do!

She ripped open the package. The parcel contained four letters, and she inhaled the scent of ink before pouring the envelopes onto her desk. Smudged, stained, wrinkled—ah yes, London's season was in full swing, and more than one woman had relationship problems.

When she'd first started, most letters came from poor girls and shopworkers, who found respite in the dramas and stories the penny magazine provided. After all, they were the paper's intended audience no matter how distinguished its name or the font that was used. As time passed, however, she answered more letters from members of the elite, who deigned to write in about their problems once they realized the responder was a member of their own class.

She sliced open a letter with her ivory-handled knife, a beautiful gift her mother had given her at the age of sixteen. Joy and sorrow were universal emotions. Problems might vary, but emotions were the same. She gave each correspondent the same attention, regardless of his or her status or position.

A knock interrupted her unfolding of a badly wrinkled letter. She laid it aside, covering it with a newspaper. "Enter."

Jones smoothed a wispy piece of brown hair that, no matter how hard he tried, always escaped his forehead. Then he set his shoulders in a distinguished way, unable to completely hide the shape of his frame, a bit like an avocado in a double-breasted black waistcoat. "Lord Bainbridge is here to see you, my lady."

She glanced at her letters, half slid under her newsprint. She would not get to them now. "Send him in, please."

He tsked, but she paid him no mind. He would rather she

take the call in the formal drawing room. Jones was finicky that way. But it was only Simon, and having spent plenty of time in the house as a child, he knew it as well as she did. Perhaps better. He certainly didn't require formalities, and neither did she.

Jones returned with the visitor.

She stood. "Thank you, Jones. Good morning, my lord."

"Good morning." After Jones shut the door, Simon strode over to her desk. He glanced under the newsprint. "A little letter writing on this fine summer day. Don't let my presence interrupt you. My life's only crumbling to pieces like last week's bread."

Amelia sighed, tucking the letter into its envelope. No work would be done right now. She gathered the other envelopes and returned them to the parcel.

"My sister detests me," continued Simon. "I need to do everything in my power to show her I care about finding George Davies's killer."

Amelia placed the parcel in her desk drawer, turning the key in the lock.

"Do you know what she said to me on my way out?" Simon didn't wait for her response. "She said, 'I hope you trip on your big feet.'" He held up a perfectly polished shoe. "I don't have big feet."

Amelia considered his foot. "Actually, you do."

"Amelia," he said in a very serious voice, a voice contrary to his odd behavior. "Are you listening to me?"

It was sweet, really, how much he loved his sister and how bad he felt at falling out of her favor. He was acting like many of Amelia's correspondents, and it was an interesting change in his behavior. If he used his usual logic, he would see Marielle was processing her grief, nothing more.

"Of course I'm listening. You said you don't have big feet, and I said you do."

His eyes narrowed into green daggers.

She'd made him suffer long enough. She stood from her desk. "Let us go find Mr. Davies's murderer, shall we?"

His face cleared, and he released a breath. "I thought you'd never ask."

Chapter 7

Dear Lady Agony,

My family has a garden, and I adore spending time in it. I'd rather cultivate flowers than anything else in the world, but my mother says I must be serious. In her day, girls did not "waste time" on flowers. They studied art and read poetry and practiced the pianoforte in preparation of finding a husband. Do you think I am wasting my time? I wouldn't want to be considered frivolous.

Devotedly,
I Prefer Flowers to People

. . . .

Dear I Prefer Flowers to People,

I don't think you're wasting your time. I think each of us knows what we like, and you like flowers. If your mother likes art,

*poetry, and music, she should attend to those instead of
harassing you. You may tell her I said so.*

*Yours in Secret,
Lady Agony*

The afternoon had grown damp, thick with clouds, but once
in a while, Amelia and Simon were treated to a burst of sunshine
that darted through the heavy sky and into Simon's carriage. It
highlighted the dark bristle on Simon's jawline, enough to remind her he hadn't shaved. It also emphasized his ebony hairline
when he took off his hat. A shock of waves was pushed back
from his forehead, and Amelia imagined he'd spent most of the
morning running his fingers through it, wondering what to do
about Marielle. She became keenly aware of his vulnerability, a
weakness she hadn't been privy to until now. It moved her—and
her heart. It did a flip-flop in her chest.

Simon caught Amelia staring, and she turned away, feeling
like a too-curious cat. She looked and went where she wasn't
supposed to. The habit had followed her since her childhood
in the excessively small village of Mells, where the traffic was
more interesting than the scenery. It had nothing to do with
Simon.

Well, maybe it had *something* to do with him. He did seem
to awaken senses she thought died with Edgar. Little did she
know, they weren't dead, just asleep, and Simon happened to
bring them back to life, like a surgeon or magician.

Putting the realization out of her head, she refocused on the
murder. The last thing Simon needed to hear was that he possessed magical powers. "When you examined the scene of the

crime, you found money in George Davies's pocket. How much, and why?"

"I can only answer one of those questions." He lowered his voice. "It was a thousand pounds exactly."

Amelia whistled. She knew it was a good deal of money but never guessed that much. It was the amount a successful barrister might make in a year. "Perhaps that's what Mr. King was looking for when he dropped by their box unannounced."

"If so, he didn't find it. Nobody did—and in this neighborhood, if you can imagine." Simon's eyes flicked to the street, where a ragtag child ran past with a stolen apple, a man quick on his heels.

"Did you discover anything else of note?" she asked. Here was his opportunity to tell her what he pocketed from the scene, the small sparkly item near George's body.

He didn't take it. "Only the money. It might have been for a bet on a horse."

Large amounts of money exchanged hands in horse racing, and George was an expert on the sport. If so, George had taken this deal to his death. "Maybe someone witnessed the exchange. The area was chock-full of the theatre crowd, not to mention peddlers. I'd like to talk to the flower vendor who sold us the violets. She was less than a block away from the murder."

"And the gin house might also provide answers." He pinched the bridge of his nose, and Amelia noted the plum-colored skin underneath his eyes. He hadn't slept well and probably rose early, forgoing his usual routine. This might be what he looked like after a bad night at sea, navigating troubled waters with great skill and care for his men. He cared just as deeply for his sister. But this storm wouldn't pass as quickly. It would take them many days to find the culprit behind George Davies's murder.

"But what of this flower vendor?" he continued. "What would she know?"

"It was something she said when we bought the flowers." Amelia remembered the detail distinctly. "She told me to avoid the alleyway. Very strange, considering George Davies was found dead in it."

"*Avoid the alleyway.*" Simon pondered the statement. "You mean to say she knew George Davies was lying dead in the side street?"

"Perhaps."

"Wouldn't she call out?" The words were hardly out of Simon's mouth before he corrected them. "Of course she wouldn't. It's best to mind one's own business in these parts."

"Head down and all that," added Amelia. "She wouldn't risk trouble for herself or inquiry by the constable. And what about the gin house?"

Simon looked out the window. "As you said, the area was teeming with people, and Mr. Davies was fond of drink. Perhaps someone saw him there."

Amelia followed his gaze as they passed Drury Lane Theatre. The portico on Catherine Street was empty, and the white facade looked plain without a spectacle of people nearby. It was as still today as it had been bustling last evening.

The carriage stopped, and Amelia descended the stairs with the help of her parasol. A rich navy color with a gold lotus flower and sturdy gold handle, it wasn't one of those thin, cotton, fringe-dripping beauties young ladies used today. It had weight to it and had brought at least one man to his knees. She never left home without it, especially when walking alone. One never knew when one would encounter a pickpocket in need of a clubbing.

The daylight did little to brighten the crowded rookeries that lay behind Drury Lane or make gladder the vendors who sold flowers, matches, and day-old newspapers for a loaf of bread or a bit of cheese. While women in ruffled gowns and men in corded silk hats poured into the theatre last night, the hardworking people of London scrambled for their living, their tenacious spirits fighting for essentials that came easily to others.

Even in the bustle of the afternoon, the flower seller from last evening was easy to spot. Her bouquets were artfully arranged, and while other sellers were bent and sly in their movements, her posture was erect and proud. The thin gray dress couldn't hide her sharp shoulders, nor did her bright eyes soften her pale face, pinched from chronic hunger.

When she spotted them walking toward her, she began packing up her bouquets as if to leave.

"A moment of your time, if you please." Amelia called out the words loudly to be heard above the crowd, and they floated along the street noise, never-ending in this neighborhood.

"That's one way to get her attention," murmured Simon.

She pointed her parasol at the vendor, who'd stopped putting away her flowers. "It worked, didn't it?"

Simon lowered the umbrella with a slow hand. "Keep your sidearm holstered, please. We cannot have this woman running for cover."

As they approached, the vendor's hand shot out. "Violets, or perhaps a rose for the gentleman?"

Simon surprised Amelia by answering, "Yes, please," and pressed a sovereign into her palm.

The woman looked at the money. "That would buy a good many roses, sir. You mistake the cost." Shockingly, she returned the money.

"We need to ask you a few questions about last evening," Simon tried again. "We talked to you, at this very spot. You sold Lady Amesbury a bunch of violets."

"I sell violets to ladies all day and night long." Her tone was indifferent, as cool as a clam under the protection of the deep ocean sand. "I can't remember every customer."

Simon was getting nowhere with his inquiry, so Amelia decided to take a different approach. "Of course not. Allow me to introduce us. As he stated, I'm Lady Amesbury, and he is Lord Bainbridge. We were with another young woman last night, and she also bought flowers." Amelia smiled. "We admired them very much."

"Now that you mention it, I do recall seeing you." Her eyes widened, revealing pretty purple irises nearly the color of her flowers. Besides her nosegay, it was the only color on her. The messy hair tucked under her rumpled hat was prematurely gray above the ears, as faded as her dress.

"Thank goodness," Amelia said. "We'd be much obliged for any information you might have about what occurred last night. Our friend, Mr. George Davies, was murdered. We only want to know what happened to him to prevent it from happening to someone else."

The woman looked skittishly from Amelia to Simon and back to Amelia. Perhaps she was reconsidering her statement of remembrance.

Amelia continued quickly. "As you know, these streets are hard enough without a murderer on the loose, Miss . . . ?"

"Miss Rainier," she supplied. "Frances Rainier. I'm sorry about your friend."

Amelia accepted her condolences. "Last night, you said something that made an impression on me. You told us to avoid the alleyway. Did you see something or someone to make you caution us?"

Miss Rainier waited for a barefooted boy in a cap to pass with his papers before answering. "I was only trying to help a lady. I didn't mean any harm."

"A lady." Amelia seized the detail. "What did she look like?"

"She, like yourself, was pretty, and dressed in a fine heather cloak. Her hair was bright, a lovely red color the likes of which I've never seen." Her eyes widened in remembrance. "A color that took one's breath away." She blinked. "She was in a hurry to catch up to a man." Miss Rainier's face pinched in disapproval. "Everyone was in a hurry, it being opening night and all. One mister tumbled my flowers."

"And the man she caught up with?" prodded Simon.

"Was in a rush, too." Miss Rainier became interested in telling the story, and the singsong quality in her voice broke through. "The alley at the corner offered a bit of space for a private conversation, if you get my meaning. That's why I warned you off. I thought they might be there."

"She was a lady. Was he a gentleman?" Amelia inquired.

Miss Rainier checked the gray sky, as if plucking the description out of the clouds. "He wore a nice suit of clothes, a silk hat, proper fitting." Her forehead wrinkled. "He had a jolly good laugh. Like a carnival, it was. That was different."

A man passed by and tipped his hat dramatically in her direction. "Good day to the prettiest flower seller in all of London. Excuse me, all of England."

She scowled, adding, "Still better than any of the blokes around here."

Simon lifted his eyebrows at Amelia. "It sounds like Mr. Davies."

"The killed man?" Miss Rainier asked. "You think it was him?"

"Yes," Simon answered. "Do you think the woman might have had anything to do with his death?"

"A lady wouldn't stoop so low." Miss Rainier's voice was full of censure. "Not one of her pedigree."

"You'd be surprised what a lady could do," countered Amelia. "If she felt threatened—"

Miss Rainier dismissed the idea. "That man looked no more threatening than Chip there." She nodded in the direction of the man who'd passed by earlier. Now he was pestering a woman selling watercress.

"I imagine you don't have the name of the woman?" asked Simon.

"I don't. I've never seen her before, and I know everyone." Miss Rainier tipped her chin with pride. "My family's been selling flowers in this area for three generations."

Simon acknowledged the declaration with a nod. "A noble tradition."

"Quite." Amelia slipped a calling card out of her reticule. "You've been most helpful, Miss Rainier. If you think of anything else, I hope you'll call on me."

"Yes, thank you," Simon added. "We appreciate the information."

"You're welcome." Miss Rainier smiled as she reached for a flower. "Now about that rose . . ."

Chapter 8

Dear Lady Agony,

Are spirits inherently evil? All ladies say so, but you're not all ladies. I'd like to hear your opinion on the subject, for I am a woman who enjoys wine and think you might be, too. Tell me, what is your estimation of the great-tasting grape?

Devotedly,
Wine, Whiskey, Whatever

. . . .

Dear Wine, Whiskey, Whatever,

I can tell by your signature you are not overly particular when it comes to alcoholic beverages. And rightfully so. Fussiness is so unbecoming when one is in the mood for a drink. Men retire to their parlors with whiskey and we to our drawing rooms with empty glasses. Wine is refreshing, and made of fruit, too, as you

*intelligently remind us. I say let it flow like the Ganges, and all
will have a fine time.*

*Yours in Secret,
Lady Agony*

After buying a rose from Miss Rainier, Amelia and Simon
continued to the nearby gin house, where Simon frankly told her
to wait outside. An argument ensued about what right he had to
tell her anything, and after all, wasn't she there to help? How
could she be of assistance standing outside the door?

"If you're worried about my female sensibilities, don't be. I
know how to handle myself around drunkards. We didn't tol-
erate them at the Feathered Nest. One poke of my parasol, and
you'll see what I mean." Amelia emphasized her point by tapping her parasol on the ground. "Trust me."

"Dash it all, Amelia. This isn't the Feathered Nest." He indicated the establishment. "This is a London watering hole that's
been upgraded with stucco rosettes and cheap mirrors. No one
will think twice about approaching you."

She set her chin, refusing to budge.

Simon's eyes darted from her to the carriage, and for a moment, she thought he'd throw her over his shoulder and carry her
kicking and screaming to the coachman. She held tighter to her
parasol in case he needed a demonstration of its effectiveness.

"Fine, but don't expect me to save you if something goes
wrong."

"Nor me you," added Amelia.

His eyes became green slits.

She shooed him toward the door.

Alternating smells of gin and ale hit her with her first step inside. She acceded his point: this was *not* the Feathered Nest. But compared to its surroundings, it was all light and beauty, with shiny mirrors, ornate wood, and enormous green and gold casks of liquor. Behind the bar stood a woman with a large knot of braided hair above each ear, her eyes half-closed in a conciliatory way at the man she served, who was dressed in plaid trousers that stopped well short of his boots. A regular customer, perhaps. The server leaned closer to him with a word, and her long necklace brushed the mahogany wood, which had been polished overnight and didn't show the abuse it would take in later hours.

That's when she noticed Simon, or Amelia assumed she did, because she straightened the neckline of her dress. She licked her lips and asked, "Gin for you, sir?"

"Yes, please."

When she didn't ask Amelia what she'd like, Amelia piped up, adding, "And if you'd be so kind, I'd like one of those biscuits." She pointed to a basket, which was covered with wicker to prevent thieves from lifting a treat.

The serving girl clucked her tongue.

Amelia wasn't sure if that meant she would or would not be getting the biscuit.

A stout man came up behind them. "Get the gentleman his drink, Ruthie. They didn't come for your lip." With an air of importance, he touched the brim of his hat. "My apologies, sir."

"Not necessary." Simon drank down his gin in one gulp, and the server poured him another. This seemed to make the man, most likely the proprietor, happy.

Amelia was not happy. She still did not have her biscuit.

"Bad business on the street last night," continued Simon. "Do you know what happened to the man they found with a knife in his chest?"

"I'm going to take a *stab* at it and guess he died," Ruthie said. The man in the plaid trousers laughed at the joke.

The proprietor cut her off. "Can't say as I do. I don't pay any attention to the comings and goings on this street. If I did, I'd knife *myself* in the heart."

"I know what happened," Ruthie put in eagerly. Her face was like a child's on Christmas morning. Her brown eyes grew as wide as if she'd spotted a present for herself under the tree. "I saw him yesterday. I told the peeler the story."

"You need to talk less and pour more." The proprietor gave her a shove toward two men at the end of the bar, waiting for a refill. "That girl has a mouth like a cesspool. Nothing good ever comes out of it."

For a second, Amelia forgot about the biscuit and readied a defense of the girl. But a moment later, Simon clasped her arm and squeezed it, silently communicating a plan. He wanted the proprietor to leave so that he could follow up with Ruthie. Arguing would delay that plan.

As luck would have it, they didn't have to wait long. A nicely dressed young man tumbled in yelling, "Gin for my friends!" The proprietor rushed over to seat them at his best table, pleased with the new business.

Simon downed his gin, setting the glass on the counter hard. Ruthie took his meaning and filled his glass immediately. This time, however, she did so silently.

"So what happened to the man?" asked Simon. "I bet you know."

"Oh, I know, but my boss don't like me saying." Ruthie wiped a spot of spilt gin with a bar rag.

"Was he here?" prodded Amelia. "Did you talk to him?"

"He was here, but I didn't talk to him." Looking at Simon,

Ruthie threw a thumb in Amelia's direction. "I don't make a habit of conversing with toffs, and he was with one. I served him, and that was it."

Amelia glanced over her shoulder. The girl couldn't possibly be speaking about her. Simon was a marquis, for goodness' sake. If anyone was a toff, it was he.

Simon ignored her confounded expression and continued with Ruthie. "How did you know he was a toff?"

"Fair hair, clean hands. Baby-soft skin." Ruthie shook her head. "Never worked a day in his life, that one. Besides, he left me a half a crown. I made good use of it, too."

"Did they argue?" asked Simon.

"The killed man was cheerful, not the arguing kind, but the toff was serious. He wasn't the type to be made a fool."

"So you're saying he hurt—" Amelia interrupted.

"I ain't saying the toff hurt him, 'cause that's not what toffs do. But he could've got someone else to do his dirty work, couldn't he? If he wanted to?"

"Yes, but why would he want to?" Amelia interrupted.

"Who knows why a toff does anything?" Ruthie spat. "I don't pretend to know. I'm just relaying what I saw, and that's all I seen."

"We appreciate that," said Simon.

She gave him a wink and turned toward the men at the end of the bar.

Amelia coughed. "My biscuit?"

Ruthie snatched the pastry and placed it in front of her, little crumbs falling to the floor.

"Thank you," Amelia called out as she mulled over their conversation. If she could figure out the man or woman who met with George the night of his death, perhaps she could solve his murder. The first person who came to mind was Thaddeus King. He'd accosted George in the theatre; perhaps he met him here, pressuring him further. But the details didn't exactly fit. Ruthie called the patron a toff, a well-to-do person who hadn't worked a day in his life. Amelia hadn't seen Thaddeus King up close, but from far away, she wouldn't have described him that way. His mannerisms were sharp, experienced. And she doubted King would have left the waitress a half a crown, unless he was paying for her silence. A bad investment indeed.

Simon took care of the bill, and they left quickly, but not quickly enough to avoid Lord Grey, who was passing outside the door. "Lady Amesbury! What an unexpected surprise."

Of all the people I might have bumped into, it must be Lord Grey. She had the devil's luck and her own. Counting to ten, she forced herself to consider an appropriate response before opening her mouth. She had the bad habit of saying the wrong thing to the wrong person, and Lord Grey was definitely the wrong person. His pond-placid face, well-groomed side whiskers, and pinched lips evoked an immediate reaction in her, and that reaction was to say the opposite of what she should.

"Lord Grey," replied Amelia. "This is Lord Bainbridge. Have you met?"

"I haven't had the pleasure."

Simon greeted him with a firm handshake.

"What brings you . . ." Lord Grey smiled at the building. "Here?"

Amelia couldn't think of one single solitary reason for being at a gin house in the middle of the afternoon, and the first thing that came into her head fell out of her mouth. "Spirits."

Lord Grey was so taken aback that his thin lips unpursed.

Simon chuckled, a smooth sound that flowed like honey

from his mouth. "What Lady Amesbury means are spirits of a celestial nature. At the opera last evening, there were tales of a ghost in gray haunting the area. We had to stop and see for ourselves on the way to the park." Simon feigned puzzlement. "It's not you, is it, Lord Grey?"

"No, afraid not," Lord Grey said with a light chuckle. "I'm stopping by the tobacconist." He leaned closer to Simon. "This might interest you. A little shop—a hole in the wall, really—but it sells the best cigarettes in all of London, Cuban cigars, and port from Vila Nova de Gaia. That's in Portugal."

"Yes, I'm familiar." A hint of irritation entered Simon's tone, and Amelia guessed he wasn't as impressed with Lord Grey as Lord Grey wanted him to be.

"It's the sort of thing a man wants to procure for himself, mind you." Lord Grey lowered his eyelids, a favorite response that made his nose appear longer and more pointed. "Although some staff fancy themselves equal to *any* task."

"Fancy?" Amelia forced a laugh. "I would say *find*. Although smoke shopping is hardly a challenge, especially for those used to hard work. And speaking of challenges, I met your daughter Beatrice this morning. A most . . . energetic girl."

"Yes," pondered Lord Grey. "I seem to remember her coming home with chocolate on her chin. So unusual for that time of day." He fastened a button on his coat. "One wonders what goes on in some houses and at what hours. At any rate, I must be on my way. Good to see you again, Lady Amesbury. Lord Bainbridge."

Amelia internally seethed. *His* daughter had a sweet tooth. *Hers* did not.

"Lord Grey." Simon touched his hat.

Amelia plastered a thin smile on her face to prevent the villainous words in her head from tumbling to her lips.

When he was gone, Simon teased, "I didn't realize I had competition for the most infuriating man in the room. Why didn't you tell me?"

"That, that . . . man!" Amelia sputtered, suppressing another word. "I can tell you right now I like you twice as much as I like him. Three times, perhaps."

Simon led her to the carriage. "Somehow that doesn't make me feel better."

"It should." Her footsteps were a steady march. "He's a cad and a scoundrel. Did you hear what he said to me?"

"I was present."

Amelia ducked into the carriage before releasing the worst of it. "He *impugned* my home."

Simon squinted, clearly confused. "With the comment about chocolate on the chin . . . ?"

"Yes, with the comment about chocolate on the chin. What else?"

He situated himself in the seat across from her and tapped on the roof. "I suppose I can see how that could offend your motherly sensibilities."

Simon is right. She shrank back in her seat with the realization. The situation with Beatrice and Lord Grey had brought forward a motherly instinct she hadn't believed she possessed. It wasn't just protective—it was overprotective. And if she admitted, a little bit hostile.

She was being one of *those* mothers. One of those mothers who wrote in to the magazine about how their children could do no wrong. How their children were angels among devils. She lifted her eyes to check if the whole world was watching her. *Whew*. It was only Simon. Thank goodness no one knew how archaic she'd been acting.

If Lord Grey wanted to insult her home, let him. In fact, she wouldn't want to live in a house of which he approved. *No thank you*. Girls, including his, would find a perfect respite in her home in Mayfair. The nonsense that went on in other houses—*Lord Grey's*—would not go on in her house. It was perfectly acceptable for them to be themselves.

Amelia dipped her chin, agreeing with her internal logic. She hazarded a glance at Simon, and he chuckled. "What is it?"

"Do me a favor."

"Maybe," she said.

"If you're ever asked to play poker, decline."

"Why?" she asked moodily.

"Because your face is like a looking glass. It will reflect your hand."

Chapter 9

Dear Lady Agony,

Do you think women should partake in strenuous games? I heard a shocking account of a woman, quite old but in good physical condition, participating in lawn tennis. I thought the tale would end with her collapsed on the green, but she thoroughly enjoyed herself and intends to play again. Her age forgives her involvement, but what about the rest of us? Do you think it wise to play?

Devotedly,
A Girl with a Ball Is No Girl At All

....

Dear A Girl with a Ball Is No Girl At All,

Allow me to correct your signature: a girl with a ball is the happiest of them all. I like nothing more than brisk physical activity, and I can't imagine other women do not feel the same.

As you state, the woman in question thoroughly enjoyed herself, and why not? A body in motion stays in motion. There's no better way to stay healthy. I'm inexperienced in the mentioned sport, but I have every confidence if it involves a net and a racquet, I would perform as well as any man and perhaps better. My advice to you and all women is: play on.

Yours in Secret,
Lady Agony

The next day, Amelia debated between a sage green or periwinkle blue dress, and decided on the sage green, for it had fewer frills and better movement. Slipping it over her head, she was happy to find it, like her walking dresses, hit just above her ankles. She enjoyed croquet and didn't want her dress getting in the way of a good time. Sure, she was going to convince the viscountess that Kitty couldn't possibly move to the country, but she might as well brush up on her moves while she was there.

She stared into the looking glass, pretending to swing a mallet. "Yes, this will do just fine."

"I like it, too, my lady," said Lettie, her maid and good friend. "It's a beautiful color on you."

Amelia donned a matching bonnet with a wide green ribbon. "Thank you, Lettie. It's nice of you to say so. However, I'm there to play croquet, not display my fashion sense."

Lettie fussed with the ribbon. "But when you can do both, why not?"

Amelia allowed her to fuss. Lettie liked fashion much more than Amelia did, and she hadn't had much fun fussing with Amelia's two years of mourning garb. The best part of being out of mourning was giving Lettie her castoffs, which Amelia made certain were still lovely and in fashion. Lettie, the imitable Patty Addington's daughter, was just two years older than Amelia but wise beyond her years when it came to style. She always made Amelia look and feel beautiful and was herself a lovely person with almond-shaped eyes, a rosy complexion, and a forthrightness Amelia had come to depend on.

"Be careful not to get . . . overly excited." Lettie stuck a pin into her hair. "It's just a game, remember."

"What do you mean, *overly excited*?"

"Remember the fiasco at Lady Andrew's house?" Lettie gently prodded.

"That," stated Amelia, "was entirely her fault. I saw her move the ball with my own eyes."

"A good many ladies do that, I'm afraid."

"They shouldn't," declared Amelia. "It's cheating."

"Maybe so, but maybe it's better to keep it to yourself when they do." Lettie secured one more pin.

"Ouch—fine. But the sport will be diminished by my silence."

Lettie lifted her eyes. "Better the sport than your reputation, my lady."

With an admiring look, Amelia met Lettie's eyes. "Touché."

Thirty minutes later, Amelia and Tabitha arrived at the distinguished house of Lady Hamsted, a sprawling mansion on Grosvenor Street. As they took their place in a row of carriages, Tabitha eyed the scene carefully, probably sizing up her competition. In her gray dress, white gloves, and dove-colored hat, she was an elegant but formidable opponent. Her cornflower blue eyes might have concealed her enthusiasm for the game, but Amelia recognized the razor-sharp focus.

Winifred had the same Amesbury focus. Once she set her

mind to something, all that was left was to do it. At Winifred's age, Amelia had been a little more slapdash. Back then, she loved nothing better than racing pell-mell through the country-side on her horse, Marmalade, Grady Armstrong trailing close behind. Grady had worked in the stables at the Feathered Nest, and his horse was neither beautiful nor fast. Like him, it was perseverant, however, and he would catch up eventually, usually in the glade.

There, they scoured old newspapers, skipped rocks, and climbed trees. They planned to leave Mells as soon as their legs would carry them. So many people passed through the small village on their way to London. Why not them? They might be clerks, merchants, or newspaper writers. Even performers at the theatre! As the afternoon grew warmer, the dreams grew bigger, like waves in the moonlight, and they wouldn't recede until the sun cooled and Amelia returned home. Then it was back to cooking, cleanup, and, if she was lucky, a game of old maid with one of the guests, a skit with her sister, or a ballad by her mother.

By the look of the stiff upper lips outside the Hamsted for-tress, no singing would occur today. Amelia's nose wrinkled. She'd be surprised if the women could play a proper game of croquet in their extravagant dresses. Some of the skirts were so full and adorned with so many flounces, the women beneath them might topple over when they reached for a ball.

Amelia slipped on her lightweight gloves as the carriage came to a stop. She would not be toppling. Her skirt had a con-venient flat front and short hemline. Thankfully her modiste was as forward-thinking as she was talented. Amelia's dress would not get in the way of a good time—or a decent game.

"If you are done frowning, we should exit." Tabitha grasped her cane.

Amelia put on her best smile. "Yes, Aunt."

Lady Hamsted greeted them. She was so thin that it was the first thing one noticed. The second was her pale eyes and jet-black pupils. They had the power to plumb situations and people within seconds, and Amelia surmised the ability accounted for their vaguely ghostly appearance. "Thank you for coming. How are you, Lady Tabitha?"

"Very well, thank you. I was sorry to hear your mother won't be joining us."

"Yes." Lady Hamsted touched her pearls, drawing attention to their exquisite whiteness. "A terrible headache. She suffers from them often in the summertime."

"We're excited to compete for the grand prize." Amelia had forgotten about the reward until she saw a large table draped in a supple gold cloth, concealing something underneath. Bending at the knees, she hazarded a low glance, hoping for a peek. "What is it this year? A timepiece? A new croquet set? A hogshead of cheese?"

The viscountess smiled, a little crack exposing the facial powder on her cheeks. "It's not a hogshead of cheese."

"Whatever it is, I'm sure it's lovely." Catching Kitty's eye, Amelia added, "And speaking of lovely, here comes Kitty."

"Ah, Mrs. Hamsted," Tabitha mused. "No one looks better in the middle of a London lawn than she." Tabitha nodded at the viscountess. "She represents your family well."

In a lavender tulle dress, an oversized lavender and white bonnet, and pretty purple boots, Kitty certainly fit in with London society, but she was better than three-fourths of it. Even now, surrounded by important duties, she never overlooked the little details—or little guests. She stopped midway to help a young girl with the ribbon on her dress. As she made a wide loop for a bow, a sliver of sun broke through the clouds, shining on her like a pot of gold at the end of the rainbow. That's how Amelia thought of Kitty, for her friendship was worth more than ten pots of gold. If she moved to the country, Amelia didn't know what she'd do. *Spend more time with Aunt Tabitha?* A nervous pang struck her heart. *Let's hope this plan works.*

"Thank you." Lady Hamsted lifted her chin. "We take great pride in our daughter-in-law."

"And rightly so," added Amelia. "No one is more trusted for the latest fashion in London. I would be lost without her example."

Lady Hamsted's eyes flicked over Amelia's modest dress and boots. "Indeed."

Amelia cleared her throat. Perhaps hers was an imperfect example, but others followed her fashion sense. Half of the women at the party had tried to replicate her style.

"You're here!" exclaimed Kitty, giving Amelia a hug.

Kitty was not only dressed in lavender but smelled of it, too, and Amelia noted the sprigs of the flower in her bonnet as Kitty released her. "Of course we're here. We wouldn't miss the Hamsted croquet tournament. Where's Oliver? Brushing up on his game, I hope."

"Unfortunately not." Kitty indicated a nearby lawn chair, where Oliver sat hunched over a book. "A new history became available, and he wanted to start on it right away."

The viscountess studied her son with unease. He was her only child; it was understandable that she coddled him. But Amelia felt as if she learned more about the viscountess in that one look than their dozen past interactions. Something was there. Amelia identified with the motherly concern. It was the same concern she and Tabitha felt for Winifred.

"What he needs is fresh air and exercise," proclaimed Lady Hamsted. "I haven't seen him stir from that chair all morning." She set her shoulders. "I'm going to roust him." She gave a quick nod to Tabitha. "Enjoy yourselves, Lady Tabitha, Lady Amesbury."

"Thank you," they said in unison.

The viscountess walked directly over to Oliver and accosted him out of his peaceful read. Blinking, he scanned the lawn as if he hadn't noticed guests had been gathering in front of his eyes. Then he stood, stretched, and yawned, tucking his book under his arm.

"Thank you, dear husband, for pounding yet another nail in my coffin," Kitty muttered in Oliver's direction. Then she turned to Amelia and Tabitha. "At this rate, I'll be moved to the country by the end of the week."

Amelia sympathized with her friend. Changing the viscountess's mind seemed futile. "Keep hope, Kitty. Tabitha already put in a good word for you."

Kitty's voice lightened. "She does put stock in your opinion, Lady Tabitha."

"As she should," stated Tabitha.

The viscountess posted the croquet teams with a flourish of her well-manicured hand. Men and women came together like pieces of an elaborate puzzle, colorful and perfectly matched. Others, who were too old or too young, watched from the lawn chairs or the snow-white canopy that provided shade and refreshments. The revelers were in for a fine afternoon; the viscountess's croquet tournament was the event of the season.

As Amelia assumed, she and Tabitha were teammates. What she didn't anticipate were their opponents: Lady Jane Marsh and Lord Cumberland, two of George Davies's guests at the opera. Amelia spun around, scanning for Kitty in the crowd. Amelia found her, and Kitty gave her a wink. *Thank you*, Amelia mouthed. Kitty always helped at the event, and despite being waist-deep in her own concerns, she had taken the time to make certain Amelia could do a little investigating while participating in the tournament. *Twice as nice!*

"How good to see you both again," said Amelia. "This is my aunt, Lady Tabitha. Aunt, this is Lady Jane and Lord Cumberland. Lord Bainbridge and I had the pleasure of meeting them at *Rigoletto*."

Lady Jane had deep brown eyes with a sleepy quality that belied her watchfulness. Her impeccable social graces must have been learned from years of astute observation, and yet one wouldn't know it. She acknowledged Tabitha with a deferential bow. "Lady Tabitha. A pleasure to make your acquaintance."

"Your skills precede you." Lord Cumberland dipped his head, displaying his perfectly slim nose. "It's an honor to share the lawn with you."

"You might prefer to wait until after the game before bestowing such a compliment." Tabitha selected a mallet.

Lord Cumberland chuckled lightly, but he was trying hard to impress Tabitha, a society doyen. Amelia had seen it before and with men more worthy than Lord Cumberland. She shook her head. *They try harder to make an impression on my dear old aunt than on me, an available woman under the age of thirty.*

"It's been said that you won the first tournament four years ago, when the sport was in its nascency," Lord Cumberland continued.

Amelia stopped inspecting her mallet for deficiencies. "I didn't know that."

"I have a few secrets of my own, you know," Tabitha whispered. "You're not the only one who can be mysterious."

"I'm not myst—" Amelia muttered, then stopped. She most certainly was.

"Shall I select one, too?" Lady Jane's light fingertips brushed a row of mallets. An accompanying flutter of eyelashes told Amelia the woman had more interest in Lord Cumberland than the game.

One less competitor to worry about.

"Let me select one for you, my lady." Lord Cumberland took great care in browsing the mallets, his deft fingers grazing each one.

"It's a stick, not a diamond," grumbled Tabitha. "Pick one and be done with it."

Lord Cumberland grabbed the mallet his hand was on.

Amelia stifled a laugh. This was going to be a good game indeed.

Chapter 10

Dear Lady Agony,

My daughter has a most unbecoming character flaw. She is increasingly competitive, and playing games with her is turning into a chore. Old maid? She silently plots her win instead of conversing. Checkers? She sneers when one makes a wrong move. Chess? The board has been abandoned altogether in our house. No one wants to play with her, and I have a party coming up. What am I to do?

Devotedly,
Games Are Not the Same

. . . .

Dear Games Are Not the Same,

Having been caught up in winning a time or two myself, I can appreciate your daughter's assertiveness. Games are inherently competitive, but some are less so. For your party, may I suggest partner games? If your daughter is forced to work with another individual, it might lessen her competitive streak. (Or cause an uprising.) Keep me posted on her progress.

Yours in Secret,
Lady Agony

Four sets of doubles set out to conquer the six croquet hoops that wound elaborately—and challengingly—around the Hamsteds' expansive lawn to the final match, where the winning team would face the winning team.

Amelia was happy to report she and Tabitha were winning.

She glanced at Lady Jane and Lord Cumberland. *No surprise there.* Lady Jane was more interested in sniggering at her mistakes than making real progress. It was insufferable, and she wasn't the only one who thought so. Aunt Tabitha had interjected several times with, "Get a move on, hit the ball, and stop giggling!" Even Lord Cumberland was growing impatient with her bad play.

It was no use. She was focused on the pretty ribbons on her dress instead of her careless hits. The bows *were* beautiful, made of exquisite silk and artfully tied, and the ribbon at the top of her dome-shaped skirt accentuated her tiny waist. *But come now! No piece of clothing is more interesting than a game of croquet.*

Amelia knew one topic that would gain her attention: George Davies's murder. She seized the opportunity to bring it up when Tabitha became distracted by an acquaintance. "George Davies's death was an unexpected tragedy. Was it not? One moment we were seated at the opera with him, and the next, he was gone."

"Most unfortunate indeed." Lord Cumberland bent down, gauging the distance from the ball to the next hoop. "With

London's increasing street crime, however, it hardly comes as a surprise."

Lord Cumberland had a gift for saying the right thing yet nothing at all. Amelia guessed they could converse for hours, and she wouldn't know him any better than when they first began.

"A dreadful place to be after dark." Lady Jane sniffed. "I wasn't well acquainted with Mr. Davies, but Lady Marielle must be devastated. She knew him quite well. It was Mr. Davies who had connections to Lord and Lady Burton, such an affable pair." Lady Jane's eyes flicked open wider.

"But his other associate." Lord Cumberland stood up straight. "The man who bombarded our box was not fit company."

Amelia took a step closer. "You mean Mr. King?"

"I do." Lord Cumberland's smooth eyebrow made a perfect arch. "The fellow used the most colorful language, even in front of the ladies. Asking about money, of all things. Highly irregular, in my opinion."

Tabitha glanced over her shoulder, obviously regretting the pause in play. It looked as if she was making her excuses. Amelia pressed on quickly. "Money? Why?"

"Mr. King seemed to believe the box seats indicated undue extravagance on Mr. Davies's part." He narrowed his gaze on the lawn, determining his next move. "I ask you what business it was of his?"

No business at all—unless Mr. Davies owed him money.

Lady Jane tipped her head, the blue-green feather in her hat exceedingly pretty. "Lady Marielle explained that equines and money always go hand in hand. She's uncommonly knowledgeable about the sport."

Deciding on an avenue of approach, Lord Cumberland positioned himself behind his ball, taking a practice swing. "Lady Marielle knows horses. She is one of the best female riders in London."

Jane Marsh pouted as he hit the ball. "It must be the reason she and Mr. Davies kept close company."

Amelia wondered if she emphasized the word *close* for Lord Cumberland's benefit. Amelia guessed Lady Jane would rather he compliment her, not Marielle.

"He had nothing else to recommend himself, except a delightful sense of humor. All the ladies thought so." Lady Jane paused a moment to clap politely for Lord Cumberland as his ball sailed through the hoop.

A new idea entered Amelia's mind. Had Mr. Davies dallied with the wrong woman, a woman attached to a jealous man?

Lord Cumberland yielded the lawn to Amelia with a self-congratulatory bow. "Mr. Davies was a half-hour gentleman," he dismissed. "Those types cast a wide net and hope for any result."

Aunt Tabitha rejoined the group just in time to poke Amelia with her cane. "It's your turn."

She doesn't miss a beat. Amelia let go of the conversation and focused on the final hoop. One small smack of the mallet, and she and Tabitha would join the other winning group to face off for the prize.

She took a mind-clearing breath and closed one eye. *Line up. Center. Imagine the ball sailing through.*

Tap went the ball, clearing the hoop.

Amelia lifted her mallet in the air. "Yes!"

"Brilliant!" exclaimed Tabitha.

Lady Jane started at their enthusiasm. "My!"

Does she not know a prize is at stake?

Lord Cumberland held out his hand to Tabitha. "My sincere congratulations." He leaned in conspiratorially. "You are indeed a fierce competitor worthy of her reputation."

Tabitha preened at the praise. "Thank you, my lord."

He certainly knows how to compliment a woman, even a seventy-year-old woman.

"Yes, congratulations," added Lady Jane. "That was fun."

But by how quickly she turned to Lord Cumberland, Amelia knew Lady Jane would have much more fun when they were alone.

"On to the winner's circle for us." Tabitha handed Amelia her mallet so that she could use her cane to walk the distance.

After a few steps, Amelia whispered, "One down, three to go."

"Two, actually." Tabitha nodded at a pair sidelined at a garden table. "It looks as if the woman turned her ankle."

Amelia glanced at the woman unlacing her leather boot and the friend helping her. "That's too bad."

"For her." Tabitha's gray eyebrows shot up craftily.

Amelia's eyes wandered to Lord Cumberland. He had found Lady Jane a glass of lemonade. "Lady Jane is uncommonly pretty, albeit a bit of a goose."

"She'd better be pretty. It's all she has to go on this season—that, and her ancient name."

Amelia frowned. "No dowry?"

"Very little," Tabitha confirmed. "Her father, an earl, squandered it in the gaming halls. Some say even their country estate in Hampshire is at risk. The best they can hope for is a wealthy American to take her off their hands. I can't imagine any young Englishman being interested in her this season."

"Even Lord Cumberland?"

Tabitha chuckled. "*Especially* Lord Cumberland. He has no need for her title. He has his own. His only want is money."

Amelia took in the couple one last time. They would have made a handsome pair, pretty and pointless, had their circumstances been different. They would have drunk champagne at all the right dinner parties and laughed at all the right jokes. At the end of the day, they would have parted with a light kiss and breakfasted in the morning on dry toast and weak tea. It would have been a charmed life—for them.

"This crowd is an ocean, Amelia, and you've only dipped your toe in the water." Tabitha trudged forward, and Amelia followed. "You have a lot to learn. But not now. Now we play."

The first game was done in an instant. The players were just as determined as Amelia and Tabitha, and there was very little conversing, except, "Nice shot, your turn, go ahead." Only once did it get heated when a woman made a roquet, hitting Amelia's ball several yards out of the way. The next shot had to *move* or *shake* Amelia's ball, and it did not. The woman was convinced it did, and a small argument ensued over the word *shake*. Amelia and Tabitha agreed *quiver* did not mean the same thing as *shake* (one implied a vigorous movement and the other did not) and eventually, the woman admitted the fault, losing the game.

Amelia was happily surprised to find their final opponents were Kitty and Oliver. First, it would be unbecoming for them to claim the prize themselves, being related to the host, so whether they won or lost, the prize should come to Tabitha and Amelia. Second, she welcomed the opportunity to convince Oliver he needed to stay put in Mayfair. And as a writer who gave advice, she could be very convincing.

"If it isn't the extremely talented, extremely competitive Amesbury women," Oliver said. "I had a feeling we'd meet you here." His hat didn't match his jacket, probably an afterthought to keep the sun out of his eyes so that he could read, and his waistcoat was wrinkled in the middle from the weight of his book.

"Flattery will get you nowhere, I'm afraid, Mr. Hamsted." Tabitha laced and stretched her fingers. "Amelia and I play to win."

"What she said," seconded Amelia.

Kitty laughed. "You two are adorable."

But Amelia wasn't fooled by her compliment. Like parties, Kitty was good at croquet. Very good. She played it with the finesse of a bank clerk counting out five-pound notes. Carefully and quickly—and before her opponents knew what was happening. Amelia noted the sly wink Kitty gave to Oliver. They, too, wanted to win, if not for the famous Hamsted prize, then for the knowledge of coming in first place in the most anticipated croquet game of the season.

The viscountess announced the start of the final game, and side conversations quieted. A few guests refrained from sipping their lemonades. Children whispered.

Lady Hamsted walked to the prize table. "And now, friends, let us see what the couples will be playing for." She laid her hand on the gold cloth and smiled coyly, enjoying the attention.

As the viscountess tossed the cover aside, Amelia felt her breath catch in her throat. It was a towering masterpiece of chocolate bonbons. White icing, dark icing, pink sprinkles, yellow sugar. The pyramid was more beautiful than anything the Egyptians had built, at least in Amelia's mind. Her mouth practically salivated, and she began imagining what Winifred would say if she saw it. *When* she saw it, corrected Amelia, for she *would* be seeing it. Just as soon as Amelia and Tabitha won this game.

Kitty was up first, and as Amelia assumed, Kitty made quick work of her turn, the ball landing near a hoop. Tabitha was next and, with a precise stroke, made a shot of a woman half her age. As the ball sailed through the first hoop, Amelia stood in awe of the older woman. Her fortitude was nothing less than Spartan.

Oliver whistled. "Well done."

Tabitha nodded briefly.

Amelia turned her attention to Oliver. "I meant to ask you earlier, How is the new book?" The question had a dual purpose. It would distract him from his shot. But it might also lead to a conversation about not taking Kitty away to the country. Weren't the most recent reads found in London? It would take time to get them in Norfolk. Best he knew all the consequences of the move before making a decision.

"It's extraordinary." Oliver pushed up his round spectacles, which kept slipping because of the warmness of the day. "The author turns the Battle of Hastings on its head. In the first ten pages, he bravely purports . . ."

Amelia quit listening. Oliver's love of reading was admirable. She'd never heard him criticize a work. He enjoyed everything he read, and he read everything. That didn't mean she needed to endure a lesson on the Battle of Hastings, however. She could understand the sentiment without the history lesson. "How fascinating," she replied. "I suppose that's one thing you'll miss at the country house."

"What?" Oliver positioned his mallet near his ball.

She waited until he was ready to swing. "Books."

The ball veered to the right.

"Oliver!" Kitty scolded.

He ignored the reproach. "Why would I miss books? I'll have an entire library of them."

Dash it all. I didn't think of that. "Of course, *old* books. But no stores or libraries within—what would you say, Kitty? A five-hour journey?"

"Six," she corrected. "On a good day with fair weather."

"I don't remember it being that far . . ." Oliver thought out loud.

"I've known people to move to the country and never come back, even for the season." Tabitha surveyed the position of the balls on the course, not directing her comment to anyone in particular. "They simply do not return."

Amelia sighed. "Dreadful."

"We came every year," Oliver refuted.

But Amelia could hear the question in his voice and was glad to have put it there. Kitty would abhor country life, and so would he. Sure, he might have spent time in the country as a boy, but that was different. He was no longer interested in fishing ponds, and he'd never been fond of hunting. Kitty told her once that seeing him with a gun in his hand struck terror into her heart, for she was certain if he ever fired it, the shot would land him on the ground in complete surprise.

It was Amelia's turn. She glanced at the chocolate pyramid and the lie of her ball, and then she took a swing. The ball sailed through the hoop, and she let out a little exclamation before receiving a warning glance from Tabitha. Amesbury women did not celebrate early. They waited until they won.

Kitty pushed up her lace sleeves and stretched her neck from side to side. Then she hit her ball through the hoop, knocking

Amelia's ball into a pit in the yard. "I believe that earns me two more turns, does it not?"

Amelia huffed a breath. She knew very well it earned her two more turns. Everyone else knew it also and was clapping.

Kitty sailed another shot through the next hoop, officially taking the lead. Not to be outdone, Tabitha took close second with her turn. What happened next, however, would be debated at croquet tournaments for years to come.

Perhaps still distracted by their previous conversation, Oliver shuffled toward his ball, not paying attention to where he was walking. A few observers moved backward, affording him room, as his last play had put him in a difficult position. Most likely he was determining the force it would take to get his ball back into the game. He pushed up his glasses with one finger, gauging the distance. That's when it happened. His foot hit the ball, moving it almost imperceptibly.

Almost.

"That's play," Amelia announced. "His foot hit the ball."

"It did not," argued Oliver. "I haven't hit anything."

Tabitha joined in. "The ball moved. We all saw it."

Kitty blinked. "I saw nothing."

Amelia admonished her with a glare.

But Tabitha went right to judge and jury. "Lady Hamsted?"

The entire lawn was silent. What would she do? What *could* she do? She'd been summoned by one of the most respected women there, and she must answer. Would she uphold the rules of croquet, which she revered more than croquet itself? Or would she take the side of her clumsy son, whom she coddled and adored? It was her game. Her tournament. Her house. Whatever she said would be the law of the land.

The viscountess swallowed, a quiet gulping noise fleeing her throat. "Lady Tabitha is correct. The ball moved. It is her turn."

Amelia had the good grace not to cheer, laugh, or smile—all the things she wanted to do when the call was announced. No, she waited to do that until she and Tabitha won the game, which they handily did several minutes later.

Chapter 11

Dear Lady Agony,

Do all sweets cause skin distress? What about chocolate? My mother has forsworn me from both until the end of the season, but I don't think I'll make it. One hour in a crowded ballroom has me dallying at the dessert table. It's better company than most of my dance partners. I swear it's true.

Devotedly,
Candies Before Dandies

. . . .

Dear Candies Before Dandies,

Indeed, the dessert table makes pleasurable company. You need not nod, smile, or compliment it. Will frequenting it cause skin distress? Your mother certainly believes so, but I do not. I've eaten a pound of chocolates without so much as a single *blotch or blemish. Yet the cruel rumor persists. If you need a break, I say a trip to the dessert table you may take.*

Yours in Secret,
Lady Agony

The next day, Amelia was celebrating her win by pilfering the tower of chocolates prominently placed in the formal drawing room. *Just one more, then I'm off.* She selected a bonbon with intricate swirls of icing, admiring the design for a quick second before popping it into her mouth. The coating cracked into a rich creamy chocolate center, melting in her mouth. *Heaven.*

"How many is that today? Three or four?"

Amelia jumped. Usually, she could hear Tabitha's cane approaching. Not today. Amelia must've been too consumed by the sheer power of chocolate to notice impending doom creeping her way. She swallowed hastily. "Three, and what does it matter? It isn't as if I need to watch my figure."

Quite the opposite. She found herself stuck between young woman and old maid. It was a difficult position, to be sure.

"Every woman needs to watch her figure, Amelia." Tabitha walked to the tower of chocolates, snatching a polka-dot masterpiece. "Under the age of sixty-five, that is."

Amelia laughed. "We were a force to be reckoned with yesterday, weren't we?"

Tabitha chewed thoughtfully, a small smile playing on her lips. "We were."

"Even if Oliver hadn't touched the ball, we would have won."

"Certainly," Tabitha agreed. "Now, if Kitty had another partner, it might have ended differently."

Amelia dismissed the idea. "I'd bet on us every day and twice on Sunday." She gathered her beaded reticule. "Speaking of bets, I'm paying a call on Marielle Bainbridge." *Be careful*, she reminded herself. Tabitha didn't know she and Simon were investigating George Davies's debts—or death. "Have you been to their home? I have not."

"Many times." Tabitha selected a rose-colored chair that had a tall straight back that suited her own. She eased into the cushion, resting her cane beside her. "It's an architectural masterpiece. Very large with a formidable staff. The duke is rarely present, and Simon will do an excellent job in his absence. He feels responsible for Marielle, naturally. Now that she's out, he'll keep a careful eye on her."

That's putting it mildly.

"And then there's Miss Pimm." Tabitha's voice lifted in a way it rarely did. "Did you meet her at *Rigoletto*?"

"No . . ."

"A pity, but you'll certainly meet her today," continued Tabitha. "So bright, well educated. A sophisticate. She was a governess for the Cavendish family before coming to the Bainbridges. A charming woman with impeccable manners."

Amelia felt a prickle of jealousy dance up her spine. Tabitha had never lavished such praise on her or her staff. "I cannot wait."

"We might consider her when Winifred comes out."

"What—why? Winifred has me—and you," Amelia quickly added.

"A girl of Winifred's considerable wealth needs to guard against fortune hunters such as Mr. Davies." Tabitha's blue eyes flicked gray, like a cloud crossing a clear sky. "Which reminds me, I don't care for your early lone walks. No woman should be about alone in this city. Start taking Lettie with you."

Jones entered, announcing the carriage was ready.

"Or Jones," Tabitha added.

Ah . . . no.

"Goodbye, Aunt." Amelia made a hasty departure.

The Bainbridge mansion overlooked Berkeley Square, and Amelia silently seconded Tabitha's high praise. The house was regal, with a towering white facade and arched windows. Popping pink roses and pale peonies softened the entrance, adding an unexpected gentleness and grace to the stately property. The sweet smell enveloped the property like a lazy summer's day, beckoning one to linger a little longer than necessary.

Amelia noted a loving touch throughout the house as she was shown to the drawing room. There, she discovered a collection of poetry displayed on a desk under a window, highlighted by a filtered stream of sunlight. Being a reader and writer, she was drawn to the desk, running her fingers across the gold type of a collection of Shakespeare plays. Someone had read these books. Someone had loved these books.

"'Doubt thou stars are fire, / Doubt that the sun doth move, / Doubt truth to be a liar, / But never doubt I love,'" said a deep voice.

Amelia spun around to see Simon standing in the doorway. "*Hamlet.*"

"No, just Simon." A smile dashed across his face; then he shrugged it off. "They were my mother's favorite lines."

Amelia's hand hovered above the texts. "These were her books."

"Yes."

"I imagined so."

"Ah." He bridged the distance between them. "You didn't take me for a Shakespeare man."

"No."

His warm laugh washed over her. "You're right. I'm no poet. I admire your honesty, Amelia. I have since the first day we met."

The way her name sounded on his lips brought quivers to her bare arms. She stared at his lips, willing him to say it again, but he didn't. She pulled her eyes to his. "What was she like? Your mother?"

"She was incredibly kind and patient, like most mothers, I suppose. But she was different, too. A musician with an artist's temperament—and passion. She cared for a great many people and causes. You remind me of her, in a way." He picked up a likeness of her, framed in ornate gold on the desk.

The woman had thick, raven curls, peach-cream skin, and dark, mossy eyes. Amelia noted something remarkable in them, something the artist had captured for all eternity. Insight? Knowledge? Secrets? It was as if the portrait had life, and the woman's warmth was familiar.

"What is it?" Simon asked. "You have something you wish to say, obviously."

"She's beautiful." Amelia shook her head, unable to put her thoughts into words. "You and Marielle look so much like her. It's . . . uncanny."

He quirked a black eyebrow. "Are you saying I'm beautiful?"

"Yes— No." She could feel the fluster start at her toes, rustle her stomach, and bubble at her throat.

He laughed his warm laugh. "Which is it?"

"She's beautiful, and you have her looks, which isn't to say I notice your appearance. Because I do not. Actually, I don't even look at you." *Stop talking, Amelia.* "You're invisible to me."

"Me, too." Marielle breezed into the room, saving Amelia from further awkward comments. "Pretend he's not even here." She took Amelia's hands in hers. "Thank you for coming."

Simon stiffened. "I didn't realize you'd made arrangements."

Marielle motioned to the tufted settee. "Please excuse my brother." She selected a chair. "He has the bad habit of thinking everything pertains to him. I've ordered tea."

Amelia sat down. "Thank you."

"Dash it all, Ellie." Simon shoved his hands in his trouser pockets. He wasn't wearing a jacket, and his waistcoat emphasized his broad shoulders and narrow waist. "I did nothing wrong. I'm trying to help you."

Marielle's chair was upholstered in violet and white chintz, which made her dark dress even more startling. In the light room, it was an ink blot on the pretty things.

Marielle peeked around her brother's large frame. "It's incredible how some people define the word *help*, is it not?"

"Is Lady Agony better suited to assist you than your own flesh and blood?"

Amelia's heart dropped into her stomach. *Oh, Simon.* If she could have picked the words out of the air and shoved them back into his mouth, she would have.

Marielle shot out of her seat like a cannonball, glaring up at him. "And how would you know I wrote to the magazine?"

Simon looked to Amelia for help.

Amelia focused on her lap.

"Yes . . . well . . . I notice things." He cleared his throat. "Large things and small things. It's my duty as your older brother."

"Is it your duty to follow my correspondence? To spy on me?" Marielle's stormy eyes matched her dark dress.

Amelia watched the volley back and forth. Black hair, set jawlines, blazing green eyes. *They could be twins.* But Marielle seemed the more passionate of the two, perhaps because of her youth or his experience. Amelia could imagine Marielle's dark curls springing from her plaited coiffure any moment. Simon's demeanor, on the other hand, was cool confidence.

"What would you have me do?" he asked. "Allow you to run off to Gretna Green and ruin your reputation and this family's?"

Marielle jerked back as if bitten by a snake. "You scoundrel. You wretch. You horrible human being. You read my letter."

"Of course I read it, Ellie. I'm not going to apologize. I'd do it again." His voice wavered, and he swallowed hard. "The person lying dead on Drury Lane might have been you!"

The door opened, and a maid brought in tea.

"Let's sit down, shall we?" Amelia suggested, although she was already seated. "This looks lovely." It looked like any other tea tray in London, with tea, sugar, cream, and lemon slices, but no matter, that. She needed them to move past their accusations—and high emotions—if they were ever to find George Davies's killer.

Marielle plopped into the chintz chair.

Simon eased in next to Amelia.

Amelia beamed at the maid. "Wonderful."

Simon and Marielle continued glaring at each other.

When the maid was gone, Amelia searched for common ground. "Lady Marielle—you wrote to Lady Agony for advice. That much has been ascertained. I assume you respect her opinion. May I ask if she responded?"

"She said not to go." Marielle took a quick sip of tea, leaving the cup perched near her lips.

"And why is that?" Amelia gently nudged.

Marielle replaced the cup noisily onto the saucer. "Apparently, nobody thinks Gretna Green is a good idea, even the daring Lady Agony."

Daring. Amelia appreciated the adjective. "Did she give a reason?"

"She said my family might see something in my suitor I did not," Marielle grumbled.

"Ha!" Simon interjected. "She agrees with me."

"We cannot know with whom Lady Agony agrees or disagrees." Amelia added one more sugar cube to her cup of Earl Grey.

Simon lowered his lashes at her, his eyes turning smoky. "I think we can."

"You would be the last person to think for Lady Agony, Simon." Marielle uncrossed her ankles as if she might jump up and sock him in the arm. "You're a brute of a man. She's an autonomous woman with independent thoughts and ideas."

Although Amelia enjoyed hearing Marielle sing Lady Agony's praises, she knew they were not bringing the brother and sister any closer to reconciliation. In fact, Simon had taken another step in the wrong direction when he'd revealed that he read Marielle's letter. "Then we can assume Lady Agony's answer had merit. Might there be something to your family's concerns? Was Mr. Davies in any trouble of which you know?"

A large white clock ticked loudly as a minute passed.

"Possibly financial trouble," Marielle finally admitted. "Mr. King implied if Mr. Davies had money enough for the opera, it should have been spent elsewhere."

"Where?" Simon asked.

Marielle directed her answer to Amelia. "I don't know where. I assumed he owed Mr. King money."

Amelia remembered Mr. King was a bookmaker. "Did Mr. Davies belong to any clubs?"

Marielle named a popular jockey club. "Why do you ask?"

"It's an idea I have." Amelia sipped her tea. "He might have an outstanding balance there. It's an avenue for me to explore at any rate."

"*You?*" Simon paused, his teacup looking ridiculously small in his hands. "If an avenue exists, I must explore it. Women are not allowed in gentlemen's clubs."

"Which is nonsense," Amelia shot back.

"Utter rot." Marielle crossed her arms. "If anyone needs a refuge, it's women."

Simon took a breath. "Nevertheless, you need me, Amelia."

Amelia didn't disagree. She understood how well the words rang true.

Chapter 12

Dear Lady Agony,

Which is the greater sin, to lie or disobey one's parents? I look forward to your opinion.

Devotedly,
Are All Sins the Same

. . . .

Dear Are All Sins the Same,

As you know, I am not a priest. Nor a pastor nor a nun. If I were, I might point you to the Ten Commandments. Being a mere giver of advice, I can only mention their position on the divine list. Honor thy mother and father is fifth. Lying is addressed in number nine. You might use the ranking to determine their importance.

Yours in Secret,
Lady Agony

By the time Marielle, Simon, and Amelia had finished their tea, the conversation was almost cordial. And then the duke dropped in unexpectedly, and the animosity returned.

From the start, Christopher Bainbridge was not what Amelia expected. Like Simon, he was tall, but where Simon was mass and muscle, the duke was lean and agile, moving about the room like a very large cat. He had coarse blond hair, combed close to his head, and steel blue eyes. As he greeted his son, his stylish mustache twitched, giving him a devilish look she recognized in Simon.

Simon introduced her. "This is Lady Amesbury."

"It's a pleasure to meet you, Your Grace."

The duke acknowledged her with a warm smile. "Lady Amesbury, Edgar's widow. The pleasure is mine. Your late husband's service was commendable. He was one of the finest seamen I knew."

"Thank you." Amelia felt her insides warm at the compliment. Coming from a man whose family had dedicated themselves to Her Majesty's Royal Navy, it meant a lot.

The duke turned to Marielle, his brow furrowing as he glanced over her dress. "Why are you clothed like that?"

The warm feeling in Amelia's stomach curdled.

"Like what, Father?" Marielle tipped her chin, looking like a Greek warrior. Her voice held a challenge in it.

"In mourning clothes."

Marielle's tone turned as dark as her dress. "Our dear friend Mr. Davies was murdered two nights past. You must know he was knifed down the same evening we attended the opera."

"I do know, and it has nothing to do with you—personally. He was a former employee. That's all."

Marielle's lips parted, revealing surprise at his cool observation.

"We never treated him as such. You, most of all. How can you say such things?"

"Go change," the duke continued. "Please."

Marielle went from Greek warrior to chastened child. Simon reached for her hand, but she dismissed the action, sulking out of the room with only a bob toward Amelia.

When she was gone, Simon glared at his father. "Was that really necessary?"

"You know what he was. We both do." The duke was still staring at the door, a sadness in his eyes that Amelia could not name. He blinked it away before turning to Simon. "As much as it pains me to say so, Mr. Davies was a liar and a cheat. Why I ever let a man such as that into my confidence, I cannot say."

"I do not think it pains you at all." Simon's voice held a challenge. "I think you are glad he is gone."

The duke retrieved a timepiece from his pocket, staring at the watch's face. It was hard to know what he was thinking, the look impenetrable. Like Simon, he had the ability to mask his reactions. When he returned the watch to its place, his countenance was vague. "He will no longer be pursuing your sister, and that brings me relief. Surely, you share my sentiment."

"You and I share nothing."

Amelia winced. The comment was a blow to the duke, but if it affected him, he did not let it show. Instead, he let out a harsh chuckle.

"Ever righteous." The duke shook his head. "But I am not so righteous that I cannot admit that the murderer did us both a great favor." His eyes caught Simon's, and the gaze charged the room with electricity.

She sucked in a breath.

"I apologize if I've affronted you, my lady," he said. "I forget myself. Our families have gone back generations. I assumed I could speak plainly in front of you."

Their history didn't give him warrant to speak so freely in front of a lady, and she wondered at the language. Maybe he lost his temper, or maybe he wasn't as good at masking his reactions as she thought he was. "No apology necessary, Your Grace."

"That gives you no right, and you know it." Simon's hands were two fists at his sides.

A beat passed, and the duke's blue irises flashed navy. "You're such a boy, Simon. And a fool." He turned to Amelia. "It was truly a pleasure to meet you. Unfortunately, I have an appointment and cannot be waylaid." He made a gallant nod, giving her the look of a duke like an unexpected bouquet, before walking out of the room.

A great void was left by his absence. Silence conveyed what words did not. Where a father-son relationship should be, there was only hurt. It went deeper than Amelia realized. She wondered when the bad feelings began—and why.

She touched Simon's elbow. "Are you all right?"

"I'm fine." He unclenched his fists. "I'm sorry for his behavior. It seems even company can't censure his hatred of me."

"He doesn't hate you."

"You wouldn't know." The comment came out harshly, and he apologized again. "Let's refocus our efforts on Ellie. Shall we? Ours is one relationship that might be salvaged yet."

Amelia understood he was upset. Too upset to make sense of what had just happened. She nodded. "Marielle mentioned a possible debt. We know Mr. Davies was found with a good deal of money on his person. It may have had something to do with his murder."

His green eyes lightened, seemingly happy to be off the sore subject. "She also mentioned his club. Someone there might know about the obligation."

"We should go at once."

Simon ushered her out of the drawing room, down the stairs, and through the front door, where the June air hit her like a godsend. She hadn't realized how oppressive the house had become when the duke entered the room. Closing her eyes, she inhaled the soft scent of roses, allowing their freshness to wash over her like a spring rain. It was good to be rid of the heaviness.

When she opened them, she realized Marielle was also outside—and in a different dress. Following her father's advice must have stung, for she, like Simon, was bullheaded. Still, she looked prettier in soft gray than dull black, and more her age. She stood beside a woman and a man who was vaguely familiar.

Amelia guessed it was the perfect Miss Pimm before Simon's introduction left his mouth. Neither too young nor too old, she wore an understated peach dress and a spoon hat with deep orange flowers that accentuated her oval face. Her posture, like her appearance, was beyond reproach, and when she spoke, it sounded as if she were reciting a book of Lord Byron's poems instead of saying *good afternoon*.

"Delighted to meet you, Lady Amesbury." Miss Pimm dipped her head.

"And you remember Mr. Hooper," continued Simon.

"The son of the famous pirate capturer," Amelia said.

Mr. Hooper smiled at the remark.

"His brothers serve, also," Simon added. "I had the pleasure of sailing with his older brother Tobias for an entire year. A fearless man with an impeccable record."

"I'm the proverbial black sheep, I'm afraid," said Mr. Hooper. "An early bout of pneumonia left me in poor health and ruined my chances of service." His voice was quiet but steady, revealing a certain strength, like his eyes, which were steel blue.

"And *improved* my chances of gaining a friend." Marielle looped her arm in his, and his face brightened. "Mr. Hooper's been kind enough to agree to a ride in the park. Miss Pimm thinks it's a good idea to clear my head."

"Nothing better than fresh air to focus one's mind," Amelia agreed.

Marielle nodded. "It's best to stay out of the house when—"

"When the weather's such as it is," Miss Pimm supplied smoothly.

"Indeed." Marielle hiked an eyebrow in Amelia's direction, telling the story words couldn't. She didn't like being in the house when her father was home, and Amelia didn't need an explanation why.

"I can't think of a better way to spend the afternoon." Mr. Hooper indicated his house next door. "If my father had his druthers, I'd be stuck inside poring over the ledgers." He crinkled his nose. "I hate numbers, and I daresay it's all I'm good at."

Marielle pulled his arm forward. "Let us seek respite from our families in the park, shall we?"

"Present company excluded," Mr. Hooper said to Simon over his shoulder. "Goodbye, Lady Amesbury. It was nice to see you again."

A small smile lifted the corners of Miss Pimm's mouth as she watched them march off. "I knew it would be good for her to get out of the house."

"You know what's best," said Simon. "I cannot thank you enough for your devotion to my sister. Now that she's out, she needs your wise counsel more than ever."

Lady Marielle's debut had been a smashing success. Every

young man at the Smythe ball was eager to meet her. They weren't as eager to meet her overprotective brother, however. In fact, it was Aunt Tabitha who eventually made Simon back off the suitors. Her exact words had been, "Do sit down. You're making yourself a nuisance." Amelia had relished the older woman's power to do the unimaginable—make him behave.

"Thank you, my lord. I do my best." Miss Pimm tidied the bow of her hat. "Lady Marielle *does* like her horses." She sighed. "Any activity that involves riding improves her mood, and Mr. Hooper has such a pleasing temperament. It will be a fine afternoon."

"Enjoy the day," Simon said with a wave, and Miss Pimm hurriedly followed after the pair.

Simon and Amelia set off in the other direction, climbing into the Bainbridge carriage to inquire at the jockey club to which George Davies belonged. *Simon will complete the inquiry. I won't be allowed entry.* Frustrated, Amelia tapped her fingers against the handle of her parasol, wondering how she would pass the time. She'd figure out something.

Meanwhile, she needed to ask Simon about their conversation with his father. It had been awkward, to be sure, but if she adhered to the murder and not the angst, she might be able to reconcile the duke's comments.

"Your father stated the killer did both of you a favor," said Amelia. "And to some extent, he is right. The killer resolved the problem between Marielle and George Davies forever."

"She would have come to her senses—eventually. I know it."

Amelia was less certain. Marielle seemed secure in her devotion. "And if she hadn't? Would the duke have gotten rid of George Davies?"

Simon stiffened.

"If the idea crossed my mind, it surely crossed yours." Amelia caught his eye. "The toff mentioned by the bar wench? He could have been your father. His hair is light."

"You know I appreciate your honesty, Amelia. I understand it to be one of the reasons Edgar chose you for his wife." He lowered his voice. "But you cannot utter that suggestion to another living soul. I cannot guarantee the duke's actions if it gets back to him. He's fiercely protective of our family's name and legacy."

"Which seems like further evidence against him," Amelia added.

"Leave me to deal with my father. I promise, if he's done something wrong, I will be the first one to find it."

Maybe that was true, but not for the reason he mentioned. He was keeping a secret, too, and she'd been waiting for him to reveal it. The night of George's death, he'd removed an item from the scene of the crime. What was it, and why hadn't he told her? She studied his eyes. Around the emerald green iris was an amber ring, like a fire in a forest. Not perceptible until now. How many other enigmas might she discover if she looked deeper?

She wouldn't push him, yet. But she wouldn't ignore evidence, either. Marielle had come to her—Lady Agony—first. Instead of advice, she'd received a heartache greater than any broken engagement. If Simon was standing in the way of justice, Amelia would find out why.

Chapter 13

Dear Lady Agony,

Men's clubs are so very popular, and my husband frequents his nearly every day. His mother says my home's inadequacies are to blame, and if I made our house more hospitable, he might not leave so often. Is that true? And if so, how do I resolve to make it better? I have never cared for decorating, and needlework is a bore. Yet, I don't like sitting alone if I can help it.

Devotedly,
No More Needlework

. . . .

Dear No More Needlework,

Rest assured, your fingers won't suffer the prick of my advice, for what is it that makes a house a home? Is it the fabric in the corner or the paper on the wall? Certainly not. It's the

companionship one finds in the room, and I can only assume
you enjoy your husband's company, or you would not be writing.
So have an honest conversation with him. Ask him why he's
attending the club so frequently. If you don't care for his answer,
find a hobby that takes you out of the house. A taste of his own
medicine might be just what he needs—and resolve the problem
of your sitting alone.

Yours in Secret,
Lady Agony

Amelia didn't understand what all the fuss was about. The club on St. James's Street was like any of the other buildings except for the large bow window, which was *the* spot to see and be seen. If a man sat there, he was important. This afternoon, the curtains were closed, so she could see no one. But Amelia didn't need to gain entrance to know that beyond the plush barrier, men smoked, read, drank, and placed bets on everything from sporting events to social affairs. After all, the wealthy needed a way to spend their time—and money.

George Davies wasn't part of London's upper crust, yet he had something they wanted: knowledge. And knowledge was power—at least in Mr. Davies's case. He knew everything there was to know about horses: breeding, grooming, racing. His success had taken him far. Yet he craved more. He wanted it all, including the lavish lifestyle of the elite.

Amelia hitched a thumb over her shoulder, indicating the club. "Mr. Davies came a long way from the stables."

Simon surveyed the building beyond the window. "George Davies was motivated by money, plain and simple. His father was a blacksmith, an honorable man dedicated to an important trade. But George set his plan in motion the moment he began working for us."

"What plan?" she pressed.

His eyes snapped back to hers. "To embed himself into our family. The leisurely rides, the racehorses, the bets. They were all ways to ensnare my sister into a love match and my father into indebtedness."

"Your father must have enjoyed some success." Many titled men participated in the sport, hoping to win honor and glory for their families. And one of the men at the opera had mentioned the duke giving them a fighting chance next year with his retirement.

"With Mr. Davies's help, my father won the Derby two years ago, the pinnacle of his achievements. But he lost many more races than he won, investing a fortune in horses and training. It was mere months ago that the duke realized Ellie's affection for Mr. Davies and the consequence of having him around. He participated in his final race this spring."

Which brought Marielle's affection to a crescendo, hence her letter to Lady Agony.

He moved toward the carriage door. "I see you grasp the timeline."

"Yes." Without the duke in his life, George didn't have a reason to visit the Bainbridge mansion—or the duke's daughter. He no longer worked at the stables, and if he wasn't training the duke's horses, he'd have no reason for making frequent stops. The duke's action had brought forth a reaction, and they were all still reeling in its reverberations.

Amelia slipped on her gloves.

"Oh, no." Simon stopped. "You're not coming with me. We'd

never get past the front door nor find out anything of value about Mr. Davies. They'd be too busy escorting you out. *No* is my final answer."

The conceit of this man! "I wasn't considering the idea, although had I wanted to, I would find a way in. Be sure of it."

"I'm sure of many things," Simon retorted. "Your obedience is not one of them."

She glared at his back as he descended the carriage steps and walked into the club.

She craned her neck out the window. A person leaving the area caught her attention. Two people. One was tall and muscular with a neck full of veins. *Mr. King!* He was the intruder in George Davies's box the night of the opera. Mr. Wells had mentioned he was a bookmaker at the club. She pressed her face closer to the window for a better look. Could he be the fair-haired toff the waitress described? *Only one way to find out.*

Amelia crept out of the carriage, following them. She kept her steps light, her focus straight ahead. From this angle, it was impossible to tell what color the man's hair was. He wore a close-fitting hat with a silk band. She quickened her pace for a better look.

Tall men meant long strides, but she herself was a walker and had no trouble catching up to them. They spoke in low tones, and she strained to hear.

"Fine, but be quick about it. I have a race to be at." That was Mr. King, speaking in short staccato sentences. He walked with an aggressive gait, like a tiger.

"Not more than two minutes, boss." That was the other man, whose shorter legs put him at a distinct disadvantage. He was practically jogging to keep up with Mr. King.

The pair paused in front of a hat shop, and she skidded to a stop, stumbling a little but catching herself with her parasol. They were going inside. *What luck!* Mr. King would remove his hat, and his hair color would be one thing learned from the expedition. She gave herself an invisible pat on the back.

Mr. King glanced over his shoulder. Amelia zeroed in on a nonexistent wrinkle in her dress. In her haste, she hadn't been as subtle as she usually was. She and Kitty had been known to slip through the smallest crack in a fence undetected. Or Kitty had. Amelia's hips were a little too wide. The point was, they had gotten the information they needed, and Lady Agony was able to out one of the worst dressmakers in London. Since then, the dressmaker paid her seamstresses twice as much in wages and provided comfortable lodgings as well.

Amelia was disappointed to learn the person picking up a hat was not Mr. King but the man with him. He was retrieving an indulgent top hat that was way too tall for his small face, but he seemed pleased with the purchase. Mr. King, on the other hand, regretted the delay and hurried him along.

Her eyes flicked to a pair of self-important men making their way toward clubland, no doubt. Their voices held a congratulatory tone for who knew what reason. *Probably being born.* Simon would be departing Mr. Davies's club soon, and time was running out. If only she could summon the wind like Zephyrus, lifting Mr. King's hat off his head. She tapped the handle of her parasol, thinking. An idea came to her. Like Tabitha's cane, she suspected her parasol might have magical powers.

When Mr. King came out, she would open the parasol, accidently knocking off his hat. His hair color would be revealed, and she would have an opportunity to talk to him. *Question him.*

The plan went off pretty much as she anticipated, except she poked Mr. King in the face, and his hat didn't fall off but moved backward enough to reveal his hair color, which she would call light brown. Not exactly fair, yet not brunet, either. An unremarkable discovery.

"I'm sorry, sir," Amelia apologized. "Please forgive my clumsiness. The sun is growing warm, and I needed shade."

Mr. King pulled his hat low over his forehead. His face was gaunt, and his eyes were hard black pebbles. His cheek twitched as if he was physically controlling his response. "Excuse me—" His eyes widened briefly. "I know you. I've seen you before." His voice removed any notion of courtesy.

She dipped her parasol over one shoulder. At least she had one bit of luck—an entry into conversation. "Oh? Where was that? Perhaps you can refresh my memory."

"I never forget a face."

"That's right. You never have," his friend agreed.

Mr. King chastised him with a look before returning to Amelia. "You were at the opera with Simon Bainbridge."

"Yes, of course." She feigned surprise. "Forgive me for not recognizing you sooner. You were with his sister and Mr. Davies. For a short time."

"His sister." Mr. King slid a sly look at his friend. "That explains it."

"Explains what?" She noticed his friend took a step closer to her.

"It was Bainbridge's sister who was caught up with Davies, and Davies owed me money."

She stepped back, wishing she hadn't divulged the familial relationship. "George Davies is dead. He was murdered the night of the performance."

"I'm aware, but that don't mean I'm not owed money." Mr. King's black eyes narrowed on her. "Why were you following me?"

"I was doing nothing of the sort." Even though she was on lovely St. James's Street on a bright afternoon, it felt as if she were in a dingy, out-of-the-way tavern. "I'm on my way to the cheesemonger. For . . . cheese." She cleared her throat. "Why did Mr. Davies owe you money?"

"For the same reason he owed everyone money. He wouldn't lay off the horses. Thought he was gold, he did."

His friend snickered. "No Midas touch in that one."

"He bet on a horse race?"

Mr. King jerked his chin at her, talking to his friend. "Listen to this one and her questions." He dropped his smile as he turned to her. "I have a question for you, little lady. Who is Bainbridge to you?"

His hard eyes turned the blood in her veins to ice, and an inkling of fear froze her limbs. "Lord Bainbridge? Oh, he's nothing to me. An old family acquaintance. Hardly that, even. I don't know him well at all." She swallowed.

"That's somewhat disappointing," said a deep voice behind her.

She spun around to meet Simon, just succeeding at not throwing her arms around his neck. Her fear inched backward. "Sim—my lord!"

He crossed his arms, putting an end to any notion of an embrace, and aimed a reply at Mr. King. "I heard my name. What is it I can help you with, gentlemen?"

"Me and your friend here were just talking about a mutual acquaintance, George Davies." Mr. King's voice was a low growl, and Amelia understood a war was being waged with the sound.

"As she stated, she's not a friend, and Mr. Davies was no acquaintance of mine."

Well, that's uncalled for.

"An acquaintance of your sister's, then," corrected Mr. King.

"Again, I'll ask, what is it you require from me?" Simon dodged the claim, refusing to acknowledge his sister had anything to do with Mr. Davies. Amelia was impressed by his steadiness under the threat of the crook. He would not be intimidated, even by an intimidating man.

"Your sister's friend owed me money," Mr. King explained. "A thousand pounds, to be exact."

The same amount that was in his pocket, Amelia thought. Was George Davies going to pay off his debt to King, and how had he come by the money? It was too much of a coincidence not to make a connection.

"Are you asking me for a thousand pounds?" Simon was blunt.

"I'd never ask such a thing." King jeered at his friend. "It wouldn't be gentlemanlike."

His friend guffawed.

"But Davies was no gentleman, and I can't see as any decent family would want their kin connected to his name." The cold look in King's eyes was back. He had no shame—and no fear. It didn't matter that he was in the middle of St. James's, speaking with a marquis. He would get what was owed to him, somehow.

Simon replied with a dangerous look of his own. "I don't take well to blackmail, and certainly not in the presence of a lady." He held out his arm to Amelia. "May I escort you home?"

"Y-yes," she stammered.

They turned in the direction of the carriage.

"Remember what I said, Bainbridge," King called out.

Simon didn't reply.

Chapter 14

Dear Lady Agony,

My friend and I, who are bachelors, have a disagreement and wonder if you might clear it up. Could you tell us, are you married? He says you are, and I say you aren't. I can't imagine any man in his right mind marrying you. I'd have your head on a stake before I'd see your letters printed. At any rate, let us know. We can't see how telling us will disclose your identity.

Devotedly,
No Wife of Mine

. . . .

Dear No Wife of Mine,

What an unpleasant thought from an unpleasant person. As I prefer my head on my neck, I think I'll keep the answer to myself. But I will give you some solicitous advice. Women

don't like being told what they can and cannot do. Talk less,
listen more, and you might find an actual wife instead of
censoring a hypothetical one.

Yours in Secret,
Lady Agony

"I cannot believe you refused to acknowledge our friendship."
Amelia had waited only for the carriage door to shut before
chastising Simon. "King might have killed me and left me for
dead. It would have made no difference to him—or you, apparently."

"You madcap." Simon tugged off his gloves. "The leeches
might rid you of your passion. You must know I was going along
with your proclamation. You should have never left the carriage.
You promised you wouldn't."

"I promised I wouldn't enter the *club*," Amelia corrected. "I
saw King, and I had to follow him. It was my only chance to find
out his hair color."

"And did you?"

She swished the answer around in her mouth, not wanting to
let it out.

But Simon was a patient man and would wait until the
Thames froze over for an answer.

"It's brown," she stated. "Light brown. Brown with some
blond in it."

"That helps considerably."

She jerked her chin. *How dare he criticize my efforts.* They
wouldn't have learned what they had without her quick action,
and it was much more than they had an hour ago.

Simon leaned in. "Furthermore, I didn't acknowledge our

friendship because I didn't want King coming after you. As you witnessed, the man's not beyond harassing a woman, and if he gets nowhere with me, he might try his chances with you."

It made sense. *Simon always makes sense.* "Do you think he'll press you for the money?"

"I do."

"Will you give it to him?" she asked.

"Never." He leaned back. "It would be an acknowledgment that Marielle did something wrong, and she did not. Besides, he wouldn't stop at a thousand pounds. He would continue to force payments from me and my family."

"But what about Marielle? He implied there would be . . . rumors about her." She hated saying the words aloud, but Marielle's reputation might be in danger if they didn't act swiftly.

"Then he will face the consequences of such rumors." His jaw clenched. "Personally."

Any brother would have defended his sister's honor. Of course he would have. But Simon didn't obey conventions, and neither did Mr. King. That knowledge made the situation implicitly more dangerous.

She changed topics. "What happened at the club? Did you find anything there?"

"I did," said Simon smugly.

She tapped her toe. He was testing her patience today. "And?"

He settled into his seat, crossing his arms. "And I can see why you're not married. Patience is not your strong suit, and it's practically a requirement of the institution."

"Me?" she huffed. "I've *been* married, and remember how that turned out. You, on the other hand, won't even condescend to kiss a woman since the *fabulous* Felicity Farnsworth." She rolled her eyes. "And heaven forbid actually courting one. Why, I've seen salamanders warmer than you—"

Simon interrupted her harangue by taking her hand and kissing it firmly. His green eyes were teasing. "There."

She glanced at her hand, where the feeling of his lips still lingered. He wouldn't get off the hook that easily.

"Not quite." She kissed him then, her lips brushing over the mystery that was Simon Bainbridge. A mystery she'd wanted to uncover since forever. Or at least a month.

Time seemed to stand still as she relished the discovery. Soft, smooth, salt-swept. Like an ocean wave. *Exquisite.*

He pulled her closer, his arm stealing around her waist. Her lips parted in surprise, and the kiss deepened. His warm mouth heated every inch of her, starting with a tingle on her lips and radiating throughout her body. She understood the danger now, why he'd held back. The feeling was electric. It loosened every inhibition and made her wish for more. More of this. More of Simon. Which would never happen.

She pulled back, opening her eyes.

He stared at her. "Now are you satisfied?"

"No." The honest answer shot out before she had a chance to check it. She slapped a hand over her mouth. How was it that she lost all inhibition when she was with him? The careful responses, the correct actions, the meticulous manners. Everything Tabitha had taught her flew out of her head the moment she saw those bottle green eyes and reckless smile. It was like she was home, but a new home. A home where she could be herself absolutely.

"Do you have to know everything, Amelia?" The question seemed to really bother him. "Is it in you to leave *anything* alone?"

"I'm a naturally curious person." She touched her lips as if they were someone else's. "But just one question, and I'll leave off the subject. I promise."

He closed his eyes and, after a second, nodded.

"Are all kisses like that?"

He was coming up with the right answer, the reasonable answer, but she just wanted an honest answer. After what appeared like an internal debate with himself, he answered. "No."

"Would you say it was better or worse?" she prodded.

"That's two questions."

It was better than the kisses she'd sneaked with boys behind the inn, but that was an eon ago. And her kisses with Edgar didn't even register. They'd been friends, not lovers.

He turned the question on her. "What do you think?"

She thought back to the moment, tapping her chin. "I'm afraid I don't have adequate experience. I was married to a sick man who turned much sicker. Our pastimes included cold cloths and bone broth. Not exactly a friendly environment for romance."

Her answer seemed to pain him, and his face darkened momentarily. His green eyes turned smoky, concealed by thick black eyelashes.

"But I think it was warm. Sweet . . . *Thrilling*."

He studied her lips as if physically recalling the kiss. "I think I agree with you."

She left off the questions then. She didn't want any more answers. Actually, she did, but knew only one way to truly find out, and that wasn't going to happen. At least not with Simon Bainbridge. And he was the only man who brought these ideas to the surface. He was the only man she'd been close to since Edgar's death. And even before, if she was honest.

"So, the club." She cleared her throat. "You were about to tell me everything."

This time, he didn't jest. He explained that George Davies's gambling habit well exceeded his income. Not only was he in debt at the club, he also owed money to several individuals, one whom they knew already: Thaddeus King. The only reason Davies was still a member was a recent bet against a horse favored to win the Derby. He bet instead on a little-known horse called Bright Eyes, who took first place. It was a great upset, and everyone wondered at his luck. Except Samuel Wells, the owner of the favored horse. He had a notion that George somehow injured the animal during a training session.

That was one question, at least, to which she could find an answer. "Samuel Wells. He was at the opera the night Mr. Davies was murdered."

"Indeed. He breeds horses at his country estate, south of London, but is in town for the season." Simon steepled his fingertips. "His champion horse lost, and with it all hopes of reward. He had a good reason for wanting Davies dead." His face lifted. "This might be the break that puts me in Marielle's good graces."

"And brings Davies's killer to justice," she added. "A man was murdered. Remember that this isn't just about you."

"How could I forget?" he questioned. "You remind me at frequent intervals. What you conveniently overlook is the fact that the man was a scoundrel, and we continue to find evidence of that at every turn. Why won't you admit it?"

Part of her wanted to believe he wasn't a scoundrel. Part of her wanted to believe it was Simon's prejudice. George Davies had been allowed into London's upper echelons, and how? Through hard work and perseverance, something she understood. But she'd seen his behavior at the opera—and his roving eye. She knew what he was. "Scoundrel or not, Marielle deserves an answer. I will find her a resolution. And closure."

They rode the rest of the way to Mayfair in silence. It wasn't until Simon helped Amelia out of the carriage that they noticed Mr. King following them in a hackney cab. Seeing him there in the open conveyance made her stomach lurch. It was no secret where she lived, but having King know her address bothered her. It bothered Simon, too. He took several large steps toward them, but the driver turned the corner just at that moment, and the hackney disappeared.

Simon returned to Amelia. "He's following us."

"You knew he would."

He shook his head. "I knew he would harass *me*. I didn't know he'd harass you."

"Perhaps it was on his way home." Amelia gave him a small smile, trying to lighten the mood with a joke.

It didn't work.

He clasped her arm, leading her protectively to the front door. "Be careful, Amelia. If anything should happen to you—"

"—it won't." She raised her parasol. "Rest assured, I'll be on guard for the unpleasant Mr. King."

That didn't mean she wouldn't be acting on the latest information on Mr. Wells, however. There was one place a horse lover was sure to be spotted during the London season, and that was Rotten Row. Even as she bid Simon goodbye, she was devising a plan to go.

Rotten Row was the place to see and be seen in London May through July. Men and women dressed in their finery, promenading up and down the sandy track in Hyde Park in high fashion. There, horse enthusiasts showed off everything from riding skills to riding habits. Amelia had known women to pressure friends for introductions to tailors after spotting an original garment or particularly beautiful fabric. It was what tailors hoped for, despite already working long hours. One mention of his creations could bring him business for years to come.

Kitty's tailor, indeed, was in very high demand.

Which is why I require her help with my plan.

It would be easy to recruit Kitty, who liked participating in her inquiries. Plus, Kitty was eager for Amelia to try anything *fashionable*. She rarely did anything vogue. Amelia was dining at Kitty's house this evening, with Lord and Lady Hamsted. She was looking forward to a hearty meal, a hefty glass of wine, and a nice visit.

Two hours later, however, she could hardly describe the visit as *nice*.

Oliver was still sore about her and Tabitha's win at the croquet tournament and took little jabs at her throughout dinner. At one point, he accidently brushed her wine goblet and asked, "Oh no! Does that disqualify me from dessert?" She fanned the flames by replying, "Yes, and whiskey and cigars, too."

Kitty covered a smile with her napkin, and Amelia fought off a bout of laughter. Oliver was being a bad loser. He didn't care a whit for the game, preferring books to sports, so what did it matter to him? He'd lost fair and square. His mother would have never made the call if it wasn't just. She was *always* correct.

Lord Hamsted joined the laughter, but without warning, his amusement turned into coughing, and he reached for his water.

"Dear, are you all right?" Lady Hamsted sounded little like herself just then. Her cool, nasal voice turned high-pitched, and seconds later, she pushed back her chair. "Oliver! Help him."

Oliver's father put out his hand to let his son know he was fine.

"Are you certain?" Oliver asked.

His father nodded, patting his throat.

"He's fine, Mother," Oliver assured. "Something went down wrong. That's all."

Lady Hamsted stared at her husband. "Are you sure?"

Lord Hamsted nodded again, taking a sip of water.

Amelia had never known the viscountess to lose her composure. Her level of concern for her husband was surprising. The Hamsteds were an aristocratic family. Amelia was sure they loved one another, but they never showed it, and certainly not in public. But the viscountess was anxious for her husband, and while she might have been embarrassed by her overreaction now, the moment had endeared her to Amelia. No longer was she a cold-blooded amphibian and society mouthpiece; she was a caring wife and mother, too.

At least for a few minutes, until she started speaking again.

"What is the status of your packing? It appears as if you might need help." Lady Hamsted's intelligent eyes bounced from wall to wall.

Kitty hazarded a glance at Amelia. "You only informed us of the move a few days ago."

"The estate needs repair immediately." Lady Hamsted sipped her wine. "There is no time to lose."

"The roof," Lord Hamsted added, clearing his throat. "Rain's coming in the south corner."

Oliver smiled at his father. "It always gave us trouble."

"It did." He and his son shared a smile, looking more alike than Amelia had first realized. "With upkeep, though, the estate will last for another hundred years."

Obviously, the estate meant a good deal to the viscount. Why was he so eager to leave it?

After dinner, the women retreated to the drawing room, the viscountess making a detour to powder her nose. Amelia seized the opportunity to tell Kitty her new plan.

Kitty was delighted. "I adore Rotten Row, and you never want to go. I have a brand-new riding habit I've been dying to wear. Cashmere blue, Hungarian basque. And the cut—so smart and practical." Seeing Amelia's uninterest, she waved her hand. "Never mind. You'll see it tomorrow."

"I'm glad you're amiable to the idea." Amelia smiled.

Kitty linked arms with Amelia. "When it comes to your investigations, I don't have much choice."

Chapter 15

Dear Lady Agony,

I'd like to visit Rotten Row, but no one will ask me. I haven't been blessed with a good face or figure, and my clothes are last season's. If my fate doesn't change, I will never see the track from the top of my horse, which is a shame since he is a skilled beauty, and I am an excellent rider. How might I entice a gentleman to take me?

Devotedly,
Rotten Row, Can't Go

. . . .

Dear Rotten Row, Can't Go,

You most certainly can go. What is preventing you? Your figure and face? Last time I heard, neither was required to ride a horse. Nor was a gentleman. Saddle up, silly girl, and go.

You might just catch a man's fancy with your skill, and if you don't, no matter. You will have a good time still.

Yours in Secret,
Lady Agony

The next day was the kind of summer day that happened once in a season. The sky was cloudless, bright azure blue with strong streaks of yellow sunshine. Perfect weather for a noonday ride on Rotten Row—after Amelia dashed off a quick note to her editor, Grady. Suffice it to say her last response didn't go over well with male readers, and she had to make her explanations.

She tucked the note into the envelope, giving it a stamp of sealing wax. Even cheap papers pandered to male readers, despite the majority of the column's audience. Amelia had news for them: women's problems were important, too. And the magazine and her column provided respite.

"Are you busy?"

Amelia looked up from her desk to see her own dear Winifred standing in the doorway. "I'm never too busy for you."

Amelia rushed over to give her a hug, taking a moment to savor the smell of strawberries that always followed the girl. She looked so much like an Amesbury with her fair hair, ice-blue eyes, and long lashes. She might have been Amelia's own daughter had she and Edgar decided to have children before he passed. Yet, she and Winifred were as close as any mother and daughter, their relationship as strong as blood. They'd weathered the tragedy of her parents' and Edgar's death together and grown close in a short amount of time.

Now, however, Winifred pulled back.

"What is it? Do I smell? Please tell me I don't. I'm riding in the park with Mrs. Hamsted in a quarter hour, and she has very exacting standards."

Winifred giggled. "It's not that. Beatrice and I are going to Kensington Gardens, and I don't want to be wrinkled."

"And you won't wrinkle in the park?"

"We're not *playing*." Winifred spoke the word as if the activity were beneath her.

"What are you doing, then?"

Winifred's eyes widened with excitement. "Lord Grey is taking his model sailboat to Round Pond. It's well known for being the best and fastest boat on water. We're going with him."

"Oh, I see." But Amelia didn't see what was so special about Lord Grey's sailboat. "I'm not sure if you know, but I'm fairly good with boats. I haven't made one in some time, but I could build something in a jiffy." Amelia's questionable construction skills flashed in her mind. It was her little sister Margaret who was good at building things. "Or buy something," Amelia added.

Winifred bit her lip. Was she holding back a laugh? "Another day. You have your ride with Mrs. Hamsted, and Lord Grey is taking us for ice cream afterward."

Amelia scowled. A boat race and ice cream? The bar had been set.

"You don't mind, do you?" Winifred asked.

"Of course I don't, dear. I hope you have a wonderful day. Perhaps next time, I can take you and Beatrice for a girls-only afternoon."

"Would you?" Winifred stepped closer, lowering her voice. "Me and Bee would love to go to Fleet Street."

"Bee and *I*," Amelia corrected. "And what do you want with Fleet Street?"

"It's the heart of the literary world, and Bee likes books." Winifred checked the door, presumably making sure Tabitha wasn't hovering outside. "Sweeney Todd? His barbershop was on Fleet Street, you know."

"And your mother is the person you ask to take you past a murderous—albeit fictional—barbershop?"

Winifred blinked. "Yes?"

Amelia laughed and tweaked her chin. "I love you, Winifred."

"I love you, too."

The butler interrupted, clearing his throat. "Mrs. Hamsted is here, my lady."

"Thank you, Jones." Amelia walked with Winifred to the hallway. "Be on your best behavior."

"I will." Winifred turned and skipped up the stairs, past Tabitha, who was standing on the landing.

"Rotten Row at the fashionable hour?" Tabitha descended slowly like a bird of prey. "What has you forgoing luncheon for that spectacle?"

"Kitty Hamsted," Amelia said. "She has a new riding habit she insists on displaying." Amelia rummaged through her memory, trying to remember the details. "Blue cashmere, Hungarian basque—"

Tabitha held up her hand. "That woman and her clothes. It's a wonder Mr. Hamsted has a halfpenny left for books. I imagine she's anxious to wear it in the unlikely event she's forced to leave London. Has she made any headway with the Hamsteds?"

"I'm afraid not." Amelia adjusted her hat, a green beauty that dipped low on her forehead. On one side was a sweeping blue feather that matched her necktie. "In fact, last evening, Lady Hamsted asked why she hadn't begun packing. Repairs are needed at the estate, and she wants them done this summer. If something doesn't change, the move might happen sooner than we think."

"Be patient." Tabitha readjusted Amelia's hat, tipping the brim slightly. "Enjoy your time together today. It may be an opportunity to prove Mrs. Hamsted's value in London."

"Yes!" exclaimed Amelia. "Rotten Row is the perfect place to exhibit Kitty's riding skills. And I'm a decent horsewoman myself. I took the blue ribbon twice in Mells."

Tabitha put a hand on Amelia's shoulder. "London is not Mells, and Marmalade is not Rotten Row caliber. He trots instead of canters. You'd do better to take one of the other horses."

A twist of anger surged through her. She and Marmalade were friends. To leave him behind would be the ultimate betrayal. "I will do nothing of the sort."

Tabitha shook her head. "Stubborn girl."

Stubborn yourself, she retorted safely inside her head. What she said out loud was, "Goodbye, Aunt."

Tabitha muttered a farewell, and Amelia was out the door, her groom in tow, to greet the day and Kitty, whose riding habit was more stunning than she described. *Or I didn't listen carefully enough.* The blue cashmere was supple, and the sleeves closed at the wrist but slashed midarm, displaying a white and black undersleeve. Her hat also displayed black and white plumes and was tipped at the perfect angle to highlight her bright eyes, the angle Amelia had tried and failed at. Atop a black Spanish mare, Kitty was indeed a vision.

"If I looked as pretty as you do on a horse, I would ride every day." Amelia's groom helped her into her saddle, and Amelia patted Marmalade's neck, a warm chestnut color. *You are pretty, too, dearest. Never mind what horrible Aunt Tabitha said.*

"You're no slouch yourself in emerald. Where have you been hiding that habit?"

Amelia smiled a secret smile as they set out for Hyde Park. "It's new."

Kitty's brow furrowed. "You went shopping without me?"

"Don't be angry. I saw the material in the tailor's window, and I had to stop." Noting Kitty's protestations, she hurried along. "I know how much you love the color on me and would approve the purchase."

Kitty's face relaxed a little. "It's divine with your skin tone."

"How did last night end? Did Oliver's mother start removing portraits off the walls and packing them into crates?"

"Very nearly," Kitty said. "I don't understand why she's adamant about the move happening in the middle of the season."

The estate was a gift to Oliver, a large gift that involved a major change. It wasn't something that could be undertaken without planning and consideration. The staff were maintaining the property; it was being cared for. What was the viscountess's motivation for moving now? "Neither do I, Kitty. Maybe today's promenade on Rotten Row will convince her you need to remain here in London. I'm certain the Hamsteds' popularity will triple when everyone sees you in that dress."

Kitty smiled demurely. "Let's hope so."

They left off the subject as they entered the park. Rotten Row had eyes and ears, and people gathered at the fence line to watch the spectacle. Ladies and gentlemen paraded down the sandy bridle way on the south side of the park on black horses, white horses, and bay horses, the horseflesh as diverse as the costumes. Open chaises, moving fashionably slow, displayed riders in top hats, straw hats, and ostrich plumes.

Amelia and Kitty slowed, too, looking for Mr. Wells. With

a penchant for fancy dress, he should have been easy to spot—except in this crowd. Dandies were out in droves. Towering top hats, fancily knotted cravats, brilliant waistcoats. Even Mr. Wells's red opera cape might not have distinguished him here.

Unfortunately, the slow pace allowed for their approach, and they were delayed by several ladies asking after their tailors. Or Kitty's tailor. Still, Amelia was awarded several compliments. After two years of mourning garb, it was nice to have her wardrobe praised.

Waiting for Kitty to finish with a young woman, Amelia caught a strong whiff of cigar and spirits. She turned in time to see Thaddeus King trot past with Lord Burton. As they did, Mr. King touched the tip of his hat and smiled, one of his teeth shining gold.

"Lady Amesbury."

Amelia didn't acknowledge him. She was too afraid for Marielle to be afraid for herself. What was Mr. King doing with Lord Burton? They were both fans of horse racing. It must be the reason. Yet the Burtons were incredibly influential. Mr. King might say something to Lord Burton about Mr. Davies and Marielle. He might try to harm her reputation with gossip.

"What was that about?" Kitty asked.

Amelia waited a few paces before she answered. "That was Thaddeus King, the man I told you about."

Kitty watched them for a beat. "I don't like that he's here."

"Nor will Simon."

Kitty turned to Amelia. "Do you think the meeting has anything to do with his sister?"

"It might."

Kitty swallowed. "Or you?"

Amelia reached out and patted Kitty's gloved hand, attempting to assuage her friend's fears. "No." Then Amelia picked up her reins. "Come along—and do try to look less pretty. We have much ground to cover, and if one more person stops us for your tailor's name, I'm going to scream."

They rode several minutes, scanning every rider. Tall, short, handsome, homely. Good riders. Bad riders. Riders who shouldn't own horses. All were in attendance, but where was Mr. Wells? They glanced into carriages, from the very old to the very new. Amelia was starting to wonder if they'd forgotten what he looked like when they passed a group of noisy picnickers. A man in a green hat caught her notice. She squinted and asked Kitty if she recognized him.

"Yes." Kitty spurred her horse on. "That's his voice."

Amelia followed Kitty's lead. Mr. Wells's voice had a tinny quality that wasn't exactly pleasing but was distinct. It carried well, as did his cologne, a bright sandalwood that was too strong to be natural. As they approached, it settled over them in a fragrant cloud.

"Mrs. Hamsted, Lady Amesbury." Mr. Wells smiled. "What a pleasure to see you here." Perfectly poised and dressed in a green coat, a white cravat tied to one side, close-fitting white breeches, and yellow kid gloves, he looked as if he should be painted for a portrait. He had the fine features for it, including a shapely nose and distinguished chin. He also had a passion for horses.

"And you as well," replied Amelia. "Your steed is magnificent."

He coaxed his white gelding into a high step. "Thank you. He took the Derby five years ago."

"And this year's Derby?" Amelia asked.

His forehead was high and smooth, but consternation creased it now. "You've heard about that. Yes, Dancer is my pet project. A gorgeous animal, as graceful as he is strong. I carefully planned his debut, pouring every ounce of time and money I had into his training. He is built for winning. And he would have won this year if I'd been more attentive."

"What happened?" asked Kitty.

"I suspect he was injured by our dearly departed Mr. Davies just before the race." Mr. Wells sighed. "It's rude to speak ill of the dead, but I should've never let him on my horse. His training program was commendable, but he was too friendly with Bright Eyes's owner. That's the horse that won this year's race. Rather convenient, if you ask me."

Amelia stopped. "What are you suggesting? He injured your horse on purpose so that Bright Eyes would win?"

He stopped as well. Good manners prevented him from allowing his horse to pull ahead of theirs. "Mr. Davies wasn't above using any means or method to win. It was how he got where he was. Did he injure Dancer on purpose?" He shrugged. "He's gone now, so we'll never know for certain. But I do have my suspicions."

Although he seemed unperturbed, Amelia wondered. He, like Mr. Davies, enjoyed winning a good deal.

"Now, *your* horse, Lady Amesbury." Mr. Wells cleared his throat. "He's an interesting fellow."

Amelia tipped her chin. "He's faster than he looks. We won two blue ribbons a few years ago."

"You mean ten years ago?" Kitty swallowed a chuckle. "Against Clydesdales?"

Mr. Wells shared the laugh.

"Not Clydesdales," Amelia fumed. "Swift horses, like yours."

"I know you love Marmalade, but he's older now. He couldn't make it to the fence without a snack." Kitty's eyes lingered over the horse's middle. "He could never keep up with my horse, Zephyr."

"I bet he could."

"I'm sorry," interrupted Mr. Wells. He tilted his head, his pointed chin emphasized by the angle. "Is that a wager? I love nothing better than a good race."

"I could beat you with one hand tied behind my back," declared Amelia, her competitive nature showing up when she least expected it. "Just like croquet."

Kitty stopped laughing. "What did you say?"

"You heard me."

"I accept the challenge," Kitty stated. "Hang the no galloping rule." She tightened the delicate bow on her riding bonnet. "I'll have you know, my governess prided herself on well-roundedness, and I studied equestrienne history and methods for two years." Her eyes took on a mischievous look. "That was *before* I learned to ride from the Duke of Glastonbury."

Amelia felt her jaw slacken. The Duke of Glastonbury was known as the best horseman on their side of England, perhaps all of England. Leave it to Kitty to learn from him.

Amelia took a breath. Well, she'd learned from a solid horseman herself: her father. And she would show them what a girl from Mells could do.

"There is a slight decline near the end of the track," Mr. Wells reminded them. "Watch for it when you make your turn. The first one to pass this green hat"—he took off his hat and waved it like a flag—"wins. Any questions?"

"None," Amelia answered.

Kitty shook her head.

Mr. Wells started the race with a shout, and they were off and running. Amelia's hat, which didn't have ribbons, was the first thing to go, followed by her hairpins. Lettie had been right, as usual. Amelia did need to put more effort into her hair—or hair clips. Her auburn locks swept about her face like an Amazon, and she couldn't see Kitty, except to know she was in front of her.

Amelia had underestimated Kitty's small stature and weightlessness. Even with her extraordinary dress, she practically flew over the track like a sandpiper over water, touching down here and there to make certain the ground was still beneath her feet. But then, as luck would have it, her bonnet began to tip backward just as she rounded the corner to return to the starting point.

Amelia had known Kitty to wade into the banks of the river Thames for the sake of a hat. Hats were her weakness. Amelia felt the tides turn an inkling in her favor.

Kitty pressed the bonnet hard on her head, losing just enough momentum for Amelia to catch up. As Amelia rounded the corner and passed Kitty, she almost forgot where she was—and who.

She crouched low, whispering into Marmalade's ear. "Come on, boy! You can do it! Show 'em what you're made of!"

Marmalade answered by taking thick breaths through the nostrils, his sides heaving in and out steadily. The sound brought her back to a race against a village boy years ago whom Amelia outsmarted by riding through the woods, where he got caught up in a low-lying thicket of bramble. He rode home with prickles in his breeches and a newfound respect for her horsemanship.

Now she and Kitty were neck and neck, and Kitty's hat, all

but off her head, was dangling by one colorful ribbon. Kitty reached for it, stuffing the hat under an armpit, her face an unwavering masterpiece of skill, determination, and beauty. In that instant, Amelia admired her more than ever. She was so much more than one of the *ton*'s favorites—she was a brave woman, friend, and coconspirator. If she left London, Amelia didn't know what she'd do.

The thought caused Amelia's heart to hurt and her muscles to hesitate, and Marmalade slowed at just the wrong time. Kitty pulled ahead, swiftly passing under Mr. Wells's feathered green cap to the cheers of several onlookers.

Catching her breath, Amelia congratulated Kitty. "After all this time, you continue to surprise me. Well done."

Kitty accepted the felicitations with a smile, her blonde curls bouncing up and down as her horse trotted to a stop. Her groom assisted her off her horse. "I stand corrected on Marmalade. He is a fine horse, very fine." She patted his big head. "Please accept my apologies, Marmalade."

"He does." Amelia smiled and took her groom's outstretched hand. "Thank you."

"An admirable race." Mr. Wells returned his hat to his head, and Amelia noted his hair was mostly blond with some streaks of brown. Since she'd been caught up in the excitement of the race, the detail nearly escaped her notice.

"Not the Derby, but it's the most exercise Marmalade's had in an age." Amelia tried twisting her hair into a bun, but it was beyond repair. She would need Lettie—and about fifty hairpins—to overcome its untidiness.

"In my experience, the Derby's overrated and expensive." Mr. Wells sniffed. "Losing the last one cost me over six thousand pounds and was half as much fun."

Amelia had no idea of the amount of money the Derby winner took home. George Davies had cost him a considerable sum if what he said was true. Not to mention the prestige, which he obviously cared for a good deal.

Behind her, a squeal sliced through the air, and Amelia didn't recognize it as Kitty's until she turned and saw her friend doubled over in pain. Amelia ran to her side. "Kitty! What happened?"

Kitty didn't answer.

"It's her foot," her groom explained. "It slipped when she stepped off the stool."

Amelia followed the direction of Kitty's outstretched finger to the lovely white boot stuck in the mud. "Oh no."

Kitty looked up from her ankle and cried louder. "My shoe!"

Chapter 16

Dear Lady Agony,

A fire can be drenched with water, but what of anger? My husband's ill-timed remarks are causing me to lose sleep. They drop from his mouth like rotten apples from trees, and my brain gathers them into a basket I tip out at night. I love him, but his brain . . . At times, it seems disconnected from his mouth.

Devotedly,
Jibber Jabber

....

Dear Jibber Jabber,

A good many wives suffer this fault patiently, and some husbands, too. Other authors might say to have him count to ten before opening his mouth. I say counting to one hundred wouldn't fix the flaw in some people. In them, the faulty mechanics between brain and mouth grind eternal. However, I *do know a remedy that might take the sting out of bedtime: brandy. A snifter just might make a difference between a horrible or harmonious evening.*

Yours in Secret,
Lady Agony

Kitty's ankle started to swell immediately, and Mr. Wells summoned a hansom cab posthaste. At the Hamsted house, a maid tended to the foot while Amelia avoided answering Kitty's pressing question: How bad did the ankle look? Indeed, it looked awful, turning a purple-blue color with a light green hue settling into the sole of her foot. Kitty's toes were like little pumpkins hanging off a log. Amelia studied the white boot still on the other foot. Those boots wouldn't be coming on again anytime soon.

"I asked you how it looks," repeated Kitty.

"It looks . . ." Amelia swallowed. She and Kitty didn't lie about things big or small. How was she to get around this question with an ounce of hope?

"Ow!" yelped Kitty as the maid took off the compress and left to make it cool again.

"It looks better than it feels?" Amelia tried. It had to be true. Kitty was in a great deal of pain. Her face was twisted into a grimace.

"It looks fine, Kitty." Oliver, who'd been patient with Amelia until now, glared at her. "But what's not fine is the constant danger Lady Amesbury seems to put you in. How does it happen, my lady? Are you two separate people? One countess and one harbinger of hazard?"

Harbinger of Hazard . . . it has a poetic ring.

"How dare you blame this on Amelia when it's my own error that turned my ankle into—" Here, Kitty sat up and gazed upon the ugly purple mass. "This! Oh dear heaven, help me." She fell back on the chaise cushions.

For a moment, Amelia thought she'd fainted.

But she sat back up, pointing her finger at Oliver. "Not one. Single. Word."

All conversation ceased, and another maid entered with a snifter of brandy.

"There, there." The maid came to Kitty's side. "This will help the pain."

Kitty took the glass and drank down its contents in one big glug.

Oliver couldn't speak, but he could glare, and Amelia focused on the ceiling to avoid his glower. Maybe he had a point. Maybe she'd put Kitty in danger once too often. But in this instance, Kitty's injury had nothing to do with her secret pseudonym. *Although my goading her into a race didn't help matters* . . .

Kitty had won the race and looked beautiful doing so. Her skills would be much talked about among the *ton*. Amelia hoped the compliments would fall on the viscountess's ears, for the viscountess loved nothing more than praise of her family. How could she receive any with Kitty in the country? Kitty would be too far from the public eye to receive notice there.

"Can I fetch you another pillow, dear?" Oliver asked.

"I'll see to her, Mr. Hamsted." The maid placed a second pillow under her foot. "Don't you worry yourself about a thing."

"Yes, *dear*." Kitty lowered her lids. "Go. I'm fine, and I know you must have work to do."

Oliver trudged out of the room like a scolded child, and Amelia couldn't help but feel bad for him. For both of them.

They never fought. They were always kind. And while their love-sickness was sometimes nauseating, it was also admirable. Amelia hoped to find a love as strong—and blind—as theirs.

The maid laid a blanket over Kitty's lap. "Anything else I can get you?"

Kitty shook her head. "No thank you."

"I'll fetch your sewing basket." The maid stood. "That'll take your mind off your trouble."

Kitty's nose crinkled after she left the room. Kitty hated sewing as much as she hated mud.

Amelia pointed to her empty glass. "If you need me to refill that, just say the word."

Kitty smiled. "I'm fine. Truly."

"I'm sorry about the accident."

"Nonsense." Kitty waved away the apology. "You had nothing to do with it. It was my own clumsy blunder. Tell me what happened with Mr. Wells. I hope my fall was worth some information at least."

Amelia filled her in on the details.

"So George Davies was his horse trainer?"

"At one time," confirmed Amelia.

Kitty raised herself up on one elbow. "Maybe Davies did injure the horse. It sounds as if a lot of money was at stake. Almost seven thousand pounds." She winced and lay back. "Dash it all! That hurts."

The exclamation was Amelia's clue to leave. "I'm going to let you rest, Kitty. We can talk later."

"The brandy *is* making me sleepy." Kitty briefly closed her eyes.

Amelia pulled the blanket up to Kitty's chin. "Send me a note tomorrow. I want to know how you're recovering."

Kitty promised she would, and Amelia let herself out.

After a short walk, Amelia was back at Amesbury Manor. She bypassed the house, making her way toward the stables. When she and Kitty left the park in a hansom cab, her groom had led Marmalade home himself. Amelia wanted to make certain Marmalade was safe and secure in his stall before going into the house.

The Amesbury stables were small, as were most stables in the city, but she felt very lucky to have personal transportation at her disposal. Only the wealthy could afford to house their horses in London, and she was fortunate to count herself in that group.

As she drew closer, the smell evoked childhood memories of her summer pilgrimages to the stables at the Feathered Nest, where she helped out when needed or stole a few minutes reading behind a haystack. While she loved the bustling inn, she also loved the quiet adventures reading brought her. How many places had she traveled to behind that barn? How many lives had she lived? She could be queen, conqueror, or consort. Reading had been her sole means of escape.

She took a deep breath. Perhaps she missed country life more than she liked to admit. A visit to Mells might be what she needed. The smell of horse dung infiltrated her nostrils. She coughed. *Or maybe not.*

The cough gained her attention, and one of her best stablemen, Brooks, quickly appeared. He took off his cap, displaying thick brown hair stuck flat to his head with sweat. "My lady. I didn't see ye come in."

"I only just arrived." Her eyes landed on Marmalade's soft chestnut coat. She smiled. "I wanted to make certain Marmalade returned safely."

"He sure did." Brooks stuffed his pitchfork in a pile of hay.

"He had himself a nice snack, too. I heard he gave Mrs. Hamsted's horse a run for her money."

Amelia beamed with pride. "He did." Her brow furrowed. "How did you hear?"

"Your groom. He said Mr. Wells was as surprised as he was at the old man's speed."

"Marmalade is not an old man," Amelia defended. She walked over to the horse and smoothed his coat. "He's middle-aged at best." He nuzzled her hand.

Brooks, in his forties with bowed legs and callused hands, appreciated the difference. He snorted a laugh.

"Mr. Wells told me his horses have been to the Derby." Amelia looked up from Marmalade. "That his horse, Dancer, was slated to win this year but suffered a last-minute injury."

"By whose hand?" Finished wiping his brow, Brooks picked up the pitchfork. "His own?"

"Explain what you mean."

He leaned into the handle. "He pushes his horses too hard, and men who treat animals like that—" He shrugged. "You have to wonder."

"I think I understand," said Amelia. "Winning means more than the health of his horses."

He nodded. "He might have expected more from Dancer than he should have."

The heat was growing oppressive, and Amelia decided to take her leave so that he could finish his work. "Thank you, Brooks, and take care you don't exhaust yourself. It's warm out today." Amelia patted Marmalade's head goodbye.

A moment later, she was free of the heat and smell of the stables. The information she'd gleaned didn't surprise her. Mr. Wells was used to winning—perhaps at any cost.

She thought back to him in his green-feathered cap on Rotten Row. He'd been a perfect gentleman, hospitable and kind. Gracious even. But when a wager entered the conversation, he'd changed. Was he more addicted to horse racing than she supposed? It was a bet she couldn't make—yet.

Once inside the house, she was greeted by Winifred, who was only too happy to share the results of the boat race with her. She'd just rung for tea when Winifred bounded through the drawing room door, pink cheeked and out of breath.

"Lord Grey won!"

"Of course he did." Amelia tried to keep the irritation out of her voice.

"And that's not all." Winifred's eyes grew wider and bluer.

When it came to Lord Grey, Amelia could only imagine what other wonderful thing he'd done.

"Mr. Armstrong brought you a package." She rubbed her hands together. "He said it's not a present, but it's quite large. And it's square. We put it in the library."

Winifred wanted to see what was inside, but Amelia knew it wasn't a gift. It must have been something from the magazine, but what? What was so large he needed to bring it himself? "Thank you, Winifred. I'll see to it soon. But first, tea! Will you join me?"

Miss Tabor entered with a silver tea tray. Petit fours were one of Amelia's favorite treats, and she counted one, two, three selections: vanilla, chocolate, and buttered rum.

She hadn't thought she was hungry, but now she found she was starving. She poured the tea, inhaling the spicy scent and allowing it to invigorate her senses. Then she handed Winifred a chocolate confection, and selected one for herself.

Winifred sneaked a glance at the door. "This is my second today."

Amelia dusted off a stray sugar sprinkle. "Some days require more chocolate than others."

"I like the way you think." Winifred giggled, and they toasted with their cakes.

After tea, Amelia headed into the library, where the oversized parcel perched on her chair. Walking past, she sized it up like an opponent. It could be only one thing, but how—and why? She used her letter opener to peek inside.

It wasn't one letter, or two, or even a dozen. At least a hundred letters were stuffed into the parcel. She quickly closed it. Then she shut the library door and tore open the rest of the package. Letters, letters, more letters. She thumbed through the correspondence. They had one thing in common: all were written by men.

I must have said something they really didn't like. Which could have been anything. Men were so touchy. Emotionally frail. She'd read dozens of letters about childbirth, and not one of the women mentioned how taxing it was. It was always, *Will my child get on? When will I heal?* And her personal favorite, *Do I have to do this again?* Yet, one mention of men shutting their mouths, and a deluge of letters arrived at her door, for she was certain it was that which had garnered the responses.

She opened the first letter, confirming the theory. Then the second and the third. She sighed. Now she would have to write a response to clear the mess up.

Moving the box, she plopped down in her chair. She wasn't going to read all of them. That would be bad for her health. Outspoken, ill-mannered, outrageous—that summed up their criticism of her. But what to say back? She selected her blue feather quill like a soldier selecting a weapon. Yet, the onslaught didn't come.

She waited, and waited, and waited. Sometime later (she suspected after the cake took effect and the sun poured over her like a warm blanket), she tired of waiting and closed her eyes for a moment, and that moment turned into an hour. At least that was the indication on the clock when Simon Bainbridge woke her up with a laugh.

In her sleepy brain, she thought the men from the letters had come to life, that they'd created a merry band, found out where she lived, and were there, laughing at her. After blinking away the sleep in her eyes, however, she discovered it was only one mirthful man in the flesh.

"I'm sorry," Simon apologized. "I told Jones I could find my own way to the library. I didn't mean to wake you."

She stretched. "Yes you did."

"You're right, I did." He pointed to the box on the floor. "What is that?"

"A treatise on manhood."

"Shall I read it?" He selected a chair across from her desk, a smile still twitching on his lips.

"I wouldn't recommend it." Amelia stretched again. The nap had revitalized her. "You might think less of your sex."

He crossed a foot over his leg. "I called earlier, and you were out. I wondered where, and then I heard at the club. It seems you and Mrs. Hamsted had a very public race on Rotten Row, where some say your hair came crashing down like the waves of the Atlantic Ocean after you took an overzealous corner in an un-ladylike bid to win."

"What's unladylike about wanting to win?" Amelia said. "Marmalade's pride was at stake. I wasn't about to let a little thing like my coiffure prevent his victory."

Simon picked a nonexistent piece of lint off his impeccable trousers. "Indeed. I'm sure it was about Marmalade. I'm sure it had nothing to do with your competitive spirit." His voice dripped with sarcasm.

"Actually, it had more to do with our investigation into George Davies than anything else." He looked up from his trousers, and she tipped her chin, glad she had his attention.

"Well, don't be coy." He leaned toward her desk. "Tell me what you found."

She told him about Mr. Wells, the Derby, and her stable hand's comment. He seemed pleased—until she mentioned seeing Mr. King at the park.

He clasped the desk. "He was following you."

"We can't know for certain." She lowered her voice. "He was with Lord Burton. I'm worried for Marielle's reputation."

"I will deal with King. I promise you that." The amber rings around his irises flamed yellow, like a stoked fire. He would burn down all those who endangered his friends and family.

Trying to douse the flame, she brought the subject back to George Davies. "At any rate, Mr. Wells is another man who might have wanted George dead. The injury of his horse might affect him more than he lets on."

"We're supposed to be eliminating suspects, not adding them," Simon grumbled. "Did the man have *any* friends?"

His words put an idea in her head. "You bring up a good point. We should find the people who knew Mr. Davies best. Ask them about his affairs. What do you know about his family?"

"His father is a blacksmith. He made our horses' shoes for many years. It's how we came to hire his son. He has a forge shop near Covent Garden." He paused. "Or used to. I haven't seen him for some time."

"It's a place to begin." She straightened the papers on her desk. "We might go now."

"An excellent idea." He slid back his chair. "I have questions about the knife used in George Davies's murder. His father might be the person to ask about it."

"What about the knife?" she prodded.

"I cannot say, exactly. It was dark, and I was too preoccupied to examine it properly." He closed his eyes as if darkness might better help him recall the evening.

Without his eyes on her, she lingered over his face. His defined jawline, his pensive lips. The lips she'd tasted for herself. The strong creases around his eyes from his time on a ship. She was surprised to discover deeper shadows beneath his lashes. He was still anxious to regain Marielle's trust, and she was anxious to help him. If only they could make some headway with their new direction.

"The handle was peculiar." His eyes opened. "As if I've seen it before."

Perhaps in your father's bureau? She kept the thought to herself. "If George's father is a blacksmith, he must be familiar with knives. As you said, he's sure to have an idea."

He stood. "Let's ask him."

Amelia acquiesced.

Simon indicated for her to lead the way. "I told my driver to wait."

She threw him a look over her shoulder, appalled by how confident he was in her dropping everything to go with him. *He knows I would travel to the ends of the earth to find George Davies's killer.* And Covent Garden? Even the words put spice into her step. She loved the neighborhood.

Amelia's excitement was squelched by the stiff rustle of Tabitha's petticoat. Some women flitted, some women floated, and other women—like Tabitha—forged ahead as a train on a timetable. She stood determinedly, her cane out at one side. "Good afternoon, my lord. How was Rotten Row, Amelia?"

It was a test, and Amelia worried she was going to fail miserably. Less was always more in these situations. Tabitha had been here all day. It wasn't as if she'd heard about the race. "Good. Very refreshing."

"Refreshing." Tabitha clumped her cane thrice. "You, the antithesis of popular opinion, found Rotten Row refreshing."

Amelia frowned. "'Antithesis' seems severe. I know how to enjoy myself like everybody else."

"Oh, I know you know how to enjoy yourself." Tabitha tsked. "Lady Sutherland informed me just how much you enjoyed yourself, racing down the row today like a common jockey or stable boy. Good heavens! Think of the Amesbury name."

Amelia's response was immediate and childish. "Mrs. Hamsted was racing, too!"

"And that improves matters how?"

"I know many riders who race before dawn," Simon interjected. "It's one of the few places to get exercise in the city."

"And at the noon hour?" Tabitha pressed.

Simon was silent.

"I thought not." Tabitha's reproach was second only to her look of censure. Standing next to her, Amelia felt the full force of her dour appearance. "Winifred is getting to the age where she will follow your lead. Be careful which direction you steer her."

The direction I will steer her will be her own. The words were said safely inside Amelia's head, but it didn't make them any less true. Amelia refused to be a mother who molded her daughter for society and nothing else. Winifred was a daughter, a niece, a friend, a musician, an artist. Many things besides a debutante. If she wanted to race in Hyde Park, so be it. Amelia would be at the fence line cheering her on.

"Lady Amesbury has been quite helpful with Marielle of late," Simon put in. "I'm certain she'll be a fine example for Winifred."

Tabitha raised her silver eyebrows, and Amelia smiled at his attempt to improve Tabitha's mood.

He continued more convincingly. "Marielle's had some trouble this season, and Lady Amesbury's assistance has been most commendable."

Tabitha's anger subsided long enough for her to give him a reassuring pat on his shoulder. "You're a good brother to watch over her so—and a good friend to defend Amelia." Her look changed from concerned grandmother to scathing matriarch. She pointed her cane at Amelia. "*You* be on your best behavior the rest of the day."

"Rest assured I'll blend into the crowd, Aunt," Amelia declared. "No one will even glance my way."

Simon nodded to her hair. "Uh-hum."

She grabbed her largest hat from the hall tree and shoved it onto her head. "Or they won't now."

Tabitha harrumphed a goodbye.

Chapter 17

Dear Lady Agony,

I have two left feet, and they keep getting in the way of a good time. A dance in the ballroom turns into toe-smashing trouble. A walk in the park turns into a stumble in shame. My mother says if I do not cultivate poise, I will end up like the flowers in our garden—wilted and forgotten. Might you tell me how to get some grace?

Devotedly,
Two Left Feet

. . . .

Dear Two Left Feet,

So much is made of girls and grace. Give me a woman who can knit an army of clothes, cook a meal for ten, or shoot a straight arrow. They are the women I want to know. So you are uncoordinated. Can you swim oceans, bake cakes, or create art?

Whatever it is, cultivate that. Leave the book balancing on heads to those who have time for it.

Yours in Secret,
Lady Agony

Covent Garden was one of Amelia's favorite places, where every sight, sound, and color of the city was represented. As she descended the carriage steps, she inhaled its energy, absorbing it through her pores like a salve.

On market days, Covent Garden overflowed with flowers, fruits, and vegetables, and three o'clock in the morning was not too early to see sellers readying their wares. From sunup to sundown, the streets were full of possibilities, from the wholesome to the wicked. Women balanced large baskets on their heads, donkeys pulled bountiful carts, and children darted between them both with the quickness of cats.

The farther Amelia and Simon walked, the stronger the sounds and scents assailed their senses. Sweet peaches, heady roses, earthy potatoes, and turnips fought for Amelia's attention like the sellers who sold them. Men carried crates as large as themselves, their loud whistles likely reaching even the far-off passersby.

As they rounded a corner, an unhappy sound cut in, stopping her abruptly. She tripped over her feet, stumbling several steps before catching herself.

"I thought you two weren't friends."

Amelia spun around to find Thaddeus King, following them like a mad dog. He was alone, which shouldn't have made him scarier, but it did. His eyes were black coal, without warmth, and his lip curled into a smile at her surprise. She wondered how long he'd been following them and what he'd heard. The throngs of people had cloaked his pursual. Like a ghost at the bewitching hour, he'd appeared out of nowhere.

"Mr. King." Simon's voice was tight. "Are you following us? Because I know you've been following Lady Amesbury, and that ends today. Now."

The response was spoken with the same refinement Amelia was used to from Simon, but something new lurked in his tone, a menace Amelia didn't recognize.

Obviously, Mr. King didn't detect the threat, because he ignored the question. His smile widened, showing a lip full of chewing tobacco. "It appears you're *good* friends. So why'd you lie to me?"

"I never lied." Amelia swallowed a quiver in her voice. "I said Lord Bainbridge was a family friend."

"Like Mr. Davies." King stared at Simon. "Who was a *close* friend of your sister's, a fact that might be forgotten for repayment of a debt."

Simon stared back. "They were not friends."

"One thousand pounds, to be exact." The way King talked, Simon might have been any debtor who owed him money, not a former navy officer and certainly not a marquis.

Like a mad dog with a bone, thought Amelia.

Simon let out a harsh breath. "Mr. Davies was our stable hand, an *employee*."

"Your sister didn't see it that way." Mr. King spat on the ground. "She thought of him as much more, and maybe it's time the whole world knows it."

"Are you threatening my family, King?"

"I'd never do that, *my lord*." King wiped his mouth with the back of his hand. "I'm merely suggesting a payment that leads to a mutual understanding."

"And if I repay Davies's debt of one thousand pounds, you won't come near me, my family, or Lady Amesbury again?"

There was that tone again, the one King was oblivious to. Amelia tensed. A storm was coming, and Simon was a fast-moving rain cloud.

Mr. King's brow lifted in happy surprise. "That's right. You *do* know what I mean."

Simon grabbed the lapels of his coat, his fists crushing the silk material. Amelia was surprised by their size and strength. His hands had brought her comfort in times of trial, but here, on the streets near Covent Garden, they became weapons, ways to destroy Mr. King and his rumors.

"If you ever say my sister's name again, even in passing, I will make sure you never conduct affairs in this town again." Simon's green eyes searched Mr. King's face for understanding. "Every horse, every race, every bet will be taken elsewhere. I will make certain my peers know your name and avoid you like the black plague. And Lady Amesbury?" He gave a quick glance in her direction. "If she so much as sees you on the street, she will tell me, and I will come after you with everything I have."

Mr. King blinked. He was stupefied into stunned silence by the turn of events. The blackmailer was being blackmailed himself. And it wasn't a veiled threat. Simon would keep his word. He'd demonstrated that he wasn't above physical violence.

Simon grabbed the lapels tighter. "Do you understand me?"

"Yeah . . . yes, my lord."

Simon let him go, and Mr. King jerked down his coat.

Amelia glanced around. No one had taken notice of the

encounter. Or if they had, they weren't obvious. Covent Garden was perhaps the only area in London that afforded such freedom, with workers, sellers, and thieves.

Mr. King touched the tip of his hat. "Lady Amesbury."

Then he was gone, moving away at a near sprint, leaving Amelia to gawk after him.

"Shall we?" Simon held out his arm.

She turned back to him. "I, er. Sure."

"I hope I didn't frighten you," he added after a moment.

"Oh, you didn't frighten me."

"Remember what I said about cards? Your face tells all." He let out a breath. "At least I hope you understand why I did it. Men like King don't respond to manners or logic. Brute force is the only option. I know he thought I was above it." He gave her a side glance. "Maybe you did, too. But I'm not. I'll use whatever means necessary to protect those I care about."

He was right; she had been afraid. Not of him, exactly, but of his physical strength. It was incredible how she hadn't noticed it before. His hands had tied ropes, knots, sails. They were large. They were coarse. They were powerful. And yet, they'd touched her with only the softest caress.

Maybe she was one of the people he cared about.

The idea was too powerful to consider, and she forced herself not to linger on it.

"I do understand." She took his proffered arm. "Completely. And I'm glad you did it. I would have done something myself— if I'd had my parasol."

The joke lightened the mood, and they started again toward the shop of Mr. Davies.

The store was off Bedford Street, around the corner from the iron forge, and not far from Drury Lane. Above the door read DAVIES. IRON WARES, and METALWORKS was below in smaller letters. In the front window hung a handsome display of knives, several small tools, and a few birdcages that drew Amelia's interest. On the whole, it appeared a very nice place of employ, which brought her to another mystery: Why hadn't George Davies apprenticed under his father? She asked Simon.

"He liked the horses, not the labor." Simon tightened his cravat, which was constantly blown open as if he was still a captain of a ship and not a marquis in London. The tussle with Mr. King had made it worse than usual. "Even as a young man, he wanted to better himself. Blacksmith was not the title he desired." Frustrated with the complicated knot, he jerked it looser instead of tighter.

"Let me do that." Being good with intricate work, Amelia tied it easily. "I take it *lord* was the title he sought—if his attention to Marielle was any indication."

He checked the knot in the store window, looking pleased with the results. "I've often thought that myself."

"It's time we find out."

Simon asked for Thomas Davies, and the clerk quickly fetched him from the forge. Like his son George, Thomas had red hair, a bright copper color streaked with gray at the temples. His blue eyes crinkled with a smile when he spotted Simon. His hands were dark with grease from iron- or metalwork, and Amelia wasn't sure it was a stain ever completely removed, though he wiped his hands on his apron before greeting them.

"Simon Bainbridge! What a nice surprise. I haven't seen you in . . ." He ticked off the time on his thick fingers. "Too many years to count." Thomas's voice was deep, like the creases in his hands, and although he was an older man, he was full of vitality. "What brings you in, my lord?"

"I wanted to tell you how sorry I am about your son George," said Simon. "I appreciated the work he did for us."

Amelia expressed her sympathy, too.

"Thank you." Thomas's smile waned. "If only he would've been content at your stables, he might be alive today." He tsked. "Never was satisfied, that one. Always wanted more."

"Was he involved with something he shouldn't have been?" Simon asked.

"The officer said no. Said it was random street violence. But I know George was in trouble." Thomas smoothed the once-red hair at his temples. "He never came to me for money. Knew I couldn't abide his running after the finer things in life like a beggar. But he stopped by the week before he was murdered, needing money. He must've been desperate if he came to me."

Simon gave Amelia a glance before turning back to Thomas. "Did he say how much?"

"A thousand pounds."

"Did you give it to him?" Simon pressed.

"No, sir. I didn't have the ability and wouldn't have even if I did. He would have thrown it away on a race or a girl."

Amelia didn't fail to notice the amount was identical to the notes George had had in his pocket. George had received the money, but if not from his father, whom?

Thomas shook his head. "He could shoe a horse faster than any boy in the shop. And he could ride like the wind. You know he could."

Simon nodded in agreement.

"Why'd he go and use his skills for bad?" Thomas continued.

"A blacksmith isn't much, but it's better than being dead. I know that."

They were silent. Anything was better than being dead.

After a moment, Simon spoke. "His reputation as an excellent horseman was well known. You can take pride in that, Mr. Davies."

The old man's eyes lifted at the compliment, and Amelia felt her heart take another step in Simon's direction. Beyond his tough exterior lay a careful, considerate human being. He put away his own feelings about George's relationship with his sister to give Thomas a bit of peace.

Simon indicated the front window. "I noticed some fine knives out front."

"Yes, sir. The finest in the city. Are you in the market for one?"

"Maybe." Simon waffled. "I'm looking for one with a special handle."

"We got every kind of handle and blade, and if we don't, I can make it." Thomas led the way to a locked cupboard. "Junior!" he called to the store clerk. "Bring me the key."

It was a family business, and the younger man must have been the brother of George Davies. Unlike his father, Junior was a careful dresser, and his hands, although callused from work, were clean. He must've managed the store while his father worked the forge.

Thomas Davies snatched the key from Junior, who was slow to a fault. "Give me that. I'll do it. I know what the marquis wants."

The first drawers were filled with usual knives, mostly pocketknives or hunting tools. It wasn't until Thomas opened the third and fourth drawers that Simon looked more closely at the blades.

Some had ivory handles; others had designs. Thomas said most could be inscribed with initials or words.

"This one, for instance." Thomas picked up a shiny silver knife with a wide wooden handle, managing it carefully. "It'd make a nice gift for you or a member of your family."

Simon turned the knife over in his hands. "Very nice. Do you have any larger ones, with a grooved handle—more ornately designed?"

Thomas scratched his faded whiskers, which covered his face and hid its roundness, except for the bright apples of his cheeks. "Not here. What you're describing might be foreign. Or a collectible."

Simon nodded. "Might you know of such a knife?"

Thomas moved his hand to the back of his neck, thinking. "The only thing that comes to mind is a facon, but where to find one in London?"

"That's an idea." Simon's voice hovered over the possibility.

"Excuse me," Amelia interrupted. "What's a facon?"

"It's a Spanish knife—about the size of a carving knife," Thomas added for her benefit. "Used by gauchos in South America. The handle is ornate, and its sheath is decorative, too. You could try the knife collector on Piccadilly—Heusen's. He has many nice blades and swords."

"Thank you, Mr. Davies." Simon seemed pleased with the new information. "You've been most helpful."

"You're mightily welcome." Thomas pulled his gloves out of his back pocket.

"Mr. Davies, may I ask one more question, about your son?"

Thomas paused. "Certainly, my lady."

Amelia waited for a customer to pass before asking the question. "Do you know if your son was courting anyone? I only ask because I met him recently at the opera. I wonder if he mentioned the woman he was with."

"The *op-e-ra*." Thomas pronounced the word in three distinct syllables. "That sounds like my George. He had fine lodgings on Warwick Street—I'm to pick up his things tomorrow—and a girl near there. Maybe that's who you saw." He winked, looking like his son for a second. "George said she was a bonnie lass." He slapped his gloves against his palm. "Margaret. That was her name. I never had a chance to meet her, though."

Amelia sucked in a breath. Her intention had been to determine whether Thomas knew about his son's possible elopement to Gretna Green with Marielle. Never did she imagine George was courting a woman besides Marielle. She checked Simon's reaction.

His dark eyebrows knitted together, signaling a dangerous retort ahead.

Amelia ended the conversation quickly. "Yes, that was probably her." Another customer walked in, and she was glad for the intrusion. "We'd best not take up any more of your time. Thank you again."

Once they were inside the carriage, Amelia put a hand on Simon's forearm, trying to calm his anxieties. "It's obvious Thomas Davies was not close to his son. He might be mistaken about Margaret. Perhaps he remembered Marielle's name wrong."

Simon's eyes narrowed, looking like green blades of grass.

"Or George could have courted the woman before your sister." Even to her own ears, the excuse seemed fumbling and weak. "The elder Davies is collecting George's belongings tomorrow. That means the staff is there today. We could ask them."

Simon gave his coachman new directions and sat back, his jaw clenched.

After a beat, she tried again. "It's probably not as sordid as it seems. It all might be a misunderstanding."

"I've found that nearly everything is as sordid as it seems. Life, in fact, is a rather sordid affair."

She frowned at his skeptical comment. It was unlike him.

He raked his fingers through his dark hair, looking more sea captain than marquis, and replaced his hat. "I'm sorry, Amelia. This situation with Marielle is driving me mad."

"I know."

"I can't stand my sister thinking ill of me. The rest of this town be damned, but she's the only family I have, except my father, and you've met him."

She nodded. "You never got on?"

"We used to get on better than we do, before my mother passed."

She wanted to ask him for details but didn't dare. Aunt Tabitha told her the duchess had been killed in a train wreck with her lover beside her. Obviously, marriage hadn't been fulfilling for her. Had it been for the duke? She didn't ask. Instead, she said, "I'm sorry."

"It's no one's fault but his own." Simon glanced out the window. "He drove my mother away. It's no surprise that he would do the same to Marielle and me."

"May I ask why they married in the first place?"

"It's a familiar story. He had a lofty title but a dwindling bank account. She had a lofty bank account but no title." He shrugged. "The families came together in one of the largest weddings London has ever seen. He kept his promise, like a perfect duke." He let out a bitter chuckle. "But nothing more. He was gone more often than not, and in his absence we grew close. Mother spent most of her time with us, and we relied on each other for everything. We were her children, and she loved us, but she had desires like anyone else. She filled them outside of marriage, which, as you know, isn't unusual in our circle. He resented it."

Like he resented George? The question flew through her mind before she could stop it. The idea was impossible, yet there it was, hanging like a low-hanging fruit from a nearby vendor's cart. Could he have done something to the duchess? "Tabitha said it was a terrible train accident."

"It was. An axle broke, a wheel slipped, and the train jumped the track." He looked out the window, staring as if somewhere in the distance were the train, or his mother, or both.

Amelia determined to stay focused on their new information. He and his father had enough problems without her adding suppositions that she couldn't prove. One murder was bad enough. Two was unthinkable. That didn't mean it was impossible, however. Dukes wielded unimaginable power in society. They could make wheels—and people—disappear. She shelved the idea in the back of her mind for future reference.

Chapter 18

Dear Lady Agony,

Between the two sexes, we are told, men are more informed. Why, then, when I need information, do I go to my female staff? They possess the details not to be found anywhere else. Can you reconcile the discrepancy? I cannot.

Devotedly,
Only Women Know

. . . .

Dear Only Women Know,

We have been told many things, some of them true, many of them false. Both men and women possess knowledge. Women, however, often possess an additional skill that's often overlooked: listening. Listening is its own education, one not always found in schools, books, or—ahem—men. It may be the reason your female staff has the information you need.

Yours in Secret,
Lady Agony

Amelia and Simon identified George's house on Warwick Street from its state of overhaul. Two men, perhaps valets, were moving a large trunk inside, where a fussy housekeeper fretted near the entry. The movers insisted the rear entrance wasn't wide enough for the trunk, yet the housekeeper worried they would damage the door on their way in. When she realized they weren't stopping, she finally stepped out of the way, onto the front stoop, only to shriek at them when one bumped into something inside.

She fisted her hands at her ample waist. "Watch where you're going!"

Simon and Amelia shared a smile before waving off Simon's footman and exiting the carriage, deciding the housekeeper would appreciate a direct approach.

The woman noted their movement, and her demeanor immediately changed from commanding officer to welcoming housekeeper. She had soft gray eyes and a matching knot of thick gray hair peeking out from her white cap. When Amelia handed her their calling cards, she acted as if they were fleeing a snowstorm instead of a warm summer's day. "Oh my goodness." She motioned them inside. "Come in, come in."

"Welcome, welcome! I'm Mrs. Unger." Her voice had a brightness that reminded Amelia of spring, all happiness.

"Thank you," said Simon. "I understand Mr. Davies let this

residence. He was under my employ several years ago, and I wondered if I might ask you a few questions about his time here."

"Of course, my lord." After glancing up the staircase and being satisfied with the progress of the trunk, she led them to a comfortable parlor. It contained two small tables, an assortment of worn but respectable furniture, and a single bookshelf. She motioned to one of the chairs surrounding the larger table. "Will this do?"

"Yes, thank you." Amelia sat down. "We appreciate your taking the time to talk with us."

"My pleasure, my pleasure." She straightened her crisp dress, and Amelia believed nothing could be too straight for Mrs. Unger. From the evenly spaced books to the crease on her sleeve, she obviously valued symmetry.

"I assume you knew Mr. Davies well," Amelia continued.

"As well as a housekeeper knows her master, I suppose." Mrs. Unger's smile indicated that she was informed on most subjects, including this one, however. "My job is to do and not know, but in my ten years, I've never seen so many people come and go in a season. Mr. Davies was quite popular." The last words were said with a hint of pride.

"His knowledge of horses gained him some notoriety, certainly," Amelia agreed. "He knew people from all walks of life. It's the disreputable people who concern me the most, however. Perhaps one who visited him here?"

"This is a respectable house." She puffed up a little at the suggestion of it being otherwise. "My employer is meticulous about to whom he lets his property."

"And whom he allows to *manage* his property." Simon gave her one of his smiles, the one that made him look most like a marquis.

Mrs. Unger was pleased with the compliment, settling into her chair a bit more comfortably. She folded her dimpled hands on the table.

"I believe what Lady Amesbury is referring to is the criminal nature of Mr. Davies's death," continued Simon. "As you must know, Mr. Davies was murdered near the theatre. Most likely a victim of random street crime. Yet we have to ask if he argued with anyone here, if anyone wished him harm?"

Mrs. Unger considered the question a moment. "He had strong opinions about horses and races, but so did the men who enjoyed his friendship. They had spirited discussions on the topic. Mr. Davies was well versed, and they deferred to his authority. He was absolute in his opinions."

Sounds like many men I know, thought Amelia. "And how did he get along with the staff?"

"Like most gentlemen get along with their staff, my lady." She twisted her hands, looking at them, not Amelia. "He had high expectations and wanted them met. Demanded, even."

That was interesting since Davies himself had been part of the working class. One might think he'd be more considerate of his help. Yet, Amelia knew some who had risen above their stations to treat others with disdain, wielding their authority like a loaded gun. So, too, might have been the case here.

"But the ladies!" Mrs. Unger gushed. "He always had a smile or joke for them." Perhaps she was one of the women he'd been kind to. "They adored him. Nothing but honey flowed from his mouth when he was in their presence. A true gentleman."

Amelia nodded, and Mrs. Unger seemed pleased with her consensus. "He was affable to me and the other women the night I met him at the opera. His father mentioned a particular admirer of his, Margaret?" Mrs. Unger lifted her brow, and Amelia noted even the lines on her forehead were parallel. "Do you know her?" continued Amelia.

Mrs. Unger ticked off people in her mind. This was a woman who stored information and dates like dishes in a cupboard. "That must have been Lady Margaret from the Reynolds family. A very musical girl. Her gift for the pianoforte was incomparable. They moved here from Sussex and rented a place nearby until they bought their home in Belgravia. Mr. Davies was quite taken with her at the time—a year ago already! Her father was an earl. And a horse enthusiast, too. I imagine they lost touch when the family left the area. Last I heard, she was studying classical music abroad."

Lady Margaret. That was interesting. She, like Marielle, had her own title. And her father was a horse enthusiast—same as Simon's father.

A maid who dawdled in the hallway now cleared her throat.

"What is it, Louise?" Mrs. Unger gave Amelia and Simon an apologetic look before she stood and marched toward the door. "Is it the trunk? I told them it wouldn't fit." She continued the conversation outside the room.

Simon whispered, "Did you hear her? The man sounds like a regular—"

Amelia made a shushing noise. Both women were walking toward the table.

Louise bobbed a curtsy. She was a young woman with lovely blue eyes hidden by thick lashes and a shy demeanor. But it took only a glance to recognize her prettiness.

"It seems Louise here is privy to some information about Mr. Davies. She *happened* to overhear us discussing the subject of Lady Margaret while cleaning up a broken vase." Mrs. Unger shot Louise a reproachful look. Louise shrank several inches under the gaze of the housekeeper.

"Good afternoon, Louise." Simon dipped his chin, which caused a tiny ripple of a smile to cross the girl's face. "Thank you for coming forward with more details."

"My lord," murmured Louise.

"Please join us," said Simon, pulling out a chair.

Louise perched on it lightly, keeping her eyes on the table.

When she didn't say anything, Mrs. Unger prompted her. "Well, get on with it. Say what you came here to say."

"Oh!" She raised her eyes from the table. "What I wanted to say is . . . What I hoped to add was . . ." Mrs. Unger harrumphed, and Louise swallowed and tried again. "Mrs. Unger is right. Mr. Davies *did* quit seeing Lady Margaret, but not because he wanted to. Lord Reynolds insisted upon it."

"When you say *insisted* . . . ?" Amelia prodded.

"I mean he put an end to Mr. Davies's advancements by leaving immediately," clarified Louise. "They would have remained the full year, but the courtship caused a hasty departure. The earl did not want his daughter near Mr. Davies."

Mrs. Unger crossed her arms. "And you know this how?"

"Christine told me," Louise whispered. "The Reynoldses' maid."

Mrs. Unger sighed. "You girls. You're not to gossip about each other's houses."

"I'm sorry, but it's true." Louise's soft chin quivered. "I thought they should know."

"We should, and we thank you." Amelia digested the new information. George Davies wanted to be a gentleman and all that name guaranteed. Yet, he went about it by unsavory means, perhaps courting ladies for their titles. Plenty of peers sought matches for money, and many had gambled away entire estates at the racetrack. In some ways, what Mr. Davies was accused of was a pastime of the London season.

"Yes, thank you." Simon's calm voice reassured the girl, and she released a breath she'd been holding. "I assume the family was able to resume life normally after the difficulty?"

"I assume so, my lord, but I don't see Christine like I used to." Her wide eyes drooped. "Now that she's moved."

"You've been very helpful." Simon smiled at Louise, who'd confirmed his long-held suspicion that George was a scoundrel. The kindness didn't go unnoticed by her, and the corners of her mouth ticked up into a smile. "Thank you both for your time." Simon stood, and Amelia did the same.

"If there's anything else you need, please ask." Mrs. Unger ushered them into the entry. "The next few days will be busy, but Mr. Davies deserves justice. If I can help rid London of a filthy criminal, rest assured, I will." Her gray eyes were concerned— until a noise happened above. Then they snapped to the staircase with anger.

Simon and Amelia quickly made their exit.

Amelia could almost feel the righteousness in Simon's steps as they walked to the carriage. Each one seemed to say, *I'm right. I'm right. I'm right.* When the footman closed the door behind them, Simon confirmed it by saying, "I was right. George Davies was after my sister's title, just as I thought he was." He loosened his cravat, as if his ego was so large, he had to remove a piece of clothing.

"That may be, but what man won't be interested in a duke's daughter for much the same reason?" Amelia regretted the comment the moment she saw his look of consternation. Of course it would remind him of his personal problems. Hadn't Felicity

Farnsworth become engaged to him for one reason and one reason only: to become the future duchess?

"You're right." His voice was quieter. "Marielle may never marry for love."

"Or she may." Amelia cleared her throat, trying to sound cheerful. With the heaviness of the subject, it wasn't easy. "One never knows what life has in store."

Shaking his head, he paid the comment no attention. "Your point need only go as far as this carriage to prove its rightness."

She loved their disputes, their disagreements, even his disapproval. The deeper the divide, the more alive she felt. If she could bring the line between his eyebrows to life, even better. Someone had to prove to the marquis that he didn't have all the answers, and it might as well be her. She reveled in her wins, tallying them like points in a boxing match.

Which was why it felt so odd, for once in their relationship, to wish she was wrong.

Chapter 19

Dear Readers,

It's a truth universally acknowledged that a man in possession of a dull opinion must be in want of advice from a woman. I've received many letters of late from men who disliked my response to No Wife of Mine, asking me to retract it. Unfortunately, I cannot do that. First, my marital status has nothing to do with the advice I give correspondents. Second, I stand by my suggestion. One would think the true troublesomeness of the letter lay not in my advice but in the writer's implied violence toward women. Yet not one word about this. The silence, Dear Readers, is deafening.

Yours in Secret,
Lady Agony

The next day, Amelia and Grady were in the library reading her response to the onslaught of letters. Grady was reading, at any rate. Amelia was watching him rub a temple with his free hand.

He laid the paper on her desk, and she noticed a dark smudge on the side of his face where his fingers had been. She smiled. When it came to Grady, two things remained constant: his stubby fingers were always black with ink, and his spine was always bent from work. No matter where he was, he looked as if he were in the middle of a newsroom or hunched over a printing press, a smattering of dishwater blond hair sticking out from his flat cap.

"Are you trying to get me fired?"

Amelia leaned back in her chair. "I thought you were the boss."

"Not for long if this keeps up," he grumbled.

"You disagree with me?" she challenged.

"No. That's the bloody hell of it." He folded the response and stuck it with the others in his bag. "They deserve every word of it. I'm afraid it'll cost us some readers, though."

"Or gain some," she put in.

He gave her a boyish grin that reminded her of their shared childhood. "You were always good at looking at another side, Amelia. I like that about you." He patted his bag. "Other men? Not so much."

"Thanks, Grady. I appreciate it." She took a sip of coffee. Many afternoons, like this one, Grady insisted upon it when he visited. Overworked and undervalued, he was in constant need of a pick-me-up and didn't believe tea provided the energy he needed to survive the day. "What of George Davies's murder? Have you heard any news there?"

"Too many murders to keep track of them all." Grady guzzled his coffee like water. "I know you and the marquis have a special interest in this one, so I've kept my ear to the street for updates. But it's all routine so far as I've heard. Stabbed in the street, very clear-cut—no pun intended. One thing bothers me about the ordeal." He set down his cup, dunking a scone haphazardly into the dark brew. "If the knife was distinctive, as you say, why would the murderer leave it in the body?" He took a bite.

"Good point. One would think it might be more easily traced to its owner."

He dipped the remainder of his pastry in and out of his cup, thinking.

"He might have been interrupted," Amelia hypothesized, but another idea had been materializing in her brain, and the forgotten knife added to it. Simon had removed something shiny from the scene of the crime. It was small, the size of a piece of jewelry. What if the item belonged to a woman? Could that be why Simon had taken it, to avoid incriminating a lady, or to shield Marielle from further heartbreak? Simon would take any means necessary to protect his sister. "Grady, what if the killer isn't a *he* at all but a *she*?"

Grady chewed his scone thoughtfully, then washed it down with his coffee. "It's possible. Men and women alike grub for their food on that street, and you said the flower vendor acted suspiciously. It could've been a robbery gone wrong."

"Except for the thousand pounds Simon found in his pocket." She shook her head. "I have a feeling this murder wasn't random. It was personal. I *know* it."

"If you know it, you know it." He slapped his hands on his knees. "I won't try to dissuade you." A smile played on his lips, turning them into a lopsided grin. "But I will remind you of *The Taming of the Shrew*. It didn't go quite as you planned."

A hand flew to her mouth. Oh my, did she remember. Then, too, she was certain of an outcome. Unfortunately, the result hadn't been what she expected.

At her insistence, her parents put on the play at the inn—with one major revision. At the time, she was feeling the pressure of growing into a young woman in rural England. With each passing year, she felt the eye of the small town on her, wondering which young man she'd choose for her mate, or who would have the courage to choose her. Her only good choice—her dear friend Grady—would leave for London the moment he could. But before he left, he helped her produce the play, which included one key difference, starting with its name.

The Taming of the Tyrant, as they aptly named it, turned the play on its head. Instead of Katherina being the shrew of the play, Petruchio was the tyrant who must be put in his place by Katherina. Amelia and her sisters had great fun performing as sisters, with Grady as Petruchio and his friends as Lucentio, Hortensio, and Baptista. And their costumes! Mother spent weeks on them. They all thoroughly enjoyed the production. But a few townspeople did not. One man left in the middle of the performance. Two hissed. Others booed. Thus, her debut as a playwright was thwarted by a few angry men in the crowd.

She glanced at Grady's bag. She hoped her career at the magazine didn't end the same way. "Yes, I remember. A very important lesson learned there."

"About men and women?"

She scratched her head. "No, about wool trousers. They are dreadfully itchy. I don't know how you put up with them. Though in comparison . . ." She frowned at her voluminous skirt. "You don't have it so bad."

Laughing his warm, deep laugh, he stood, pointing to her new stack of letters. "Go easy on the correspondents today, all right?"

"I will." She fingered the letters. "These are all from women."

"I don't know how you did it." He pulled his cap low over his brow. Still, a few hairs stuck out like shards of glass. "I never thought I'd see the day when more men wrote to the column than women. Nothing short of a miracle."

"Maybe I should call myself Saint Agony?" She lifted her eyebrows suggestively.

He tossed her a glare over his shoulder. "Don't even think about it."

For the next hour, she worked on the letters, happy to be on familiar ground with busybodies, ball gowns, and bad haircuts. Goodness, women suffered during the season! It was deplorable how young women had to account for their every move. Over-bearing aunts (she could relate), eager mamas, and elderly chaperones were just a few of the problems in today's batch of mail. Not to mention hassles with undersized dresses, unmatched slippers, and flat curls. As she folded the last response, she realized how lucky she'd been to avoid a season herself. With the protection of Edgar's title and money, she could enjoy the beauty of the London summer without a care in the world for the opposite sex.

Except when their letters flooded her mailbox.

Jones's soft shuffle sounded at the door. "Mrs. Hamsted is waiting for you in the drawing room, my lady. I didn't want to interrupt."

Amelia smiled. "Thank you. I'll be right there."

She quickly tucked away her work, eager to see how Kitty was faring. The last time they'd talked, Kitty's ankle was the size of a peach, and Oliver was angry about the injury. Had he forgiven Amelia? She was about to find out.

Despite her recent troubles, Kitty looked par excellence. She wore a light gray dress with royal blue stripes and a bonnet with a blue bow so large it concealed most of her jawline. *Stunning*. If Amelia tried the same creation, it would end up with soup stains.

"Kitty, an unexpected surprise!" Amelia selected the chair across from her as Kitty's dress enveloped most of the settee. "How is your ankle?"

Kitty lifted her dress to reveal a barely-there slipper. The peach-sized ankle was now the size of a plum. "Much better."

"And your riding gloves?" Amelia thought they might've been damaged.

"They had to be discarded." Her button nose wrinkled with irritation. "Such a waste."

Amelia admired her friend's frugality. Though Kitty was one of the best dressers in London, she always made good use of her clothing and was never afraid, like most ladies, to wear an article more than once. When she did retire an item, she often reused the material to make a scarf, shawl, or reticule. "Do I dare ask about the status of the move?"

"Oliver has laid off the topic, for now. His mother, however, has not. She insists we move immediately."

Amelia puzzled over the problem. "Don't you find it odd she suddenly wants the estate transferred? What's the motivation for the timing?"

Kitty raised a pretty blonde eyebrow. "I don't find anything she does odd anymore. And it's not as if she's giving it to a stranger. Oliver knew sooner or later it would be his. I just hoped it would be later."

Amelia scratched her head, thinking she was missing something.

"But I didn't come here to talk about my problems." Kitty smoothed the hem of her dress, frowning at her unfashionable slipper. "In fact, I'm bored by my problems. Catch me up on your progress with George Davies's killer—and Simon Bainbridge! Please tell me they're not exclusive paths."

Amelia admired how easily her friend sneaked in a question about the relationship. "I have news, on both fronts." She tilted her head. "Really, I cannot believe I forgot to mention it before."

Kitty picked up her gray reticule and swung it at Amelia's knees. "You'd better start talking, or I'll beat it out of you."

Amelia gave up her pretense with a laugh. "Fine. I kissed Simon."

Kitty's brow furrowed. "You mean, Simon kissed you."

"No. Well, actually, yes. He *did* kiss my hand, in a jest, and I kissed him back. I, however, was not jesting."

Kitty covered her eyes as if she didn't want to see the truth behind the statement. "Goodness, Amelia. You didn't."

"I did."

"What did he say?"

"He admitted to liking it." Amelia's lips tingled at the memory. "Of course, this was after I told him I thought it was pleasurable, so perhaps he was just being nice."

"Let me get this straight." Kitty sat up as if to emphasize the point. "You not only kissed him. You asked him if he enjoyed it."

"That's correct."

Kitty let out a sigh. "What am I going to do with you?"

"Figure out how to find George Davies's killer?"

Kitty crossed her arms. "Fine. Bring me up to date."

Amelia filled her in on the details she didn't know: Lady Margaret, the facon, and her new theory of a female killer.

Kitty surprised Amelia with her speedy agreement. "We know two women were in the area. The flower seller and the lady she described, who perhaps disguised herself with a red wig. If the facon is as large as you say it is, anyone might have felled a man with it. And Mr. Davies was on the small side." Kitty's voice grew more convinced the longer she talked. "In a moment of passion, a woman might have left the knife behind. A man who's killed before wouldn't likely make that mistake. And Simon is still withholding that piece of evidence . . ."

Amelia was becoming more convinced, too.

Kitty folded her tiny hands determinedly in her lap. "This is what we should do. Engage the flower seller for the garden party. Get to know her personally. With effort—and, more important, money—she might reveal knowledge of the crime. Perhaps even her involvement."

"That sounds like a wonderful plan, Kitty, but what garden party do you mean?"

She stood. "Yours, silly."

Chapter 20

Dear Lady Agony,

I enjoy garden parties, but I can never get the mood right. They always come out fussy instead of fun even though I provide the necessary food, music, and entertainment. What makes a good experience?

Devotedly,
Fussy Not Fun

. . . .

Dear Fussy Not Fun,

Garden parties should be fuss-free. Being outdoors among friends should be fun enough. Perhaps you are forcing too much into the day. Try planning less and enjoying yourself more. Cake and conversation are all that is needed for a good experience.

Yours in Secret,
Lady Agony

On the way to Drury Lane, Kitty explained that Amelia would be the one throwing the party. Amelia needed to figure out who killed George Davies, and bringing together the possible culprits might end in new information. Furthermore, Amelia deserved a party. Hadn't she been in mourning too long? Yes, Kitty answered before Amelia could debate the question, she had. Nothing signaled a return to society like a well-done garden party. The season was in full swing, and better still, rain wasn't forecasted in the near future.

Amelia was amenable to the suggestion. She hadn't had a party since she'd been out of mourning. Winifred's recital was the closest they'd come to having a real event at the house, and Winifred had enjoyed it immensely. She was growing into a young woman and had been through much. A garden party with a few of her friends was just what she needed. And Amelia needed it, too.

She, like Winifred, was finding out there was more to life than existing. She wanted again to be a participant, and that meant engaging in not only work, but life. Often, she'd focused on readers' lives instead of her own. Indeed, her work at the penny paper had been her only outlet for two years. Now she had others, and the garden party would be one of them.

"It need not be formal," Kitty assured her. "In fact, the less formal, the better. It should feel as if the hostess has gathered a bunch of posies, a basket of cakes, and a handful of her dearest companions and thrown them together for a joyful afternoon."

Amelia slid a glance at her friend. Kitty made it sound so easy, but Amelia wasn't as good with domestic details as Kitty was. Indeed, if she mixed the three things together, it might look like a cyclone happened upon her backyard.

As if reading her mind, Kitty continued, "I will help you, and Tabitha will be there. The first thing you need is a guest list—"

"—which must include my suspects."

"Leave it to you to throw a party of merry murderers," Kitty grumbled.

"Not just murderers. There will be cake, too." When Kitty didn't smile, Amelia nudged her. "I'm only kidding. We'll keep it small so that I can watch over everyone's movements. Safety is my utmost concern."

"If the first murder was committed in passion, which seems likely, further violence is improbable. But one can never be too careful"—Kitty switched gears—"when it comes to flowers. We'll ask the flower vendor what she suggests, and what she can get in, but I'm thinking sweet peas. Lavender, white, and pink in the daintiest vases you've ever seen. Snow-white teacups. And a tower of cakes with rosewater frosting."

Just like that, the conversation changed from murder to pastries. Celebrations were in Kitty's blood. Like walking or breathing, events came easily to her. If Amelia wasn't careful, the entire *ton* would descend on her garden just to be seen at the impromptu event.

She wished only that her family could be there. Recently, she'd written her mother with the news that she was out of mourning, completely. Her mother was thrilled and promised a visit soon, but Amelia understood that *soon* might be a while. Summer was the busy season at the Feathered Nest, and the family rarely left home this time of year. And with Amelia's work at the magazine, returning to Mells was out of the question. At least right now.

Frances Rainier was in the same spot Amelia and Simon had found her before. She stood proudly, her shoulders mere blades beneath her dress, and perspiration clung to her throat from the late-afternoon sun. Like one of the flower bunches in her myriad baskets, she sparkled in the light, her violet eyes matching the hydrangeas of the same color.

"Stunning," Kitty whispered. "I've never seen dahlias that color."

Amelia glanced at her friend, wondering how much help she was really going to be on this expedition. If hats were her first weakness, flowers were her second, with shoes coming in a close third.

"My lady." Miss Rainier's voice raised in surprise. "You've returned."

"Miss Rainier," greeted Amelia. "I've brought my friend with me, Mrs. Hamsted."

Before Miss Rainier could acknowledge her, Kitty inquired about the flowers. "I must say, I've never seen dahlias so brilliant. A cross between pink, purple, and red. May I ask how you achieved the miracle?"

Miss Rainier's mood changed from cautious weariness to eager talkativeness. Squatting near the basket of flowers, she explained her process in depth, and Kitty, joining her, gobbled up every word. Miss Rainier handled the flower like a chalice, twisting it slowly for Kitty to admire. A sigh of delight escaped Kitty's lips.

Impatiently, Amelia waited for the conversation to cease so that she could go on to more important things—like throwing the garden party and finding George Davies's murderer. Marielle and Simon were counting on her to uncover the culprit. If she couldn't, she would disappoint two very dear friends.

But Amelia held her tongue and foot silent, realizing Kitty was achieving something with Miss Rainier she and Simon hadn't: trust. She kept quiet until they were finished, and her patience was rewarded. A genuine friendship seemed to have sprouted, like flowers, between the two women.

"If I may, I'd like to take this basket with me," said Kitty, standing. "It will be the envy of Mayfair."

"Of course, Mrs. Hamsted." Miss Rainier beamed, taking the coins from Kitty's outstretched hand. "I know it will be in good hands."

"I also need a favor." Kitty leaned in, in a way that always made one feel part of her intimate group. "Lady Amesbury is having a small fete, a garden party, and I'd like to decorate in purple, white, and pink sweet peas. Is it possible on short notice?"

Miss Rainier delayed a moment, causing some angst in Kitty's face. Then, in a sweeping motion, she uncovered a steel bucket of said flowers. Her face was radiant. "It is." Her fingers brushed the tips of the flowers. "I was just tucking them away for the day."

Kitty sighed. "They are just what I mean. Let's see, I'll need . . ." She counted on her fingers. "Eight bouquets for the tables, two for the gate, some of these lovely hydrangeas for the walk, and a dozen roses for the musician."

"Musician?" Amelia interrupted.

Kitty waved away the question. "Someone always sings at these things. You know that."

Amelia guessed she did know, but not as instinctively as Kitty. In her first year of mourning, she had been shut out of society altogether. The second year, she attended events sporadically. And the Feathered Nest hadn't exactly prepared her for life in London. Obviously, she had some catching up to do. But Kitty was the perfect teacher.

Kitty returned to Miss Rainier. "It's extraordinary of me to ask, and I hope you don't mind, but could you—would you—

manage the party?" Seeing the flower seller's reluctance, she continued quickly. "Lady Amesbury's gardener is not accustomed to parties. While he's very astute, he's also very old."

"It's true," Amelia added. "I'd hate to see him exert himself."

Miss Rainier chewed her bottom lip as she contemplated the proposition.

"It wouldn't take more than a day, two at most," Kitty promised. "And then after the party, you'll be right back on Drury Lane."

Miss Rainier chortled. "As if it's worth coming back to." She held out her hand. "You got yourself a deal, Mrs. Hamsted. When and where do I report?"

Kitty and Amelia smoothed out the details. Miss Rainier should arrive tomorrow afternoon, two days before the party, ready to work. With the help of Amelia's gardeners, she would refresh and decorate the area. It was short notice, certainly, but not uncommon for garden parties in London, where the weather changed event details as often as Kitty changed hats. Amelia had the staff, and her friends had the time. An impromptu party was just the thing for a summer's afternoon.

After taking their leave of Miss Rainier, Kitty and Amelia continued the discussion on the way to Kitty's house. Kitty was treating her like a small child, going on about the invitations, the food, the entertainment. She must have believed Amelia to be completely incompetent. After hearing her go on for a few minutes, however, Amelia wondered if it was partly true.

"The invitations must go out today and say something to the effect of, 'In light of our recent spate of favorable weather, I would like to invite you to an informal gathering in my garden day after next.'" Kitty steepled her fingertips. "'Please oblige me by coming as you are with the intention of wandering through freshly cut hedges, listening to joyful music, and drinking lemonade.' Or something as such." She clasped her hands nervously. "On second thought, maybe I should just write them."

"May I remind you that I write a dozen letters every day?" Amelia tsked. "I think I can handle one little invitation."

Amelia was beginning to question her declaration an hour later, however, when she tried and failed to recall the exact words Kitty had used just that afternoon when none of her own came to the paper. *Soirée? Party? Fete?* What had Kitty said?

"Lady Marielle is here," announced Jones. "Shall I say you're occupied?"

"Heavens, no!" Amelia was glad for the distraction. "Bring her in, will you? I have a question that she may be able to answer."

Marielle entered the pale blue morning room with a delightful expression on her face. Like Simon's, her eyes were green, but leaned more toward hazel, full of energy and light. They flicked from wall to wall, pausing on the floral art and towering windows. "What a beautiful room. I adore the color."

"Thank you. I like to think it matches the sky on an ideal spring day." She motioned to the chair near her small writing table. Like the woodwork and drapes, it was white. The other chairs were green chintz. "Please sit. I need your help."

As Marielle took the chair, a black tendril fell from her coiffure and crossed her forehead. She brushed at it youthfully. "Of course. Anything."

"I'm giving a small garden party—you're invited."

"Wonderful!" she gushed. "I love outdoor parties."

Amelia smiled. It was easy to get caught up in the young woman's enthusiasm. "Yes, me, too. But the invitation . . . I need to get it right. Should I use *party, fete,* or *soirée*? It's been a while since I've thrown such an event." Her smile faded. "Actually, I never have."

Marielle considered the question. "*Gathering*, I believe, is the word for which you're searching."

"Yes! *Gathering*," Amelia interjected. "Thank you." It was just the word Kitty had used, and she wrote it down immediately. "It's two days from today. Will you and your brother be able to attend?"

"I cannot *presume* to speak for Simon." Marielle lingered over the utterance like a curse word. "He does what he likes, as you must know. But my neighbor could escort me. We're good friends, and he's always home, buried in bookwork."

"Perfect." Amelia thought bringing Mr. Hooper was a grand idea and one that would keep Marielle's mind off her problems. She cleared her throat, preparing to change topics to one more unpleasant. "I've found out more information about the night of George's death."

Marielle reached for Amelia's hands across the desk, giving them a squeeze. "I knew you would."

"Simon helped," Amelia added.

She released Amelia's hands from her clasp. "By *helped* do you mean *interfered*?"

"I can certainly relate to that sentiment." Amelia sighed. "His help is not always helpful. This time, however, we were able to find out something about the knife that was used in George's murder. It's a large, ornate knife. A facon. Do you recall seeing it? Perhaps on the hip of one of George's acquaintances? It might have had a decorative sheath."

She shook her head. "I don't believe so. It sounds like a knife one would remember."

"What about money?" Amelia pressed. "Do you remember seeing money in his coat pocket the night of the opera? Enough to make you curious?"

Her face twisted with confusion. "Are you saying he was robbed?"

"Not exactly . . ."

"You're saying he's a thief, then." Marielle was incensed, her voice deeper, like her brother's, and her eyes darker.

Amelia held up her hands, pleading innocence. "I don't know what I'm saying. All I know is that he had a thousand pounds in his coat the night he was murdered. I'm trying to figure out why. Did he have a bet at the club earlier? Or a race he was wagering on later?"

"Not that I'm aware of. That night, he came by the house, talking to Father while I finished dressing. Lord Cumberland and Lady Jane arrived with her aunt in a carriage, and we left shortly thereafter."

"Your father was present?" Amelia asked.

"Yes, he's a great fan of Lord Cumberland's," Marielle explained. "Lord Cumberland's uncle knows my father. They played together as children. If Father had his way, I'd be engaged to Lord Cumberland straightaway. He thinks theirs is a grand family."

Amelia needed to get closer to the duke, to find out about his conversation with George Davies and what, if anything, it had to do with his death. The only connection she could make was money. George didn't have much, and the duke had a great deal. He'd employed George at one time. Perhaps work was the connection. "Do you think it's possible George was working for your father again? That the duke gave him the money?"

"Never." Marielle's answer was firm. "After the last race,

Father was finished—with George and racing. He didn't appreciate the attention George was paying me. He wanted him as far away as possible."

"Ah." Amelia sucked in a breath.

"What is it?" Marielle paused. "Oh, I think I understand. Father wanted George to stay away from me." She shook her head. "You wonder if the money was a bribe. To get George to leave."

"Perhaps." Amelia watched Marielle's face change with the emotions washing over her: surprise, confusion, anger, sadness. The betrayal of a family member stung worse than that of any friend or foe. It was the fatal poison that killed relationships, changing the course of everything.

"Oh!" Marielle's mouth turned into a perfect circle. "But if the money was in George's coat, it means he accepted it."

Which suggested George didn't love Marielle as much as she thought he did.

Chapter 21

Dear Lady Agony,

How can you pen letters for a cheaply produced paper? The articles are scant, and the stories are overly dramatic. If you really are a lady, you are above this magazine. Stop embarrassing us with your writing.

Devotedly,
A Proper Peer

. . . .

Dear A Proper Peer,

It's always nice to hear from peers. I never tire of telling them, as I will you, that I will not put down my pen. Personally, I find the magazine's articles fascinating and the stories entertaining. It is your drawing rooms that are the greatest bore. Perhaps if they were more interesting, I would visit them

instead of these pages. Until that day, friend, you may find me
here, scribbling outside the lines.

Yours in Secret,
Lady Agony

The next day, Amelia was eager to pay a call on the Bainbridges. Before Marielle had left, she agreed to ask her father
about the money, and Amelia was grateful. Amelia didn't trust
Simon to get to the bottom of the matter.

That wasn't exactly true. She trusted him; she just didn't trust
him to tell her all the details. When it came to his father, he was
keeping a secret, and Amelia wasn't sure why. But she and Marielle had one goal, and that was to find George's murderer, the
duke be damned. Marielle had agreed to tell Amelia what she
found out today.

Which was why Amelia was growing impatient with Winifred and Bee. She was eager to commence their outing so that
she might return in time for tea with Marielle. She tugged on
her dress. For their afternoon shopping excursion, she'd allowed
Lettie to select a yellow frock with a fashionably full skirt, so
fashionable Lettie insisted on an expansive wire crinoline and
petticoat. Amelia was in a hurry and didn't resist, but now the
girls were nowhere to be found. She'd checked Winifred's room,
the nursery, even the mews. Nothing. She made her way toward
the garden, where Miss Rainier had begun work on the gazebo.
It was a favorite spot of Winfred's, especially with the party taking place.

Indeed, the stage was being set for a beautiful event, and
Amelia surveyed the area with admiration. Not until now had

she realized what the Amesbury staff was capable of. One utterance of the word *gathering* was all it took to set people in motion, and everyone from the groundskeeper to the stable boy was pitching in to help. The terrace was a delightful mix of oversized plants, potted flowers, and chairs arranged in gathering nooks. The sprawling courtyard, just three steps down, had been trimmed to perfection. Every shrub and flowering bush had been cut to show off its geometrical shape, and the hedges were maze masterpieces. The fountains were in the process of being cleaned, and as Amelia passed by her favorite, Aphrodite arising from the foam, she noticed it glistened white.

The gazebo had changed from white to lavender with Miss Rainier's purple wisteria. The result was a stunning, secluded hiding spot, perfect for Winifred and Bee. But all the flowers in the world couldn't conceal their giggles, which Amelia detected from several yards away.

She smiled as she spotted them sitting inside on the bench, poring over some sort of paper or book. She glanced about for Miss Rainier and located her at the nearby pond, where she was reconfiguring stones.

Amelia crept up on the girls and poked her head in without warning. "Good afternoon, ladies."

"Oh!" Winifred shrieked. "You scared me."

Bee tucked the paper under her arm.

"I'm sorry." Amelia laughed. "I didn't mean to scare you. It's just deserts for making me wait. I thought we were going shopping."

"I guess we lost track of time," Winifred apologized. She shot a smile in Bee's direction, and Bee tucked the paper farther under her armpit.

This was the second time Amelia had come upon them reading something they put away quickly. A little too quickly, in her opinion. "What are you reading?"

"Nothing," Bee answered immediately.

"What's that under your arm?" Amelia tried again.

"It's a . . . a . . . something we found." Bee darted a glance at Winifred.

"Right, we found it," Winifred confirmed. "Discarded."

Amelia was genuinely confused. "You know I don't mind what you read as long as you're reading. So why don't you show it to me."

No one moved.

"Come now," prodded Amelia. "Let's have it."

Bee peeled the paper from her armpit.

The type, the title, the illustration. *Is that what I think it is?* Of course it was. She would recognize Lady Agony's column anywhere. A little exclamation escaped her. "Oh!"

"It's our housekeeper's magazine." The words fell out of Bee's mouth in a rush. "She reads it every week. She must have been finished, because I found it by the trash. But I'll bring it back. I promise. Just please don't tell my father." Her face pinked at the prospect, her freckles appearing darker, and her bottom lip quivered.

"Why would I tell Lord Grey?" Amelia asked.

"It's inferior literature." Bee twisted her braid nervously. "Ladies aren't supposed to read it." She glanced up from her lap. "But the stories are so good."

"Excuse me?" Even though she'd heard the claim before, Amelia felt her temper double. It sounded exactly like something Lord Grey would say. "A good many ladies read the magazine. Why do you think Lady Agony receives all those letters from them?"

"That's what I said!" Winifred chimed in.

Bee's face relaxed a bit, a smile playing on her lips. "This week, she responds to all the men who've been complaining about her advice to No Wife of Mine. It's the best response yet."

"I think it's brilliant!" exclaimed Winifred.

"I think *she's* brilliant," Bee added.

Somewhere inside of her, Amelia felt a shift. She smiled with realization. When she'd started writing, it was a way to keep herself busy after Edgar's death. A way to escape. She wasn't used to having time on her hands, nor was she used to the appropriate methods of spending it. In many ways, her secret pseudonym was a mode for her to evade the constraints. But seeing Winifred's and Bee's reactions made her realize Lady Agony was an example for all girls and women coming up against society's limitations. Every time Lady Agony refused to follow convention, it might encourage others to do the same.

"Regardless, you never have to hide anything from me, Winifred, especially your reading selections." Amelia winked at her daughter. "I myself have waited on pins and needles for that story's next installment." She nodded at the magazine. Once, she'd forced Grady to bring her the final episode of a romance five days before it was printed, but he wouldn't budge on the current issue. "I'm of the opinion that children should read whatever they want, within reason. It builds future writing and reading skills."

"That's what Bee wants to do." Winifred jumped off the seat. "She wants to be a writer."

"Maybe," added Beatrice bashfully. "Maybe I want to be a writer."

"Then you should read as often as you can." Amelia lowered her voice. "And as variously."

Winifred smiled at her friend. "I told you she is the best."

"Now, fetch your gloves and hats, and I'll meet you in the foyer." Amelia shooed them toward the terrace. "I need to speak to Miss Rainier for a moment before we leave."

The girls dashed off in the direction of the house, and Amelia walked toward the pond. If this morning's creations were any indication, Miss Rainier was proving to be an excellent designer. But she wasn't here solely for her gardening skills. The plan had been to quiz her as much as possible about the night of George's murder, and Amelia had today and tomorrow to get the details.

"Miss Rainier, I've just come from the gazebo." Amelia indicated the beautiful creation. "I love what you've done with it."

"It isn't finished." Miss Rainier kept at her task, her gloved fingers like tiny hoes working the dirt. "The girls wanted to see, so I left it awhile and started on these weeds." She glanced up, and Amelia noted a trickle of sweat sliding down her cheek. "They're everywhere."

"I'm afraid Taber, our head gardener, isn't as young as he once was, but he enjoys the pond and feeding the fish. I haven't had the heart to give someone else the task." Amelia sat down on the long stone bench. "Why don't you join me in the shade? You look warm."

Frances removed her straw hat, swept back her moist brown-gray hair, and replaced it. "For a minute. I have a lot of work to do, and I haven't started on the flower arrangements."

"Please don't fret," Amelia stressed. "It's been a long time since we've had a social gathering, and I don't expect you to renovate the entire lawn in two days. It's an ancient manor, and I actually prefer it that way."

"But it needs to be ready for the party."

"The event is small and informal." Amelia shrugged. "If my

friends can't abide the sight of a weed or two, then I need different friends."

"I like your friend Mrs. Hamsted."

"I do, too. She'll be at the party. So will Simon Bainbridge, the gentleman who was with me the night we first met." Amelia paused. "Do you mind if I ask you a question about that evening?"

Frances stiffened. "No, but I already told you everything."

"I just need to clarify something." Amelia smiled, trying to ease her fears. "You said you saw a woman in a nice dress, perhaps a lady, talking to Mr. Davies. Someone else told us they saw him talking to an upper-class gentleman." She tapped her chin. "What I'm wondering is if these two people might have been together. Maybe even a couple that split up to talk to him separately."

"I don't recall." Frances shook her head. "What'd the man look like?"

"He was fair-haired, nicely dressed," Amelia supplied.

"I didn't see a man like that."

"The waitress at the gin house told us about him," Amelia added.

Frances snorted a laugh. "Ruthie? You can't believe a word that comes out of her mouth. She'll say anything you want for a nice tip."

Simon *had* tipped her well after the conversation. Had the entire dialogue been a ruse to get into his pocketbook? Amelia didn't think so. The woman had too many details for it to be made up. Besides, Amelia had the feeling the proprietor knew something, too, but wasn't saying. It might have been the reason he dismissed Ruthie so quickly.

"If you remember anything at all, you'll let me know?"

Frances gave her a brisk nod and glanced at the pond. "I will."

"Thank you." Amelia returned to the house, where Winifred and Bee were anxiously awaiting their shopping trip. Amelia was anxious, too. Winifred was growing up. The afternoons spent with her would become farther apart, and friends like Bee would get more of her attention.

She put the trouble out of her mind as she, Winifred, and Bee scoured the West End, shopping for treasures. Regent Street, Bond Street, and Pall Mall provided brief stops for new bonnets, ice cream, and a magic show. Then, as promised, Amelia pointed the driver to Fleet Street, where the girls took in the busy newspaper hub from the safety of the Amesbury carriage. It was chock-full of men, boys, and horses, not to mention newspapers, magazines, and pamphlets. Words themselves seemed to fill every crack and crevice in the street, and once in a while, a wave of them would pour into the carriage, the important news of the day hitting Amelia's ears with hard insistence.

As they passed the building where Grady worked, Amelia peered up at the tiny windows. Right now, someone might be gathering her responses, arranging them for the weekly column. Little did they know, Lady Agony was driving down this very street with two girls in tow.

Amelia glanced at Bee and noticed she, too, was taken with the neighborhood. The smell of newsprint practically filled the carriage, and the girl inhaled the air as if it were rose scented. Maybe here was the next newspaperwoman—one who wouldn't use a pseudonym at all but her real name. Amelia bit her lip to keep in a chuckle. *Lord Grey wouldn't like that.*

The carriage turned toward Mayfair, the day complete. At

least, she thought so until she spotted a magnificent toy ship in a shopwindow. It was the handsomest sailboat she'd ever seen, with a rich brown hull, crisp white sail, and sparkling flag. She pounded on the roof. "Stop, please."

Winifred crowded close to her. "What is it?"

Amelia stuck out her finger. "That."

Both girls oohed at the vessel.

"We've been wanting a new boat," Amelia said.

"Don't you think it's a trifle . . . big?" asked Winifred. The ship was as least as tall as she was.

Bee blinked.

"It's not big. It's . . . smart." Amelia tugged at her reticule. "Let's go see it."

The footman opened the door, and off they went to the little shop with the big boat. Amelia hadn't seen Winifred this excited for an age, and truth be told, she was excited herself. Winifred examined the ship, reaching out her hand but not actually touching the sails, as if they were protected by an invisible shield. Amelia, however, couldn't resist a fleeting touch of the wide-striped cloth, beautifully starched and stretched. It looked as if the boat belonged in the ocean, sailing the high seas.

"I see you found our prized possession." A shopkeeper approached. He was tall, all limbs, and his beard was brown and square. "Like the sirens, it's lured a good many children from their destinations."

"Does it work?" Winfred asked.

"Does it work?" The shopkeeper tutted, his mustache stirring with the action. "You think we'd be selling it if it didn't?" He ran a hand over a knot in the strings. "This is the finest model ship in all of London, built by Admiral Edwards himself."

Admiral Edwards. Amelia's ears perked up at the name. He

was a friend of Simon's, one she'd come to admire in the last month. Besides working for the Royal Navy, Admiral Edwards owned a shipbuilding business, Fair Winds. *If his model boat performs as well as his real boats, we are in for a real treat.*

She gazed at the ship. Before her eyes appeared Victoria Park. A sunny day, a calm wind, a beautiful regatta of boats. Her boat was in the lead. Lord Grey's was at the shoreline. Winifred was cheering her on. She smiled. *Lovely.* "I'll take it."

The shopkeeper's mouth twisted open in surprise. "My lady?"

"Yes, that's right. I'd like to purchase it." Amelia opened her purse. "How much?" He named the price, and she put away her reticule. "If you could so kindly send the bill to me, Amelia Amesbury."

"Certainly, my lady. We'll deliver it today."

"No need. I have my carriage." Amelia motioned out the window, and her staff came forward. "My footman can help you."

The men wrapped the boat in brown paper and loaded it onto a cart while Winifred and Bee clasped hands to keep from jumping up and down. They were giddy about racing it in the upcoming regatta at Victoria Park. Amelia was giddy, too. Never in her life had she had such a toy, and she felt like a girl with a peppermint stick about to taste it for the first time. Her childhood had been all work and no games, except for those that included entertaining guests. But now? She looked on at Bee and Winifred and their happiness. She could revisit her childhood one boat race at a time.

Chapter 22

Dear Lady Agony,

I love the wire crinoline! It's so light and creates such a desirable shape. Plus, it has given our carpenters work to do, widening doorframes. But my aunt thinks it's unchaste, for if a solid wind whips up, a lady's ankles are bound to show. You're a sensible woman. What is your opinion?

Devotedly,
Ankles Away

· · · · · · · · · · · · · · · · · · ·

Dear Ankles Away,

My verdict on the crinoline is decidedly more mixed. While I appreciate its lightness, I worry about its real dangers, which do not include exposed ankles. These are the ones I've heard of personally: being caught on fire, being caught in carriage wheels, and being caught in machinery. And if one needs to make a

quick getaway? Forget it. One is better off hiding than making a
run for it. Readers of my column will understand which option
This Author prefers.

Yours in Secret,
Lady Agony

When Amelia arrived at the Bainbridge mansion, she was disappointed to learn Simon wasn't home, not that she'd admit it. Marielle said she expected him back later that evening, but for now, they had the drawing room to themselves. The last of her callers had left thirty minutes ago, and she uttered her relief. Miss Pimm was proud of the number of visitors, seeing it as a sign of Marielle's success this season, but Marielle was clearly exhausted. She had to pretend she wasn't grieving the death of George Davies all while entertaining company.

Marielle released a breath, and her shoulders lowered several inches. "Thank goodness that's over. You can't imagine what it's like to entertain guests while wishing you could dive under the covers of your bed and not come up for days." She blinked. "Actually, you probably can."

"I can, but my circumstances were different. Edgar and I were married, and our relationship was known." Amelia gave her a sympathetic embrace before selecting the settee. "Is the duke still insisting on complete denial of your acquaintance with George Davies?"

Marielle's eyes narrowed, and she looked like Simon then, all cool intelligence. "Worse than that. He's preventing rumors by putting me in society's eye." Her eyes flicked to the door. "Miss Pimm has been my shadow for days."

"At the duke's request?"

"I'm certain."

Amelia mulled over the response. It wasn't a bad one, from a duke's perspective. What better way to prove his daughter had no feelings for George Davies than to have her seen in public, unaffected? But as her father, couldn't he see she was hurting? Amelia understood the true extent of her sadness. Marielle had lost a man she cared for deeply. Perhaps with love's first sting.

The realization brought with it a memory of herself at sixteen years old and her devotion to Patrick Kingsley, an Irishman she was certain she would marry before he departed from the inn. He was nine and twenty, with a head of curly red hair and a thick accent that made her blush every time she heard it. Her love affair began when he described Ireland's hills as verdant vales of green. He had the words of a poet in his back pocket, awakening an Irish longing she didn't know she possessed. She had the wanderlust in her even then and would have followed him into the River Styx as long as it took her away from rural England.

As it were, he left her one Monday morning with a good-hearted chuckle when she declared her fervent wish to travel the world, starting with Ireland. He stated plainly she was much too young to have such thoughts and to stick to books for adventure. His accent sounded decidedly less attractive then, though Grady thought the rebuff supremely funny coming from a man who told them he'd left home at the age of twelve. Amelia would still like to see Ireland . . .

She refocused on Marielle. "Did you ask your father if he bribed George Davies? His answer might provide us with a new direction."

"I did." Marielle joined her on the settee, continuing at a whisper. "He turned the question on me, asking how I could be involved with someone who could be bribed. He called me fool-ish." She made tiny fists with her hands. "He isn't wrong. If George took the money, he might have been the scoundrel my family said he was. And I've been a stupid girl."

Amelia reached for her hands and gave them a squeeze. "You're a very bright woman. If George was a scoundrel, what does that have to do with you? You can't blame yourself, and maybe you can't blame George, either. Don't underestimate the power of money. To someone who doesn't have any, it's life-changing."

Marielle smiled. "Talking to you always makes me feel better."

Amelia returned the smile.

A knock happened at the door, and Miss Pimm entered.

"Lady Marielle." Miss Pimm's voice was like an early-morning bird's, energetic and insistent. "I'm sorry to interrupt, but Mr. Hooper's new filly has arrived. He asked me to share the news at once. He's quite excited. Why don't you go see for yourself?"

Marielle's eyes lit up. "Do you mind, Amelia?"

"Goodness, no." Amelia knew how much Marielle loved horses—and she had a plan of her own. "Go on. I'd love to freshen up after shopping all day with Winifred. I didn't have much of a chance."

While Miss Pimm showed Amelia where to revive herself, past the second drawing room and imposing portrait museum, Marielle darted outside to see Mr. Hooper and his horse. Ame-lia made a production of opening her reticule as noisily as pos-sible, but really, she was listening for footsteps. Once they disappeared, she reopened the door, glancing furtively left and right. The second-floor hallway was clear. One more flight of stairs, and she would be in the personal living quarters of the family.

A secret remained between her and Simon, and while she'd given him ample time and opportunities to reveal it, he hadn't, so she must see for herself what he retrieved the night of George Davies's murder. Marielle said he wouldn't be home until tonight, so, with the family outside, now was her chance to find it. The item was small, shiny, and of consequence. Otherwise, he wouldn't have taken it. Also, he would have told her. It must have pertained to his family or a friend or a woman. He was protecting someone, but whom?

Silently, she climbed the stairs. The house was massive and brick, and the hallway was dark, with only the light from a stray bedroom window illuminating the way. The rooms had been cleaned hours ago, and no maid or staff was nearby. She followed the paisley carpet like a walking path, keeping her focus on the intricate design and not her nerves.

She came upon mahogany double doors, shut except for a narrow opening that revealed an enormous bed with four posts, heavily curtained. She stopped, inhaling the slight scent of salt and ocean breeze that followed Simon wherever he went.

This is it. Don't think. Do.

Summoning all her courage, she glanced over her shoulder and ducked into the room, flattening her back against the bedroom wall. Her chest heaved. Never had she been so afraid in all her life. Well, she had, but just once when a murderer was chasing her. Simon was the second-most dangerous man she knew. She cautiously glanced around the room. *And the most virile.*

Everywhere she looked reminded her of the opposite sex. The bed was the most commanding piece of furniture in the room, followed by a dressing screen with an ornately carved hunting scene, followed by a thick bearskin rug. It was hard not to linger over what happened in the room and where. She swallowed hard.

Concentrate.

She wasn't here for herself. She wasn't here for Simon. She was here for one of her readers, Marielle, and she deserved her full attention. Simon was hiding something, and when Amelia spotted it, she would know what. Her best guess was a piece of jewelry. It'd sparkled brilliantly on the dark street. Was it a woman's? Marielle's? If so, it made sense why he hid it from the police, but why hide it from her?

A walnut box with mother-of-pearl inlay was the most obvious place to look for jewelry, and she started there. Rings, cuff links, pins—nothing unusual. In the drawer was a locket with his mother's hair inside. Pitch black like his own. She closed it quickly. It was wrong to be here, riffling through his personal effects. What had she been thinking?

She took a step toward the door and stopped. *No.* He'd forced her hand. She'd come here to find what he was hiding, and that's what she intended to do. He wouldn't keep a piece of evidence with his personal possessions. *Think, think.* Scanning the room, her eyes landed on a small desk. It was the only furniture with a lock on it. If he was hiding something, it was in there.

The lock would be easy enough to get around. She slipped a hairpin from her auburn tresses, and a few curls came undone. Plenty of guests had locked themselves out or lost their keys, and Amelia was proficient at getting people back into their rooms.

She fit the hairpin into the opening. A push and a twist, and another twist. *Success!* It opened.

Writing paper, the Bainbridge seal, naval documents. She smiled. Letters he'd saved from his mother were wrapped in a pink ribbon. She reached deeper inside, feeling with her fingers, and something moved. A panel. Her hand shook a little as she inched it open. It was a false bottom! A drawer within a drawer.

She bent down for a closer look, her skirt fanning around her in a circle of yellow sunbeams. Something sparkled in the dark. She reached for the item. "Ouch!" It was a tie pin in the shape of a horseshoe, six diamonds and three emeralds. Green and white—the colors of the Bainbridge crest. No wonder Simon hid it. Presumably, it placed his father at the scene of the crime.

"What in God's name are you doing?"

She spun around and fell on her rear.

Simon stood in the doorway.

She grasped for something to say, but words failed her. What could be told that he didn't understand already? Her movements and motive were obvious. She held the tie pin in her hand, evidence he'd withheld in the murder of George Davies. It was she who had questions. "Why are you hiding an important piece of evidence from the police? It's your father's, isn't it?"

Simon slowly closed the door. "I'm going to ask you again. What are you doing in my bedroom?"

"I saw you retrieve something shiny from the scene of the crime." She held up the pin. "This. When you didn't tell me about it, I came looking for it." She tried to inch her way off the floor, salvaging her dignity, but her skirt was too full, and she slipped. The one day she'd tried a new fashion, and it was keeping her down—literally. It was the first and last time she'd try to keep up with London's trends.

He stalked over to the desk.

He looks so much taller from this angle. Goodness, he needs a shave, too, and it's only four thirty in the afternoon.

He held out his hand.

"Thank you—" she started, thinking he was going to help her up.

"The pin."

"What? Why should I?" She put the pin behind her back. "Marielle deserves to know why you have this."

He bent at the knees, and the scent of the wind washed over her like a summer breeze. His eyes were stormy; they'd gone from bottle green to steel gray. And in his strong jawline, she noted a twitch.

"Give me the pin."

"No."

His eyes narrowed. "You know I can just take it from you."

"Not without a fight." She jerked her chin.

"Is that what you want?" His glance passed casually over her bare shoulders. "For me to wrestle it away from you?"

Her face flushed hot. Her gown had not only a full skirt but a low-cut bodice. Her bust was spilling over the top of it right now. *I should have never allowed Lettie to play dress-up!* Of course, the gown would soon be passed down to her, which was why she really wanted Amelia to wear it—and get rid of it, which Amelia planned to do as soon as this day was done.

She cleared her throat, trying to sound less amusing than she looked. "First, tell me what it is and why you took it."

"And then you'll return it to me?"

"Yes."

He sat down on the floor next to her. "I was going to tell you. I needed more time. That's all."

She clasped the pin tighter behind her back. "Time for what?"

"Time to figure out why the duke's pin was near the body of George Davies the night of his murder."

"I knew it belonged to your father!"

"He had it commissioned after his horse won the Ascot in 1854." He stretched out his legs. "He's worn it at every race since, safely pinned to his cravat. I can't imagine him giving it to George Davies."

"You're saying George stole it?"

He shrugged. "Perhaps. My father's been avoiding me, and I've been unable to quiz him. But I will."

"Yesterday, Marielle asked your father about the money in George's pocket. He didn't deny giving it to him. Instead, he asked why she would be involved with a man she suspected of accepting a bribe."

"The duke deals in obfuscation." His tone was thick with bitterness.

It confused Amelia. "What are you saying?"

"When he's involved, people you love disappear." He looked away.

Confirmation washed over her in a wave of coldness. *Simon thinks the duke did something to his mother.* Was it a child's suspicion or something more? His mother died in a train accident with her paramour beside her. The duke might make people disappear, but wreck an entire train? She didn't see how it could be possible. "Oh, Simon."

He turned to her, the mask of the experienced naval officer gone. He was a son who'd been hurt by his father, and his face displayed a youthfulness she'd never noticed before. Though his visage was well creased from his time on a ship, his eyes widened with the knowledge that she knew his worst fears. How long he'd held up an internal, solitary battle. How lonely it must be for him to wonder about his father's involvement and never ask.

"I couldn't allow Marielle to feel what I've felt since our

mother passed until I knew for certain the duke was involved, and I never found evidence. Suspicion changes a person, and not in a good way." He shook his head, and a lock of dark hair fell over his brow. "I don't want that for Marielle and me. I need her to trust me."

"Of course. We cannot rely on half-truths and suppositions. You need to ask your father about the night of George Davies's death, and I want to be there when you do."

"You don't trust me?" A hurt expression crossed his face.

"I do." As the words rushed out of her mouth, she realized she truly meant them. He'd hidden the pin from her but for good reason. He didn't want her to tell Marielle without proof of the duke's involvement. "But Marielle doesn't trust you right now. I need to be there. You need to trust *me* this time."

He nodded slowly. "All right."

She felt their relationship shift—grow—and it felt good. She'd trusted him with her secret pseudonym, and he'd trusted her with his painful past. They could be honest with each other, and vulnerable. It was a relief to her, to them—to people who were always expected to act a certain way. She handed him the pin. "I'm sorry for sneaking into your bedroom."

"Under difference circumstances, I wouldn't have minded." A smile played at the corner of his lips.

"You're just trying to make me blush again."

He tilted his head. "You look pretty when you blush."

She focused on her lap.

He stood, placed the pin on the desk, and then pulled her up. She wobbled a little, and he clasped her waist to steady her. "Whoa."

His hands seared through the fabric of her dress and into her skin, and all she could think of was his touch and their kiss. All thoughts of growth and maturity flew out of her head. She returned to the curious young woman who wanted to know more about his body, his desires, and her own. She turned away, determined not to pursue him.

He caught her face.

She didn't move. This would be all him or nothing at all.

He lowered his head, his eyes searching her own. He was asking for permission without saying a word. Finding it, he moved his hand along her jawline as if tracing the lines of a map to a destination. He lingered over her neck, inhaling softly. "Roses. I knew it was roses."

She longed for him to take her in his arms, to crush the heavy scent between them. Yet she stood still, using every ounce of her willpower to remain so.

"Lord Bainbridge," interrupted a voice from beyond the closed door. "Are you in?"

Amelia's stomach lurched. All thoughts of flowers and kisses flew out of her head.

It was the perfect Miss Pimm.

Chapter 23

Dear Lady Agony,

I have a cousin. I'll call her Excellent Evelyn. She's welcomed at fetes, balls, and musicals of people I can only pretend to know, and don't get me started on her own parties, whose invitations never seem to reach my mailbox. My mother constantly compares us, and it's exhausting. I don't see how I will ever measure up. Do you?

Devotedly,
Second Best

....

Dear Second Best,

Don't confuse popularity with excellence. Certainly, she has been invited more places, but does that make her better? It does not. Don't compare yourself or your invitations. And tell your mother to stop such nonsense, too. She's old enough to know better.

Yours in Secret,
Lady Agony

As a widowed countess, Amelia didn't have to adhere to many of the rules forced upon other women her age. She had a daughter, she had a title, she had money, and if that wasn't enough, she had Aunt Tabitha, whose reputation was beyond reproach. But being caught in a man's bedroom? That was a rule not to be broken. And yet there was Miss Pimm at the door!

"Yes, I'm in." Simon's voice wavered. "What is it?"

"I thought I saw you." Miss Pimm's self-important voice was congratulatory. "Why are you back so soon, my lord?"

"I forgot to post an important letter." He picked up a piece of paper and rustled it noisily.

"I can take care of it," answered Miss Pimm. "You need only open the door."

Amelia's jaw dropped.

Simon tried to assuage her fears by patting her shoulder. "I can't right now, Miss Pimm. I'm indisposed. Just tell me what it is you need."

"Should I send for your valet?"

Amelia shook her head violently.

"No!" Simon shouted. "No thank you. What can I help you with?"

"It's Lady Amesbury," Miss Pimm whispered into the door. "She was here a moment ago, and now I can't find her. Yet her carriage is still outside. I thought your paths might have crossed."

Amelia hid her face in her hands. If only the action would make her disappear.

"Oh, Lady Amesbury," answered Simon confidently. "I saw she was outside when I returned."

Outside? What was he thinking? How was she going to get outside undetected? That was even farther than the drawing room.

"*Indeed.*" The censure in Miss Pimm's voice was palpable. "I didn't think to look there."

"Around back. By the mews."

"She must have decided to see Mr. Hooper's filly after all," Miss Pimm said. "I'll send away the tea things, then."

Amelia heard her footsteps start and stop.

"And please let me know if you need anything at all," added Miss Pimm.

"Certainly."

Simon and Amelia waited a few moments in stone silence. When Amelia was confident Miss Pimm was gone, she whispered, "How am I supposed to get outside? Do you have a magic carpet somewhere?"

"No, but I have a balcony—and a tree. Climbed it many times myself as a young man. Very sturdy. Not too big, not too small."

Amelia peered out his double window, studying the terrain like an acrobat eyeing a tightrope. She allowed the curtain to drop. "Let me get this straight. You want me to slip out the balcony, climb down a tree, and land on a patio *three floors down*? Are you mad?"

"Not a patio. A garden hedge. And there's a balcony beneath us, too. So technically balcony, balcony, tree, hedge." He smiled. "I'll be with you the entire way."

She wasn't sure if that made it better or worse—better that he could catch her if she fell but worse if someone saw them, which was a possibility, since it was late afternoon. Yet the side of the house was concealed by tall trees. The chances of someone seeing beyond the tree line were slim to none.

"We'd better hurry if we are to beat Miss Pimm."

His words lit a fire in her. She slipped off her shoes and tucked them under her arm. "I can't possibly handle this dress and *these* shoes." She smoothed a loose hair behind her ear. "What's unfortunate is that I'm really good at climbing trees, but you'll never know it in this monstrosity." She touched her skirt.

"You don't have to be good, just decent enough to get down the tree. I'll go first." He stepped onto the balcony and scanned the area. Then he motioned her forward.

The stone balcony was long and narrow and cold on her feet. No other windows opened to it, and it acted more as a decoration to the facade than a resting place. She tiptoed to the corner, where Simon slipped down to the second-floor balcony with the agility of a cat. Or a young boy looking for a way out of the house undetected.

He's done this before. Amelia peeked over the edge, and he held up his arms to her.

"It's fine," he promised. "I'll guide you. Toss me your shoes."

It really isn't that far. Watching her shoes hit the stone balcony didn't instill confidence, however. She took a breath and swung her legs over the ledge, where his arms were waiting for her. *Hurry, ninny, before he sees your underclothes.* She slid down the length of his body, his hands following her every move. Her feet landed softly. Knocking in her chest, her heart beat so loudly she hoped he couldn't feel it. She would've been fine if not for the cumbersome dress, but it was like climbing down a ladder in a church bell. One wrong move, and she'd go from ding to dong.

Her dress was twisted, and she pulled it straight, taking a deep breath. *I can do this. I need to do this.*

"See? That wasn't so bad," he declared.

She gave him a curt nod. Now for the tree.

Simon was right. It was mature, and its branches were long but narrow. It would easily support the weight of a boy, but two grown adults and—she glanced at her dress—*this*?

Reading her mind, Simon added, "It's an English oak. We will manage."

English oaks were symbols of strength. In fact, couples used to be wed under them in Cromwell's time for that reason. *We shall test its fortitude today—literally.* "Right. Let's get on with it."

A branch hung directly over the balcony, so reaching it was no problem. It lowered only briefly when Simon put his full weight on it, which was a small comfort. It bobbled up and down as he inched toward the trunk on his knees, turning and waiting for her before he went any farther.

The confident look in his eye assured her she could do this. She focused on that instead of the ground as she grasped the branch and hung. *Plunk.* Back down she went to the balcony, where she noticed her slippers still lay. *That won't do.* How would she explain her shoes being on his balcony? She stuffed them into her neckline, hoping her corset would hold.

Pulling herself up was one thing. Pulling up herself *and* this dress was another. Even though it wasn't nearly as ornate as this season's dresses, it was much fuller than her usual gowns. *Too full.*

Simon scooted back toward the balcony. "Shall I give you a boost?"

"Not necessary. I know how to climb a tree." *Just not in this ridiculous dress.* Indeed, she had to try two more times before she had success. The nice thing was, after reaching the branch, she was able to bunch the dress beneath her knees to protect them from the hard bark. *At least it has one benefit.* Plus, the tree's leaves concealed their location, and she felt less anxious about someone seeing her than she did on the exposed balcony.

She followed Simon's lead. After a short climb along the branch, down the trunk, and onto the hedge, he waited for her under the tree. Escape and freedom seemed to be hers for the taking, and, inching along the branch, she congratulated herself on her strength and agility. *The old childhood reflexes are kicking in.*

As kids, she and Grady had climbed their fair share of trees. And barns. She recalled the time they tied a drunk man's shoelaces together, and the only place they had to go was up. They sat on the top of the horse shed until the man passed out under a tree, waiting for them. She'd never forget the feeling of her feet hitting the ground that night and the air rushing through her lungs as she ran full speed for home. She suspected it would feel just as good to be on solid ground today.

She reached for the trunk with a sigh of relief.

"Bainbridge! I didn't see you there."

Amelia froze.

"Hooper!" Simon's voice was ten times louder than it needed to be. "Hooper, our friend and neighbor. Good to see you."

Oh no! I cannot let him see me.

"Uh, same to you." Mr. Hooper fumbled a reply.

Amelia pulled back, and when she did, a satin slipper fell from her bosom. She slapped a hand over her mouth to prevent herself from crying out but heard Simon's sharp intake of breath.

"What was that?" asked Mr. Hooper.

"Nothing." Simon shuffled his feet, perhaps concealing the slipper. "A walnut, I believe."

A walnut from an English oak tree? Good Lord.

Simon cleared his throat. "I'm here to see the new filly." He was still talking ridiculously loud for Amelia's sake. "Where is she?"

"Around back. Lady Marielle is with her."

Simon chuckled. "That's not surprising. My sister is attracted to any horse in a fifty-mile radius."

"She knows her horses," Mr. Hooper complimented. "I think she prefers them to people sometimes."

"That's my doing, unfortunately. We visited the ponies so much as children that we thought of them as our friends. And when I joined the navy, I'm afraid they did become her friends."

The idea tugged at Amelia's heart. Their mother was gone. The duke was largely absent. Of course, the brother and sister would turn to the animals for friends. Finding George, a man who knew and loved horses as much as she did, must have felt like a dream come true for Marielle. And with her older, protective brother gone, George could take advantage of her vulnerability.

"Not a bad friend to have, in my book," Mr. Hooper replied. Grass crunched beneath his feet. "Shall we?"

"You go ahead," Simon suggested. "I'll be right behind you." A long moment passed, and Simon whispered, "Did you lose something, Amelia?"

"Sorry, it slipped out of my . . ." Amelia shoved the remaining slipper deeper into her corset. "Never mind. Is the coast clear?"

"Hold on." Footsteps and then a moment later he said, "For now, but hurry."

"What do you mean *hurry*?" Amelia grumbled. "I move as fast as a snail in this thing."

"It's Marielle," he said in a low voice. "She's headed this way on the new filly, and that means Hooper will be, too."

Oh no, oh no, oh no. Amelia repeated the words silently as she inched toward the trunk. At least it was Marielle. They were friends, and she wouldn't ask questions. But Mr. Hooper? She needed to get out of the tree before he spotted her. He was a nice young man and neighbor. Amelia couldn't chance him seeing her here. *Better than Simon's bedroom, I suppose.*

She reached for the trunk, and jagged bark tore at her skin. She shook off the sting. "Blazes!"

"Amelia! Are you all right?"

"It's fine," she assured. "Just a scratch." But as she clasped both arms around the trunk and pushed off the branch, she realized it wasn't fine. In fact, it was so *not* fine that her grasp released and her dress ripped as she fell down, down, down and into Simon's arms. Thankfully, he caught her—before they both tumbled backward onto the ground.

She heard his breath lodge. Then she heard someone call her name from somewhere in the sky.

It took a moment for the dizziness to leave her and her eyes to focus. She blinked. Not the sky, exactly, just Marielle sitting high above her on a horse. She squinted. *Drat.* Mr. Hooper was at her side.

Chapter 24

Dear Lady Agony,

It's my daughter's first season, and naturally, she's spent much time on the dance floor with various suitors. Although I've told her it's perfectly acceptable to ignore the unsuitable men when she meets them on the street, she insists on acknowledging them. How am I to correct this behavior?

Devotedly,
Cutting Allowed

....

Dear Cutting Allowed,

While cutting is deemed acceptable by polite society, I contend that your daughter is the better behaved for her acknowledgment. If a gentleman spent time with her the evening before, why shouldn't he be greeted in passing? I can see no harm in her

conduct. Polite society's conduct, however, could use a refresher
on the word **polite.**

Yours in Secret,
Lady Agony

Amelia had been in many tight places. She'd been at the wrong place at the wrong time while conducting research for a response in her Lady Agony column. Readers might complain about a store or a seamstress or even a street that was particularly troublesome, and she'd have to investigate the problem on her own. Quick thinking was a must in her work, and luckily her brain was able to generate plausible explanations at will. Found in an unsavory part of town? Winifred loved jam from the neighborhood's corner baker. Caught sneaking out of the house when she should be in bed? Her insomnia necessitated fresh air. Spotted riding astride instead of sidesaddle on Rotten Row? Well, that was just plain common sense, but Amelia made an excuse about bad balance. Indeed, her head was full of ideas.

But today—nothing. Maybe she'd suffered a head trauma in the fall. Or maybe the cut on her hand hurt too bloody bad. Or maybe the fuzziness behind her eyes refused to let her see what was right in front of her: Marielle and Mr. Hooper waiting for an explanation.

"Lady Amesbury," Simon squeaked beneath her.

That got her moving.

"Oh!" Amelia rolled off his chest. She heard the air return to his body.

Slowly, he sat up. He scanned her for signs of distress. "Are you hurt?"

"What happened?" Marielle asked as she dismounted the horse.

"I'm fine," Amelia assured Simon, tucking her bare feet beneath her dress.

Simon grabbed her hands. One was bloodstained from the tree bark. "That needs attention."

Marielle stared at the gash, repeating her question. "What happened?"

Amelia had the hard-earned belief that saying something was always better than saying nothing. She hoped it proved true again as she cleared her throat. "I ran into the tree."

"And into Lord Bainbridge . . ." added Mr. Hooper, as if trying to fill in a blank in his mind.

"Right," Simon agreed, helping her up. "I saw Lady Amesbury coming and tried to stop her."

"I—oh." Marielle surveyed Amelia's dress, which was torn at the hem. Her eyes landed somewhere over Amelia's shoulder. "Your shoes!"

Amelia clutched her chest, but the remaining slipper was gone.

"Are right there, where they fell off," supplied Simon.

Amelia followed his gaze. Her shoes were a few feet from her, behind the tree. She dusted off her dress, which was beautiful but going straight into the garbage after this fiasco. Being fashionable was not worth the headache—or injury. She walked to the shoes and slipped them on, Mr. Hooper turning his head as if she were putting on drawers instead of footwear. "I worried I'd miss the chance to see the new horse and took off at a run, but lucky me, here it is."

The horse whinnied as if on cue.

"It's good to see you again, Mr. Hooper," Amelia continued. "She's a beautiful filly. You're an equine enthusiast, I take it."

"Enthusiast, yes. Lady Marielle is the real expert, however." Mr. Hooper's voice was mellow and full of admiration as he took the reins from Marielle. "I'm just glad she approves of my choice."

"Approves?" Marielle petted the horse's head. "Approves and envies! She's as gentle as today's wind, especially for a young horse."

Mr. Hooper beamed at the compliment.

Amelia thought the horse was a lot like its owner, calm and quiet with an unspoken strength. Mr. Hooper's manner was unassuming, and his cobalt blue eyes had a tendency to look just above one's head, out of shyness, Amelia guessed, not conceit. Mr. Hooper was a younger son who hadn't had a lot of practice in society. He was tolerated but not as welcomed as his brothers were. The best he would be able to offer a bride was his good name and a meager allowance.

"I agree," said Simon. "She's a spectacular animal. Will you race her?"

"No." Mr. Hooper chuckled. "I'd love to, but the field is overcrowded as it is."

Amelia knew what he meant. Racing was incredibly popular with the upper classes; he would be a small personality among giants. She didn't think he had it in him to strive for more.

"Well, I think you should," Marielle put in. "The field might be overcrowded, but it's also overinflated. With egos."

Mr. Hooper's chuckle turned into a laugh, and he twisted the reins of the horse around his hand. "Walk with us to the mews? I'll tell you about my plans for her."

Simon gave Amelia a glance that asked if she was up for it. Although her head still felt fuzzy, she agreed. Her stablemen had proved most helpful, and she realized Simon's staff might be able to provide information about George Davies, too. "Yes, let's."

Simon and Mr. Hooper took the lead with the horse, and Amelia and Marielle fell in line behind them. After a few minutes, Marielle touched her elbow. "You *did* run into the tree, didn't you? My brother didn't ravage you underneath it, did he?"

The comment was so unexpected Amelia choked back a laugh. "No, he didn't ravage me." They'd hardly kissed, let alone embarked on ravaging.

"I didn't think so, but he's different around you." She hazarded a glance at Amelia. "I wanted to make sure."

"Different?" Amelia asked. "How so?"

Marielle bit her lip. "I'm not sure . . . more like himself, I suppose." She shook her head, and a lock of hair dipped over her eyes. "That's not it exactly. What I mean is, he's always the duke's son. The marquis. The decorated navy hero. Around you, though, he lets down his guard. I haven't seen him do that since Felicity Farnsworth."

Although their acquaintance was brief, it had weathered several storms. Talk of murder, marriage, and madness had a way of breaking down conventional barriers of a normal relationship. Amelia felt comfortable asking the question foremost on her mind. "He loved her, didn't he?"

"Yes." A sad smile crossed her lips. "He would never admit it, but at one time, he was a lot like our mother. Passionate. Romantic. Headstrong." She shrugged. "After Felicity, that passion turned into carefulness. Caution. Toward me, he remains unchanged, however. An overbearing brother."

The men's distant conversation filled the silence for a few beats. "Perhaps with good reason this time?"

"Perhaps," Marielle admitted.

Both the Bainbridges and the Hoopers housed their horses and the horses' caretakers in the same lovely, U-shaped area. While the Hoopers had four stalls, the Bainbridges had six, complete with upstairs apartments, window boxes, and the family crest. It was a village of horses, men, and activity.

Marielle slowed her steps. "Did you tell Simon about the money? How Father might have instigated a bribe?"

"I did, and he cautioned patience. He plans to speak to the duke himself." When Marielle started to protest, Amelia added, "I'm going to be there, and you know I will tell you everything."

"How are you going to manage that? Being present?"

Amelia waved away the question. "I'll figure out something."

Marielle smiled as they turned toward the open stall. "Somehow I believe you will."

Mr. Hooper was holding a basket of apples, and Marielle joined him, scrounging for the best piece of ripe red fruit to feed the filly. An old stableman looked on with a smile. It was hard not to get caught up in Marielle's love for horses. She looked happier here than anywhere in London, and Mr. Hooper seemed to admire Marielle's skills.

"As much as I've enjoyed this afternoon, I must go home and change before anyone else spots me in this dress," Amelia informed Marielle and Mr. Hooper. "I'll see you at the garden party?"

"We're looking forward to it." Marielle found a perfect apple and held it up like a trophy.

"Yes, quite," Mr. Hooper added. "Goodbye, Lady Amesbury. Lord Bainbridge."

"I don't see how you have time to organize a garden party in the midst of our inquiries," Simon whispered as they rounded the Bainbridge stalls.

"You're not seeing the big picture. By bringing the same people together as the night of George's murder, there's a chance we might learn something new or even apprehend the criminal."

Simon crossed his arms. "I think you and Kitty are attempting to force Oliver's hand about the move. Kitty, party, flowers? He's going to see through it, you know."

"That obtuse man? No." Amelia shook her head. "He couldn't see through a clean window. He'd have a book in front of it." She paused. "Since we're here, let's ask your stablemen about George Davies. They might provide us with new insight."

Simon agreed, and they turned toward a beautiful stone bench in the courtyard, where a man poured a cup of water from the well bucket.

Simon nodded to the man. "That's our head groomsman, Turner. He was as close as anyone to George Davies. Maybe he knows Davies's enemies."

"Or lovers," added Amelia.

Turner was a paunchy man with a sparse beard and round shoulders. His face was pleasant, and he smiled when he looked up, as if expecting to see a friend. "Taking a ride with the lady, my lord?"

"No, please continue." Simon gestured to the bench. "I didn't mean to interrupt your break. I'd like to ask about George Davies, if you have the time. His recent murder has raised some questions in my mind."

Turner sat down. "Of course. Happy to help, my lord."

"You worked with him before he left our employ?" continued Simon.

"As much as the man would work." Noting Amelia's frown, he explained. "Excuse me, my lady. Don't mean to speak ill of the dead, but the duke knew it as well as we all did. That's why he got rid of him. Davies got a taste for the finer things and wasn't the same. Training winning horses went to his head. He put himself above us."

Amelia knew another reason for Davies's dismissal: Marielle's affection for him. But Turner didn't. Professional jealousy might have spurred his comments. After all, it wasn't every day the pupil became the master. But Turner didn't seem like the jealous type.

"Davies enjoyed winning." Simon paused as a stable boy walked past them. "Perhaps too much. Maybe he made an enemy that way, an enemy who sought revenge."

"Maybe." Turner shrugged. "He was a good-timing man. More friends than foes. Everyone wants to be around a fellow like him."

"Ladies, also?" Amelia asked.

Turner's eyebrows peaked with surprise. "Why yes, ladies also. All women love a winner, don't they?"

"I'm interested in one woman in particular." Amelia lowered her voice. "A Lady Margaret. Did he mention her name, perchance, when he worked here?"

Turner sat up straighter, his round shoulders squaring. "*Lady* Margaret? Never. What business would Davies have courting a lady?"

He was so incensed at the suggestion that Amelia almost apologized.

"Thank you, Turner." Simon took a step in the other direction. "Do let me know if you think of anything."

"I will." Turner dipped his chin. "My lady."

When they were out of earshot, Simon let out a groan. "Another dead end."

"Not dead, just cold."

"We need a new direction to explore," said Simon.

"Tomorrow, at the garden party. Something will come of it. I'm certain."

His lips twitched with a smile. "Something besides a new dress for Kitty?"

Amelia looked down at her own crumpled gown. "If anyone is in need of a new dress, it is I. How will I ever explain this to Tabitha?"

"You're good with words." He opened her carriage door. "You'll think of something."

Several minutes later, nothing came to mind but a pain in her shoulder. She must have twisted something when she fell. At least the scrape on her hand had ceased bleeding. That was the good news. The bad news was Tabitha stopped her before she got past the foyer. Accosted was more like it.

"Did you wrestle with a badger, Amelia?" Tabitha leaned into her cane. "Or a kid goat?"

"I ran into a tree." Amelia placed her parasol in the hall stand. Thank goodness *that* hadn't been damaged. "Nobody saw me."

Tabitha's eyes narrowed as if to say, *I see you right now.*

"It's this dress." Amelia motioned to the absurd garment. "It was the cause of my unfortunate accident."

"Doubtful," Tabitha mumbled. "But you're right. It doesn't suit you."

"Thank you—what, why?" Amelia was incensed. "Lettie said it was *fashionable*."

Tabitha held up her hand to avoid further explanation. "Mrs. Hamsted is waiting for you in the drawing room, and while I would love to explain exactly what is wrong with your crinoline, gown, and attitude, I don't have time. *She* doesn't have time. Lady Hamsted has decided they must move immediately."

Amelia let out a little cry.

"Now go change, and meet us upstairs."

Amelia nodded, taking the stairs two at a time.

Lettie followed her into the bedroom, helping her out of the damaged dress. She gasped at Amelia's muddy slippers. "Your shoes!"

Amelia sighed. "It's a long story. Please don't ask. I never want to see *that* monstrosity again." She pointed to the yellow frock on the floor.

Lettie silently selected a dress of the simplest material.

Good. She realizes what I've been through.

Wordlessly, Lettie helped her into the dress. Amelia slipped into new shoes, glad to have the muddied pair out of reach of Tabitha's discovery. She turned toward the door.

Lettie grabbed her arm. "Your hair, my lady!"

Amelia glanced at her reflection. *Heavens.* It *did* look as if she'd been attacked by a badger. Half her hair was in pins; the rest fell down her back. Thank goodness the perfect Miss Pimm hadn't seen her leave. Her spoon hat would have bent with fright.

Lettie quickly worked her magic, and Amelia's auburn hair was done up with a couple of deft twists and turns. A dozen pins later, Amelia was rushing to join Aunt Tabitha and Kitty in the drawing room.

"I'm here," Amelia announced breathlessly. "Tell me everything."

After the telltale click of the door, Kitty divulged the details. Her father-in-law wanted to finish repairs on the roof of the country house by August—and grouse hunting season—which meant they needed someone there *now*. Evidently, the viscountess didn't want it to be her or her husband. Since Oliver didn't care for the season's activities one way or the other, he didn't object to the idea. "What he said was, 'What's one more party when you've already been to five?'" Kitty fisted her tiny hands in her lap. "He doesn't know me at all."

Amelia moved next to Kitty on the settee, covering her hands with her own. "He does. He's just being obtuse."

"His isolation has left him thickheaded when it comes to social situations," added Tabitha.

"Will Lady Hamsted be at the garden party tomorrow?" Amelia asked.

Kitty sniffed. "Yes."

"It's our last chance, then." Tabitha tapped her cane. "We need a plan, and it better be a good one."

Amelia rubbed her temples. Frankly, her plan was to expose George Davies's killer. How could she possibly solve this trouble, too? *Think, Amelia. Think. You pore over people's problems every day. This problem should be easy.* When she put it in that perspective, a question came to her. It was the one she'd ask a reader if she'd written to Lady Agony. "Don't you think the timing is strange? Lady Hamsted wanting you to leave before the season is through? I understand her wanting Oliver to take over the estate, but why now? What's behind it?"

Kitty sniffed.

"I see your point." Tabitha pointed a finger at her. "Lord Hamsted has managed the estate for thirty years. What's one more month?"

"Exactly." Amelia snapped her fingers. "Maybe we've been looking at the wrong person. Maybe the trouble lies with your father-in-law, not your mother-in-law."

Kitty wrinkled her button nose. "Perhaps, but he's the least troublesome man I know, besides my dear Oliver."

Ten seconds—a record time for Kitty being upset with Oliver.

"It's an avenue we haven't explored," Amelia continued. "One we can explore tomorrow."

She explained the plan, which was quite simple: corner the viscount, ask him what peril was keeping him away from the country house, and find out how Kitty might prepare for it.

"And your substitute plan?" asked Tabitha.

"Don't fail at the first plan."

Chapter 25

Dear Lady Agony,

My hair is red. I've tried many remedies, but nothing can correct the color. It makes me the most unpopular woman in the room, and you can see why. I've included a lock for your inspection. Please help. I am willing to try anything.

Devotedly,
Red Might as Well Be Dead

. . . .

Dear Red Might as Well Be Dead,

You are correct. The color is red. Not auburn, not gold, not strawberry. But red. Other authors would tell you to try a lead comb to darken your tresses, but I will tell you nothing of the sort. Your hair is beautiful just the way it is. Please do not let lord, lady, or louse make you think otherwise.

Yours in Secret,
Lady Agony

The next day was as lovely as any Amelia might have wished for: the sun warm, the breeze mild, and the clouds fluffy white. She opened the terrace doors like a child opening a Christmas present, turning a full circle to experience the fairy tale awaiting her outside. Miss Rainier had outdone herself. A spectacle of violet, white, and occasional pink flowers accosted her eyes. The linen-draped tables brimmed with vases of sweet peas, and the hedges were perfectly cut into zigzagged mazes that circled the courtyard, not a blade or branch out of place. And the gazebo! Amelia imagined Winifred would spend most of the afternoon in the spot turned secret hideaway.

Amelia ran her hand across the creamy tablecloth, and a familiar feeling skipped into her heart. She loved parties. She *missed* parties. The last two years had made her forget, and now she remembered. Something wonderful happened when people came together, something irreplaceable. Of course, she'd been to events. She attended some after the first year of mourning ended. And Winifred's recital had been a fine time but one fraught with the anxieties of a mother worried about her daughter's performance. But this! Amelia beamed at her courtyard. This was a *party*, and one that reminded her of family. Nothing could replace the true joy of bringing people together. Even if it was to catch a killer.

"This turned out well." Wearing a mint frock that almost matched the fernery, Tabitha joined her on the patio. She was a head taller than Amelia and easily surveyed the area. "In fact, it's quite nice, and so is that dress. I never imagined I'd like you in pink, but I do."

Amelia took her hand from the tablecloth, brushing her gown. It wasn't exactly pink but mauve, with pale pink rosettes at her neckline, waist, and chignon. Still, it was much lighter and more feminine than the darker colors she usually favored, and perfect for a garden party. Modernly full, but not overflowing. "That means a great deal, Aunt. Thank you. Have you seen Miss Rainier?"

"She's helping with the food trays," Tabitha explained. "She insisted on matching bouquets for the cake platters." Tabitha leaned closer, and Amelia could smell her expensive cologne. "I appreciate her attention to details. Wherever did you find her?"

"Drury Lane," answered Amelia. "She was selling flowers the night of the opera."

"Why does that not surprise me?" Tabitha tutted, but in a superficial way that said she didn't mind and perhaps even respected the move. "Nonetheless, we need to keep her card on hand."

At that moment, Winifred and Bee flew around the corner, looking like two colorful butterflies in their organza dresses, leaving a string of giggles behind them.

Amelia smiled at the sight.

"I see you've come to terms with the Grey girl," Tabitha observed.

"As long as she's not a proponent of child labor, I think we'll be fine." Amelia pretended to straighten a rose on her dress. "Did I tell you that I found out what they were doing behind our backs?"

Tabitha grabbed her arm, her hand like a steel hook. "You know you didn't. Tell me."

Amelia chuckled. "They were reading Lady Agony's column. That's all. Nothing to worry about. Harmless fun."

Tabitha crossed her hands on her cane. Today she sported the shiny black one that matched the geometric black squares trimming her dress. "Harmless fun? Humph! Lady Agony is responsible for half the harebrained trouble in London. Have you seen what she's done to the men? She's reduced them to sniveling babies. I can't imagine what her column might inspire in small children." Her eyes followed Winifred and Bee to the gazebo. "*Mutiny.*"

Amelia's chuckle turned into a full-blown laugh. Tabitha revered rules above all else. She liked method and order. Lady Agony challenged method and order. It was understandable why she thought Lady Agony's advice intolerable. *Which is why she must never know the truth.*

Jones stepped onto the patio, informing them the musical trio had arrived with their equipment.

"Please show them to the gate," said Amelia. "I'll meet them there."

"I'll see to the trays." Tabitha followed Jones back into the house, and Amelia met the ensemble by the entrance. A striking woman with a high forehead, red hair, and deep blue eyes; a very tall male violinist; and a bassist who might have been his brother stood at the gate. The men shared the same olive complexion, high cheekbones, and long, dexterous fingers, but the woman was definitely not related. Amelia led them to the terrace and then left them to their arrangements so she could greet her guests.

Amelia saw to the Bainbridge carriage first, which held Simon, Marielle, Mr. Hooper, and Miss Pimm. Simon was Simon, the ever-composed marquis. He gave her a knowing bow, indicating he could take whatever the day threw out. She responded with her own *come and get it* look, then turned to a more pleasant vision, his beautiful sister, Marielle.

Because the siblings looked so much alike, handsome and intrepid, Amelia rarely took Marielle's age into consideration. But Marielle was young, and today she looked it as she gazed upon the courtyard. Her cheeks matched her blush dress and parasol, her bare shoulders untouched by the sun. In this light, Amelia could understand Simon's desire to protect her from the rest of the world. She had the same desire for Winifred, and at times, it was nonsensical and overwhelming.

"Miss Pimm." Tabitha was at her shoulder to greet guests. "It's good to see you again. I do hope you'll stay in London after your assignment with the Bainbridges."

"Lady Tabitha." Miss Pimm bobbed the perfect curtsy, the one Amelia couldn't quite master. "I plan to stay in London as long as my services are required by young ladies."

"Forever, then." Tabitha smiled, obviously pleased by the response. "Wonderful news."

Amelia refrained from rolling her eyes and didn't have time anyway, for Lord Cumberland arrived next, and she had the duty of making introductions. "Lord Cumberland, welcome. You've met Lord Bainbridge and his sister, Lady Marielle."

Lord Cumberland bowed deeply, his eyes never leaving Marielle's. "It's always a pleasure."

"And this is Mr. Hooper," Amelia added.

"Yes, we've met." Lord Cumberland gave Mr. Hooper the briefest glance before turning back to Marielle. He was interested only in people who could increase his popularity, not decrease it. "May I fetch you a glass of lemonade, my lady?"

"Nice to see you again, Cumberland." Mr. Hooper's sentence trailed off as he glanced toward the refreshment table. "I'm happy to find you a glass, also."

Simon clasped both men's shoulders. "Let's all go. It's been, what? Two minutes? I know I'm parched." Marielle followed the group reluctantly, throwing Amelia a miserable look before she left.

Tabitha tsked as she watched Simon lead the men to the refreshment table. "If the marquis is not careful, he will stunt his sister's choices as much as he has stunted his own."

"Indeed." Miss Pimm lifted her eyebrows in Tabitha's direction. "Finding suitable company is an obstacle when he is around."

"I think it's honorable of Lord Bainbridge to look after his sister. He obviously cares about her a great deal." The comment came out stronger than Amelia intended. Was it her dislike of Miss Pimm or her affection for Simon that infused such emotion into her statement? Amelia hoped the former.

"So do dogs, but we don't take them to parties," observed Tabitha. She poked her cane in Simon's direction. "That's one devoted pup that might need to sit the next party out."

"My thoughts exactly." Miss Pimm smiled.

Thankfully, Kitty and her in-laws arrived next, and Amelia could make her excuses. Any more from perfect Miss Pimm would have set her own tongue wagging. Kitty was flawless in her sky blue silk organza dress, trimmed from her wide skirt to her tiny waist in swirling purple pansies. The viscountess was a stunning second with her high-reaching hair, distinct silhouette, and striking dress. If flowers bloomed in Kitty's path, they wilted in the viscountess's out of sheer intimidation. She cast an evaluative glance over the party. It would soon be known whether she approved or not.

The viscount, Amelia realized, looked a lot like Oliver. Brown hair, inquisitive eyes, easy smile. *He's a better dresser, that's all*, Amelia decided, and that was probably the viscountess's doing. Otherwise, he seemed to share his son's view of parties. Which also confused Amelia. Why was he giving up the country estate so easily? It was time for her to find out.

"Welcome, and thank you for coming." Amelia motioned to the women. "Your dresses are incomparable."

"Lady Amesbury," Lady Hamsted returned her greeting. "Who, may I ask, has turned your yard into a fairy tale? They must do mine next."

"Miss Rainier." Amelia shot Kitty a sly grin. "Mrs. Hamsted recommended her."

Lady Hamsted placed her hand on Kitty's arm. "You know the best people."

Kitty shared a sneaky smile with Amelia before turning to her mother-in-law. "I learned from the best."

After the men left to greet Simon, Amelia added, "*You* know positively everyone, Lady Hamsted. Would you mind if I ask after someone in particular?"

Lady Hamsted tipped her chin. "Ask away."

"Lady Margaret Reynolds." Amelia stated the name Davies's housekeeper had given to her. "I was told she's abroad, studying music, and you know my Winifred is musically inclined. I'm wondering if I should seek her out as a tutor when she returns."

"Is that what you were told?" Lady Hamsted tutted. "Only if studying music is a euphemism for avoiding the Foundling Hospital." Her gray eyes widened with the revelation.

Kitty gasped. "Does that mean what I think it means?"

"It can only mean one thing, dear." Lady Hamsted patted her hand, sorry for Kitty's ignorance. She, herself, did not suffer from ignorance—or mercy. She delighted in exposing the sordid details. "Lady Margaret was indeed musically gifted. As a young woman, she gave delightful musicals people actually enjoyed. But last year, the year of her debut, she disappeared after dallying with a secret suitor. Some say the affair led to an offspring, which prompted the trip. The family covered it up well, admitting nothing, and I assume we'll see her back by Christmas, her child placed with a far-off relative, and her music none the better or worse."

"The suitor's name—" Amelia started.

"I certainly wouldn't presume to know." Lady Hamsted cut her off. Her voice was as sharp as her cheekbones. "And I would never ask."

Another difference between us, thought Amelia.

"I wonder how Lady Margaret came to meet him," Kitty mused aloud.

"Lady Margaret was the season's catch, and so many unsuitable men are allowed into the ballroom these days. It's impossible to tell a real suitor from an impostor." Lady Hamsted sniffed. "Unfortunately, Lady Margaret learned that lesson the hard way."

Lady Margaret had indeed learned a hard lesson, and George Davies had been the one to teach her it. The affair was confirmation that Davies seduced women for their titles, hoping they would afford him the status he hadn't been able to gain through wins. Amelia hated to share the information with Marielle, but she would. She had to. Only when Marielle had all the facts would she be able to process her grief and move on.

But right now, Miss Rainier needed her. Near the center fountain, she hailed Amelia with a wave. From the look of the gesture, it was time sensitive. "Please excuse me. Help yourself to a refreshment."

Amelia weaved in and out of small groups to Miss Rainier, who wore a nice brown dress with silk trimming, perhaps the best dress she owned. It flattered her figure much better than the plain dress and apron she wore selling flowers, and she looked as pretty as one of the peonies she'd so carefully cut for the party.

"Miss Rainier, the courtyard is a vision. I cannot express how happy I am with the results."

"Thank you, my lady, but I need to tell you something." Frances's voice was a shrewd whisper. "That woman I saw on Drury Lane? The one in the heather cloak? She's here." She started to raise her hand, but Amelia clasped it.

"Please don't point. Just tell me where."

Miss Rainier tipped her chin toward the terrace. "She's the singer."

Amelia squinted at the trio. "The singer? I thought you said she was a peeress?"

"I know what I said, but that's her. There's no mistaking her hair. That color, remember? I couldn't forget it in a hundred years."

The singer was a one-of-a-kind beauty with a presence that commanded attention. Redheaded, voluptuous, and the voice of an angel besides. Guests paused as they passed by, as if entranced by a medium. "I remember. But I also remember you said she was in a hurry. Maybe you didn't get a good look at her. You dropped your flowers, if I recall."

"I didn't drop them." Miss Rainier frowned, as if pondering her statement. Then her eyes opened wide, and with the additional light, their color changed from violet to lavender. "*I* didn't drop them." Seeing Amelia's confusion, Miss Rainier tried again. "Don't you see? The man in the cloak. It was his fault. He caused the accident that night."

Amelia recollected their earlier conversation. What she remembered of it was the redheaded beauty. Obviously, that's what Miss Rainier had remembered, too, for neither of them had thought the cloaked man of any consequence—until now. "Another person was present the night of George Davies's murder."

Miss Rainier nodded slowly.

"Do you remember anything of his appearance? Height, build—clothes?" The questions tumbled out of Amelia's mouth in rapid succession.

"All I saw of him was the back of his cloak."

Which could have been any number of theatre patrons, masquerading in their finery. The perfect disguise if the person was involved in George Davies's murder.

The realization brought to mind Shakespeare's *As You Like It*. All the world was a stage, and men and women merely players. They had their entrances and their exits. But someone had planned George's exit carefully. Amelia would find out who, and when she did, the masks would come off, revealing the killer's true identity for all to see.

Chapter 26

Dear Lady Agony,

My sisters and I have one brother, who is loved considerably. He is wise, handsome, and best in our parents' eyes. But would it be too much trouble for our parents to acknowledge us, also? We have tried hard to be good, and while we might not be as clever as he is, we have other talents. But they seem to be blind to our skills. How might we catch their attention?

Devotedly,
Sisters of Sebastian

· · · · · · · · · · · · · · · · · · ·

Dear Sisters of Sebastian,

Oh brother! I detest letters such as these. Only sons are doted upon their entire lives, and often sisters and parents alike are caught in the trap of worshipping the young man. Nothing could be worse for his intellect—or yours. Stop it at once. And forget *seeking attention, too. Find another occupation. Like science or art. It is a much better use of your time.*

Yours in Secret,
Lady Agony

After checking on Winifred and Bee, who were enjoying three tarts, two bonbons, and one oversized piece of cake in the privacy of the gazebo, Amelia stalked the singer. Unfortunately, the singer was in the middle of a stunning aria that held half of the audience motionless. Amelia turned to the lawn. The guests who weren't listening to the trio were engaged in games, including the Hamsteds. The viscount was balancing a glass of lemonade in one hand and selecting a racquet with the other. Amelia swooped in to assist him.

"Let me help you with that, my lord," Amelia offered.

"Thank you." He gave her the drink, which she placed on a nearby table. "Have you tried your hand at this game?"

"A few times." Amelia leaned in a little closer. "I concede I'm not very good at it, though. Last time I attempted it, I nearly took Lady Tabitha's hat off, and she's forbidden me from playing it in her presence."

Lord Hamsted chuckled. "Luckily, we have plenty of space today."

"And a better hitter." Amelia smiled. "I imagine you enjoy many outdoor sports at Hamsted Hall?"

"Indeed, we do. We did. We will again." His face relaxed, turning wistful. The mention of Hamsted Hall must have evoked a memory in him, making him look younger. His brown eyes softened, and the creases around them smoothed. The viscountess had made him into a fashionable gentleman, but behind those eyes was the look of an adventurer, one who enjoyed hunting, fishing, and rural pursuits.

"I'm sure my son will take good care of the property . . ." Amelia allowed her eyes to wander to a nearby blanket where Oliver was staring at the clouds as if making dreamscapes.

Lord Hamsted followed her gaze. "Oliver was never . . . mechanically inclined. His pursuits were more scholarly in nature."

Kitty, who was sitting next to Oliver, noticed their attention. She knew of Amelia's plan to interview the viscount and hurried to join them. "I've been wanting to play this game." Kitty nodded at his racquet. "Need a partner?" She lifted one sculpted eyebrow. "Or an opponent?"

"Be careful, Mrs. Hamsted." Lord Hamsted turned over the racquet with the flick of his wrist. "I won't go as easy on you as my son."

"Easy, ha!" Kitty fisted her hands on her waist. "It is *I* who takes it easy on Oliver."

Hearing his name, Oliver stretched and wandered over, a drowsy look still in his eye. He adjusted his collar, frowning at Amelia. "Please tell me you don't intend to involve Lady Amesbury in a match, Father. She's a terrible cheat. You should see her croquet game."

Amelia let out a huff. "I am not. *He's* a sore loser."

"A game of redemption. What do you say?" Lord Hamsted asked. "Women against men?"

Kitty set her chin, perhaps angry with Oliver for the joke or the viscount for his dismissal of her skills. "You're on."

After selecting racquets, Amelia and Kitty positioned themselves on one side of the net, and the viscount and Oliver positioned themselves on the other. Oliver reached down and touched his toes, stretching.

As if that will help your game. Oliver was better at books than athletics, and Amelia had the notion she and Kitty could beat him without much effort. One look at Kitty's sly grin told Amelia she was thinking the same thing.

Lord Hamsted moved from foot to foot. He took a practice swing above his head. "In my day, I could hit anything that moved. You don't have a chance—" He released a little cry and dropped his racquet.

From across the lawn, Lady Hamsted made an exclamation. Looking very unlike herself, she hoisted her skirts, revealing her ankles and a good portion of her legs, and dashed over.

Amelia held back her own surprise. She'd never seen the viscountess walk fast, let alone run. And in public? Most of the guests were listening to the trio; otherwise, her actions would have garnered more attention—and not in the way she was used to.

"What is it? Is it your heart?" Lady Hamsted asked. "Oliver, get a chair."

Lord Hamsted held her hands. "I'm fine, dear. I only strained a neck muscle. I haven't played in some time."

"Are you certain?" fretted Lady Hamsted.

He lowered his voice. "The children, Edwina."

Oliver returned with a lawn chair. "Somebody better explain what's going on here. What's wrong with Father's heart?"

"It's nothing," Lord Hamsted said, refusing to sit. "A little palpitation now and again. That's all."

"It's not nothing!" Lady Hamsted insisted.

"You're making a scene," warned Lord Hamsted.

Lady Hamsted took note of her surroundings. Seeing the guests' preoccupation with the trio, she continued but in a quieter voice. "A physician doesn't prescribe medication for no reason." She turned to Oliver. "You might as well know. Your father has to take something to regulate his heart—and you might someday, too, if you keep spending all your days sedentarily, reading books."

"Is that why you want us to move to Hamsted Hall?" Kitty's voice raised unnaturally high. "So that Oliver will get exercise?"

A puff of surprise escaped Amelia's lips, and she shut them tight, pretending to study her racquet. It was hard to imagine Oliver exercising or doing any strenuous work at all. Unless lifting a heavy book counted as exercise. But it would explain the viscountess's insistence on the move—and the viscount's reluctance.

"That and we need to be close to the physician in London. In case . . ." Lady Hamsted swallowed hard.

Oliver looked from his mother to his father, his face a puzzle of emotions.

"Your mother is overreacting." Lord Hamsted's steady gaze was convincing. "I promise you all men my age have little problems now and then that need tending. In fact, the physician told us we could stay at Hamsted Hall. It's your mother's idea to move full-time to London to be near him."

Kitty did not suffer from her husband's confusion. She asked for further clarification. "And what about Oliver? Will he have this problem, as the viscountess suggests?"

"The physician stated exercise can prevent the condition from worsening. He did not say it could prevent it entirely. That was speculation on my dear wife's part." He clasped her hand. "And perhaps wishful thinking."

Oliver shook his shaggy brown head. "Why didn't you tell me? Why the subterfuge? Did you think I couldn't handle it?"

Amelia noted the hurt in his tone and felt empathy for him.

Oliver was a kind man but a distracted man. His mind was always on a book or project, unless Kitty was near, and then it was on her entirely and nothing else. It was hard to engage him. Maybe he saw that now.

"We didn't want to worry you." Lady Hamsted took her hand from her husband's and touched her son's shoulder. "We wanted to keep you safe."

"Safe?" Oliver's voice was incredulous. "I'm thirty-two years old, Mother. You're treating me like a child—and my wife also. We make our own decisions, not you. Not Father. I love you dearly, but I won't be influenced when it comes to our future."

Lady Hamsted started to say something, but her husband stopped her. "You're right, son. It's your future. It's up to you to decide."

"And Kitty," he added, taking her hand.

Amelia gave him an invisible pat on the back. It was moments like these that endeared Oliver to her. He could be an absolute ninny when it came to his wife, but he was also her fiercest defender. He respected Kitty and her independence, and that meant a great deal to Amelia.

It meant a great deal to Kitty, too. She looked at her husband with new admiration, which was saying something, since Amelia had thought she'd seen every adoring look between the pair for the last two years.

"If it's exercise the physician prescribes, I suggest doubles against the women, if you're up to it, Father." Oliver put aside the chair that was in their way.

"Of all the wrongheaded—" started Lady Hamsted.

"Excellent idea," said Lord Hamsted. "It's sure to increase my heart rate."

The viscountess took in the situation with a shrewd glance. The vein on her neck strained as she tipped her chin. "I will never forgive you if something happens to your father." She lowered her lashes at Kitty. "Or you." With that, she walked away, taking long strides toward the center fountain.

"Please don't concern yourself about that, Mrs. Hamsted." The viscount gave Kitty an apologetic look before picking up his racquet from the ground. "She is doing what she thinks is best for me."

"And I must do what I think is best for us." Oliver's voice was firm.

"Does that mean you're not moving to Hamsted Hall?" asked Lord Hamsted.

Amelia heard her breath catch at the same time as Kitty's.

Oliver turned to his wife. "What would you like to do, Kitty?"

Kitty was as still as a statue. "You must know I want to stay here, in London."

"Then that's what we shall do."

Overcome with emotion, Kitty threw her arms around him and kissed him full on the lips.

The viscount averted his eyes, but Amelia was used to their indulgences and smiled at the pair. Kitty would be staying in London. That's all that mattered. She would put up with all the overt affection she must to keep her best friend nearby.

"Truth be told, I didn't want to leave the house, not yet, anyway. Grouse season is coming, and there's much work to be done on the roof." Lord Hamsted tossed a shuttlecock in the air, batting it with his racquet. "I'd like to see to the repairs myself."

After an affectionate squeeze, Oliver released Kitty and joined his father. "I figured you did."

Lord Hamsted gave him a nod of acknowledgment. "Thank you, son."

Oliver returned the nod. "When the day comes, I will be ready to take over the estate."

Lord Hamsted hit the shuttlecock in Amelia's direction. "But today is not that day."

Chapter 27

Dear Lady Agony,

I have made the worst kind of enemy—a powerful one. I worry she will ruin my chances in every respectable drawing room in London. I promise I am a good person, but she will say otherwise to punish me. My opportunities were slim before this trouble. After, they might be nonexistent. Can you tell me what to do?

Devotedly,
Friend to Foe

....

Dear Friend to Foe,

Congratulations on your disobedience. It's not easy to stand up to anyone, let alone the strong or powerful. Now to the problem of the drawing rooms. You sound like a smart woman. Be that

*instead of sorry. Have courage, and be kind. You'd be amazed
by how far those two attributes will take you.*

*Yours in Secret,
Lady Agony*

After an exhilarating game, which they won by a single point, Amelia and Kitty retreated to the refreshment table to discuss their other win: Kitty remaining in London. They were almost as giddy as Winifred and Bee, who had filled up on way too many sweets and were skipping around the lawn like tiny gazelles. Amelia wasn't worried about the behavior. Tabitha stood and walked to the edge of the terrace, and that's all it took for the girls to stop prancing through the garden. *If only Aunt Tabitha could make the murderer reveal himself as easily.*

"My concern is Oliver's mother." Kitty's happy face turned sour. "She seemed really angry."

Amelia couldn't argue with the statement. The viscountess had leveled a look at Kitty that could have frozen water on a summer's day.

"I have a hard time getting along with her when she's not mad," continued Kitty. "Can you imagine what family dinners will be like after today? I'd better take care she doesn't poison my tea."

"She *does* seem like the sort of woman who would exact revenge."

"Thanks, friend." Kitty crossed her arms. "Didn't your mother ever teach you if you don't have something nice to say, don't say it at all?"

"She said, 'Speak your mind, or someone else will speak for you.'" Amelia shrugged.

"That explains so much."

The trio started a crescendo, and Kitty and Amelia had no choice but to pause and listen. The audience was pin-drop silent, and the singer's voice was hypnotic. It had the power to stop people and time.

Amelia took the opportunity to wonder how in the devil she was going to interrupt her. She still required a private audience with the woman. She stared at the singer, pondering a way to get her to stop singing. A refreshment perhaps?

"She's incredible, isn't she?" Lord Cumberland was at Amelia's elbow, his thin lips twitching with a whisper. Mr. Wells accompanied him. "I saw her in *The Bohemian Girl*. Marvelous voice. Charming woman."

"Lord Cumberland, Mr. Wells," said Kitty. "How nice to see you again."

Lord Cumberland bowed. "Mrs. Hamsted. Always a pleasure."

Mr. Wells took off his cap in a dramatic gesture. "Good afternoon, Mrs. Hamsted. Lady Amesbury. You wouldn't believe the number of inquiries I've fielded about your race on Rotten Row. At least a dozen. How is your ankle?"

"Better," Kitty admitted. "Thank you for asking."

Amelia returned to Lord Cumberland's previous statement. "You know the singer, my lord?"

Lord Cumberland's face lifted, and Amelia understood why ladies thought him handsome. He was an open book, without complicated objectives. "I know of her talent. I assume you do as well, which is why she's here."

"I left the music in Lady Tabitha's capable hands." A thought struck as the words left her mouth. She might not be able to interrupt the trio, but she could certainly interrupt Aunt Tabitha and ask where she found them.

"Lady Tabitha is most capable in everything she does." Lord Cumberland looked for her over his shoulder. "Have you seen her? I haven't had a chance to thank her for the invitation."

Amelia was in charge of the guest list and had invited as many suspects as possible to the gathering. So technically, it was she he should be thanking. But she kept that to herself.

"I'd like to meet her," Mr. Wells added in a whisper. "I never have."

Kitty motioned toward the horseshoes. "She's there, playing a game with the Bainbridges. Lady Amesbury could introduce you."

Brilliant. Amelia would have no problem interrupting a game with a family friend. She could ask Aunt Tabitha about the singer without waiting. "Good idea, Mrs. Hamsted. I need to speak with her, too. Excuse us."

Kitty stayed behind to watch the trio as Amelia, Mr. Wells, and Lord Cumberland made their way to the grass. Amelia noted that while Mr. Wells asked several questions about the lawn and intricate maze, Lord Cumberland's attention was on Marielle. Distracted, he forgot to pause when Amelia gave an explanation of a fountain as they passed. He kept walking steadily toward Marielle, who'd just made a very good toss, and they hurried to catch up.

"Lady Marielle has excellent aim." Lord Cumberland smiled.

"Indeed," added Mr. Wells. "She seems to enjoy playing horseshoes."

"I believe she enjoys anything related to horses," Amelia said with a chuckle. "Even games."

"I must extend her an invitation to Rotten Row so that she might ride Angelica," Lord Cumberland proposed. "Angelica won the Ascot five years ago."

"Angelica," repeated Mr. Wells. "She was a fine racehorse. I was there when she took first place."

"Lady Marielle would like that." Amelia nodded to Miss Pimm and Mr. Hooper as she passed a table where they were taking a refreshment break. "Did Mr. Davies train Angelica, by chance?"

"Mr. Davies?" Lord Cumberland's brow furrowed. "He might have. I can't recall. Angelica was my father's horse. I've only recently become interested in the sport."

And in impressing Marielle, apparently. No wonder Marielle was attracted to Mr. Davies. If this was her alternative, she understood how Mr. Davies turned her head with his real experience, plain talk, and easy laugh.

"Davies *did* train her," supplied Mr. Wells. "It was one of his first major wins. He became quite popular after that. In fact, it was then that I introduced him to Quicksand." He waited for Lord Cumberland's acknowledgment, but it didn't come. "Quicksand won the Oaks the following year."

Mr. Wells was more knowledgeable about horse racing than Lord Cumberland. Mr. Wells was also more passionate about the sport, as the experience at Rotten Row had proven. Amelia imagined Lord Cumberland grew bored very easily.

Metal rang out as Marielle landed another horseshoe around the stake. Amelia clapped. "Bravo! Perfect shot."

Marielle took a little bow. "I couldn't let my brother best me—or Lady Tabitha." She frowned. "Did she practice before the party, or am I just rusty?"

"I'm afraid no sportsman or woman is safe in Lady Tabitha's company." Amelia added in a whisper, "She's a ringer when it comes to yard games."

"You're one to talk." Tabitha indicated for her cane, lying on a nearby chair. "Your competitive streak is dangerous at times."

Amelia handed her the cane. "Which is why we're such good partners."

Simon gestured to Lord Cumberland. "Try your hand at a toss?"

Marielle held out a horseshoe, and that was all the prompting Lord Cumberland needed. "Why not? Join us, Wells."

With Lord Cumberland, Mr. Wells, and Marielle occupied, Amelia took the opportunity to ask Tabitha about the trio. "Aunt Tabitha, I need to ask you about the singer. Who is she?"

Tabitha regarded the trio with pride. "Remarkable voice, isn't it? Her name is Miss Fairchild, and she often performs with the Gibson brothers. They are missing their cellist today, which concerned me, but for no reason I see now. A beautiful performance."

"Miss Fairchild," Simon repeated. "She gave Marielle voice lessons many years ago. I must remember to give her my regards."

Amelia reached for his elbow. "Why not now? I'd love to meet her."

"Contain yourself, Lady Amesbury." Tabitha pursed her lips. "It would do no good to interrupt. The song is about to end, and the final note is a showstopper."

"Oh, we will wait until it's finished." Amelia took a step toward the trio with Simon. "Don't fret, Aunt. I'll be as quiet as a mouse." Her foot landed on a horseshoe. "Yow!" She clapped her hand over her mouth. "Starting now."

After a few steps, Simon spoke in a hushed tone. His breath was warm on her ear. "I know you're not an admirer. What's the real reason for our detour?"

Amelia didn't have the opportunity to answer before being

interrupted by Lady Jane Marsh. She stepped in front of them, her placid face changed with enthusiasm. "Thank you for the invitation, Lady Amesbury. I'm so glad we've been able to get to know each other better this season."

"As am I. Thank you for coming." Amelia counted the minutes of friendly conversation they'd have to endure before moving toward Miss Fairchild. The song was growing steadily louder, and Amelia didn't want to miss another chance.

"Good afternoon, my lord." Lady Jane extended a curtsy, the frills on her white dress rustling. "Is Lady Marielle in attendance as well?"

"Good afternoon." Simon nodded. "She's playing horseshoes."

Lady Jane followed his nod, where Marielle was being entertained by Lord Cumberland and Mr. Wells. Her face pinched at the sight. "Horseshoes is such an amusing sport. I must give it a try."

Amelia sympathized. Marielle had not only a title but also wealth. Jane had only one of those things, which made even her good looks less impressive. Yet, the situation gave her one thing the others didn't have: a reason for wanting Mr. Davies alive. With Marielle's attention on him, she wouldn't have had to worry about competition.

Still, Amelia couldn't dismiss her entirely. The Marsh family had lost their fortune to gambling, an addiction George Davies frequently took part in. But what were the chances of George having anything to do with that history? The trouble was an old one, perhaps too old for George's involvement. "Yes, do try it, but be careful for your gloves," added Amelia. "I wouldn't want you to spoil them with grass stains."

"I'll ask if one of the gentlemen will hold them for me." Her drowsy eyes narrowed like a fox eyeing its prey. Then they widened again, and she flashed Simon and Amelia a quick smile. "Good day."

"A good day to be a gentleman indeed," Amelia whispered to Simon after Lady Jane left. "Not one but two titled ladies in your presence."

"And one stalwart aunt," added Simon, indicating Tabitha.

Amelia watched the game change players. "She's calling in reinforcements. Here comes Miss Pimm." Applause broke out, and Amelia realized the trio had finished their number. "Blast it! Let's go."

"What's the hurry?" Simon asked. "You never explained."

"She's the woman Miss Rainier saw talking to Mr. Davies the night he was killed." Amelia walked as quickly as her legs would take her, Simon easily keeping up. "In fact, she may be the killer. Kitty and I have been wondering if the murderer might be a murderess."

"Miss Fairchild?" Simon asked as a wave of soft laughter fell from Miss Fairchild's lips and onto the crowd of admirers that had gathered around her. They'd formed a wall that Amelia wasn't able to penetrate. The guests wanted to be close to the buxom beauty with the voice of an angel, and so did Amelia, but for different reasons. She wanted to ask her what business she had talking to George Davies on Drury Lane so late at night, and what, if anything, did the conversation reveal about his state of mind.

"What reason would she have to murder the man?" prompted Simon. "And didn't Miss Rainier state the woman she saw was a peeress?"

Amelia waved away the question. "It was dark, and one peer

looks like another, if you ask me. Mr. Davies dallied with several women. Maybe she was one of them."

"Mummy!"

Only one word would have stopped Amelia's pursuit of Miss Fairchild, and that was it. Somewhere, Winifred cried for help.

"Dear God." Amelia spun around but didn't see the child. "Winifred? Winifred?" *Think, think, think.* Where had she seen her last? "The gazebo!"

She took off pell-mell across the lawn, Simon right beside her. Her tight corset did not make the activity easy, and she bent over, catching her breath outside the gazebo. "Winifred?"

Simon parted the purple drapery of flowers so they could see inside.

Winifred was crouched next to her friend, her sky blue eyes filled with worry. "Bee has been stung by a bee!"

Amelia joined them at the bench. She knew bee stings could be serious, but that didn't seem to be the case here. The sting was on the arm and the skin around it only slightly raised.

Beatrice cried out in pain.

"The stinger should be removed." Simon's voice was calm and collected. "Allow me."

Amelia made room for him, which wasn't easy, considering he took up the entire space already.

He knelt next to Beatrice. "I've done this before. Don't be afraid. I'll have it out in a jiffy, and then you and Lady Winifred may go back to playing."

Beatrice must have seen what Amelia saw in that moment, a gentle person who could be just what one needed. He'd been the same person for her on more than one occasion, and she trusted him implicitly.

Bee slowly nodded. Simon had the stinger out in seconds.

Winifred took his place, hugging her friend. "Are you better, Bee?"

Bee nodded, and her hair fell into her eyes. "Yes, thank you. But I think I might need a new nickname."

They shared a laugh before going inside to wash the wound.

Chapter 28

Dear Lady Agony,

I passed a man on Charles Street a week ago and cannot stop thinking of him. He was walking a fuzzy brown terrier and sported a wonderful mustache. We shared a smile, but I was with my mother and could not talk. Since then, I've walked Charles Street many times without my mother, but to no avail. If you would please print my letter, he might try the street again. My only wish is to remedy a missed opportunity. My heart will break if I cannot.

Devotedly,
A Girl in Glasses

. . . .

Dear A Girl in Glasses,

As you know, my column does not provide matchmaking services, but your letter made an impression on me. Therefore,

I'm printing it in its entirety. How many of us wouldn't like a second chance? Very few. Mustache man, if you're out there, please leash up the terrier and take it for a walk. A girl in glasses is determined to meet you.

Yours in Secret,
Lady Agony

By the time Amelia and Simon washed Bee's wound and found the girls an ice cream treat, Miss Fairchild had gone on break, and Amelia's chance to interview her had disappeared. After talking to the other two musicians, Amelia discovered Miss Fairchild had been intrigued by the garden maze and mentioned a walk. So Amelia and Simon started there, entering one of many paths that crisscrossed the grounds.

Even with her purpose in mind, Amelia struggled to maintain her focus, for the maze was one of the most beautiful and complex aspects of the manor. The copper and green beech trees were arranged in color and size to mimic the Amesbury family crest. While there were several paths, only one—directly through the maze's center—brought walkers to the other side.

How well Amelia knew that detail. After Edgar passed, she spent hours trying to crack the code. The problem was, so many wrong turns led to righteous places: fragrant flowers, spraying fountains, ornate benches. Even when she took an incorrect turn, she enjoyed the detour. She only hoped Miss Fairchild hadn't made the same mistake, for there was no telling how far she might be and how long it would take them to find her.

"Do you know the last time I was in here was with Edgar?" murmured Simon.

She heard the smile in his voice before seeing it. "When was that?"

Simon's eye held a faraway look, like a sea captain in search of land. "Almost twenty years ago? We were merely children." He looked down a long stretch of hedge. "Is the curved bench still here, the one with the sea horse?"

Amelia smiled. "It is."

"Would you mind?"

"Not at all." She held out her elbow. "Lead the way."

"Edgar was a younger son and could disappear for hours without being noticed. His older brother did not have that comfort—nor did I." He stepped over a fallen branch. "But Edgar was convincing with his talk of fish and frogs and mermaids in the pond, and I spent more hours here than I should have."

"Mermaids?"

He shrugged. "We wanted to be sailors. Pirates, actually."

"I can see that." She laughed.

"He was a bad influence on me."

"Are you sure it was not the other way around?" she asked.

"I'm certain, although you probably don't believe me." They came to the bench by the ornamental pond, and he released a breath. "He and I spent hours with our boats at this very spot. He had the luxury of time—at least he thought he did."

Amelia was silent. The conversations at the garden party were a distant roar, but here, even the wind was quiet. Ominous clouds had gathered overhead, creating a gray barrier, and the croak of a frog echoed somewhere in the thick, decorative grasses.

He bent down and pointed out the initials *EA* and *SB* carved on the bench. Edgar Amesbury and Simon Bainbridge. Then he rose, looking at her for the first time since they entered the maze. "Perhaps none of us have as much time as we think."

This was the point where she should turn away, get back on track. Find Miss Fairchild and George Davies's killer. She did none of those things, however. She returned his gaze.

He was right. She felt it deep in her soul, an undercurrent beneath the surface of daily life. Always, the winged chariot of time at her back since Edgar's sudden passing. A knowledge that life was fleeting and could end despite age, experience, or circumstance. Did Simon feel it, too? Would he ever put away his stubborn notions long enough to find out?

She wouldn't be a fool. She *couldn't* be a fool. She'd been proved one before by her impetuosity, her desire to know. *Never again.* Although it took every muscle in her mind and body, she stood perfectly still, daring him to move. *But oh, those lips.* It was hard not to stare—and imagine.

He touched her chin.

She closed her eyes. Maybe if she didn't look at him, she wouldn't be tempted to pull him into a scandalous embrace. Maybe she wouldn't be consumed by the thought of dragging him to the bench. Maybe she wouldn't be lured by the knowledge that he could make her feel like a woman instead of a widow, a debutante instead of an old maid. Maybe she wouldn't—

A moan interrupted her thoughts—not a good moan.

She flicked open her eyes.

Simon was frowning. "Did you hear that?"

Another moan was his answer.

"It sounds as if someone is in trouble." Simon turned in a circle. "But where?"

That was a good question. Nearby was her best guess. The

sound wasn't coming from this path. The only way to find out was to try different paths.

Simon came to the same conclusion, and they retraced their steps. They tried another path, but the grass was untrodden, as if its location were a secret. They turned back before they reached its end and tried another route. Quickly, the new path widened into a towering center square, the tall hedge obstructing their view.

"I think the sound was closer to the house. Come on." Simon zigzagged to the next row, and she followed.

This path led to a miniature fountain of Cupid, complete with arrow and red rose garden. It was the path nearest the manor and the only one Edgar had been able to show her while he was still alive. The pungent smell of rose petals filled the air, a heady scent that could have filled the best perfumeries in London, and it grew stronger with each stride.

Simon stopped suddenly, and Amelia bumped into his solid back. She inched backward but still heard his breath heave in and out.

"I hear something," he whispered.

Another moan. A cough.

"I do, too," she confirmed. "This is the one."

They continued running, twisting through the crooked passage. Amelia had forgotten how long and frustrating the maze could be, and now more than ever, she wished for a good hedge clipper to make short work of her task. The path narrowed, then straightened. She turned one corner and then another. The rose garden came into sight as did a body that was making the moaning cries. But it wasn't Miss Fairchild's. It was a man's, a finely dressed one from the garden party.

"Lord Cumberland!" Amelia exclaimed.

He opened his eyes, trying hard to focus.

"Are you all right?" Simon asked.

Lord Cumberland rolled toward Simon's voice and cried out in pain.

"Don't move." Simon surveyed the area. "We'll find help. They'll come to you."

Amelia knelt beside him. "What happened?"

"A horseshoe flew off course. I went to retrieve it." Lord Cumberland's hat was off, and his perfect part had come unparted, his blond hair falling over his forehead. "I must've taken a wrong turn."

Amelia noted the deep red stain in his hair. She touched it gently, confirming what she already knew. "Blood."

"I must have fallen," said Lord Cumberland. "Did I fall?"

He was too far from the fountain for it to have caused the injury. He was in the middle of the grassy path. Nearby, branches bowed as if someone had cut through them. However, no leaves stuck to his jacket or trousers. "Yes, but what hit your head?" she asked.

Simon ducked into the broken hedge. "Do you remember seeing anyone?"

"Do I remember seeing anyone?" Lord Cumberland repeated the question instead of answering it.

Obviously, he was having a hard time focusing. Amelia needed to fetch help. She stood. Simon was busy looking for someone or something, but what? She asked him.

"I don't know." He lowered his voice. "He didn't get that bump from the ground."

Lord Cumberland was the least of her suspects in George Davies's murder. Why would someone want to hurt him? "Who would do such a thing?"

"We know of one person who was in the maze. We were looking for her ourselves."

"Miss Fairchild?" she whispered.

Lord Cumberland tried to sit up but fell back. "This dizziness. I cannot shake it."

"I'll find help," Amelia promised. "Mr. Dawson, in our stables. He'll know what to do."

"*I'll* find him," corrected Simon. "You stay here." He ran off before she could argue and returned several minutes later with Mr. Dawson, who treated her horses. He was the nearest thing they had to medical treatment. Several people trailed behind him, the last one being Mr. Wells, who carried a large satchel.

"A footman brought around your bag." Mr. Wells hoisted up the medical case.

"Make room," Mr. Dawson instructed. "Bring it here."

"What in Jove's name happened?" asked Mr. Wells.

"Wells? Is that you?" asked Lord Cumberland.

Lady Jane joined the gathering group. "Oh dear!"

Hearing her voice, Lord Cumberland attempted to smooth his hair.

"You've taken quite a blow," stated Mr. Dawson. "Please be still, and don't talk."

They stepped back, giving Mr. Dawson room to assess the situation. Now that other men were present, Lord Cumberland stopped making a fuss, but it was obvious the bump on his head caused him pain. He flinched as Mr. Dawson put a cloth to his head.

Mr. Dawson pulled it back, examining the amount of blood that soaked the fabric. "The head can take hard hits, and this is one of them. Lady Amesbury, another rag, please, and a bandage."

Amelia found the items in his meticulously sorted medical

bag. She was surprised to find a hammer there but then remembered he helped horses, which required horseshoes and the equipment to work with them. "Would you like me to apply pressure to the wound while you wrap it?"

"You won't faint, will you?" Mr. Dawson peeked at her from beneath bushy white eyebrows.

"Heavens, no. You know I grew up in the country. I've managed worse than this." Truth be told, it wasn't the sight of blood that made her woozy but the knowledge that the killer could be running around the courtyard right now. Of course, that had been the idea when she and Kitty planned the party, but with Lord Cumberland on the ground, the circumstances had changed. She wanted only to interview suspects, not have them come to any harm. Who would risk such an action at a garden party in the middle of the afternoon? *Someone desperate, that's who.*

But why? What had instigated the terror? Lord Cumberland was a bit of a dandy; that was his only charge. She retraced his steps at the party, but none of them seemed distinct in any way. He'd mentioned his horse winning the Ascot; she'd mentioned George Davies; then he mentioned Rotten Row. That brought an idea—or person—to mind: Lady Jane. She seemed perturbed by his attention to Marielle and was, coincidently, here now. Perhaps this crime and George Davies's murder were unconnected. Lady Jane was visibly upset. Because she'd perpetrated the accident? Amelia checked her dress for evidence, but not a flounce or feather was out of place. The person who'd hurt Lord Cumberland must have done damage to their clothes. They'd certainly done damage to her hedge.

"There now," said Mr. Dawson. "Let's take him inside. Gentlemen?"

"I can walk," Lord Cumberland insisted, but it was obvious

he couldn't. The moment he tried to stand, he swayed left and right.

"Whoa," cautioned Mr. Dawson. "Don't be foolish. Let these young men assist you." While the men from the party helped Cumberland into the house, Mr. Dawson packed up his bag.

Simon took the opportunity to ask him a question. "What do you think caused the bleeding?"

Mr. Dawson looked over his shoulder, watching the men take Cumberland down the path. "Something hard. Really hard, to cause that kind of confusion. I wouldn't be surprised if it takes Lord Cumberland a few days or longer to recover."

"You mean, *someone*," clarified Simon. "Perhaps accidently."

Mr. Dawson slowly nodded. "It might have been. I see no explanation for it."

"Mr. Dawson, do you think a . . . woman could have hit him with such force?"

"A woman, my lady?" Mr. Dawson's jowls shook with confusion. "What would make you think so?"

It wasn't what but who, for two women came to mind for the crime: Miss Fairchild and Lady Jane. Miss Fairchild was in the vicinity, and Lady Jane was, too, playing yard games. Furthermore, both were present the night of George Davies's murder. These facts suggested the idea wasn't as impossible as Mr. Dawson purported.

"I must see to Lord Cumberland," continued Mr. Dawson. "He might not be fit for traveling."

"Of course," Amelia agreed. "He's welcome to stay as long as he needs to."

Mr. Dawson turned to go, and Simon put a hand on her elbow. He mouthed the word *weapon*, and she nodded in understanding. They dallied several paces behind Mr. Dawson.

They needed to find the instrument that caused the injury and didn't have much time. An ominous rain cloud had taken the day hostage, its light pitter-patter threatening to break into a downpour. A splash hit her head and then another. While Mr. Dawson forged ahead, Simon took one side of the hedge, and Amelia took the other, searching for the item that felled Lord Cumberland. But by the time they reached the maze entrance, neither had found what they expected, except rain. It was coming down in torrents, and the entire garden party had dispersed, including the trio.

Amelia bit back a curse. Her search for Miss Fairchild was delayed yet again.

Chapter 29

Dear Lady Agony,

I have been duped twice this season, and it is only June! Once by a dance partner, who I later found out was a merchant salesman, and another by a caller who I discovered was a fifth-born son. How am I to guard myself against this sort of deceit? It appears I can be beguiled by even the most inexperienced actor.

Devotedly,
Believing Bessie

. . . .

Dear Believing Bessie,

I'm sorry you find yourself twice duped this season, but if your letter is any evidence, a third time is highly improbable. Being aware of a mistake is the first step in not repeating it. Now that you are alert, you can study your prejudice. What is it that

deceived you? Proper manners? Pretty words? Good looks?
Steel yourself against them, and in the future, you will be a
Better Bessie because of it.

Yours in Secret,
Lady Agony

As luck would have it, Lord Cumberland was able to travel, but Amelia asked Mr. Dawson to accompany him as a precaution. If and when Cumberland remembered the details surrounding the accident, Mr. Dawson assured Amelia she would be the first to know when he returned.

After Mr. Dawson left, Tabitha muttered, "Your first gathering, and someone takes a rap on the head. Why am I not surprised?"

"It's not as if *I* did the rapping, Aunt," hissed Amelia.

Simon, Marielle, Miss Pimm, and Mr. Hooper returned wearing their coats, and Amelia and Tabitha quit the conversation.

"I'm sorry the day was cut short by the weather." Marielle adjusted a creamy shawl, which matched her skin beautifully, over her shoulders. "It was a wonderful party. But poor Lord Cumberland. He had quite a fall."

Amelia was relieved to know her guests were unaware of the extent of his injuries. "Mr. Dawson says he'll recover completely."

"Did you see Miss Fairchild, by chance?" Simon asked his sister. "I didn't have an opportunity to talk to her before the accident."

"In fact, I did," said Marielle. "With all the commotion, I'd forgotten to tell you." She turned to fill in Mr. Hooper and Miss

Pimm. "She was my singing tutor long ago but, after years of tutelage, could do nothing with my voice."

"I'm sure you sing beautifully," Mr. Hooper proclaimed. "Like a bird."

"Perhaps a parrot!" she laughed. "At any rate, Miss Fairchild sings with the royal opera. She's playing the part of Lady Macbeth at Covent Garden Theatre. Isn't that wonderful? She always loved the theatre and now has a lead role. She mentioned a performance this evening."

Simon turned to Amelia. "That explains why she was spotted in the area."

"What do you mean?" asked Marielle. "What area?"

Detecting Tabitha's quizzical gaze on him, Simon changed the direction of the conversation. "Nothing of interest. Just a side topic Lady Amesbury and I were discussing. We'd best get you home and into dry clothes, Ellie."

"It's you and Lady Amesbury who are soaked," Miss Pimm pointed out. "What took you so long to get inside?"

"Indeed." Tabitha's eyes narrowed on the pair.

"I had to make certain Winifred and Bee weren't still in the gazebo." *It's not a lie*. In fact, Amelia had made sure the girls found their way inside. It just wasn't the whole truth. Not a chance she was telling Miss Pimm they were looking for the weapon that had taken out Lord Cumberland.

"Naturally, I had to accompany her." Simon put up his collar to brace himself from the rain and wind, looking very much like a sea captain. "I'll see you later this evening? For *Macbeth*?"

Amelia understood his meaning and quickly agreed. They were going to find Miss Fairchild, rain or shine. A little London thunderstorm wouldn't stop them. She checked Tabitha's reaction. Tabitha was still puzzling over the subject change. "You're welcome to join us, Aunt."

"And me also?" Marielle poked Simon with her umbrella. "I'd love to see Miss Fairchild perform, and I think you owe it to me."

"I think you're right." Simon looked pleased at the light joke, a little of their sibling camaraderie restored. "We'd love to have you. You, too, Hooper."

"Thank you, but unfortunately, I can't. My father's entertaining company this evening." Mr. Hooper's face was pinched with disappointment. "Another time, though."

"And I have an appointment with the fireplace and a good book." Tabitha rubbed the chill off her shoulders. "I won't be going out in this."

"Until tonight." Simon tipped his hat.

"Tonight."

After they left, Tabitha inquired about her plans. "The theatre again? I didn't know you were an aficionado. Is there another reason for spending so much time with the marquis?"

Amelia tilted her chin. "What reason would that be, Aunt?"

"I may be an old woman, but I am not oblivious to his charm. A young lady might have her head turned by such a man."

"I agree, he's charming, but my head is not turned." *Perhaps just sideways.*

"Good." Tabitha's voice held a firm note of satisfaction. "It would be foolhardy to fall for a man like Lord Bainbridge."

"And why is that?" Amelia had her reasons, but she wanted to hear Tabitha's.

"He has his responsibilities, and you have yours." Her perfect gray eyebrows lifted, making her blue eyes icy. "I do not see them crossing."

Which meant they would not cross if she had any say in the matter. *And she does not*, Amelia reminded herself. "I'll have the fire started and ring for hot chocolate."

"Excellent idea."

After they took refreshment and a light supper, Amelia dressed for her evening with Simon. Her *inquiry*, she corrected, for soon Marielle, too, would know of their plan. In fact, maybe she already suspected the plan since Amelia had mentioned the area of George Davies's death. However, Amelia liked to think the brother and sister were faring better and resolving the ill will between them. It might be that Marielle wanted to attend the theatre with them for no other reason than entertainment or reuniting with her mentor.

Lettie tucked a silver crown into her hair. It had a deep red ruby that matched her scarlet dress perfectly. "Stunning, my lady."

Amelia lifted her head, gazing at the stone in the reflection. It truly was. The large ruby hung from a chandelier of diamonds that reflected the twist of her auburn tresses. She hadn't worn such vibrant colors since coming out of mourning and loved how alive she looked and felt. She was glad she'd decided to embrace her role of wealthy countess, a lesson Miss Fairchild had taught her.

Miss Fairchild had been so believable in her role of Lady Macbeth that her outfit convinced Miss Rainier she was a lady, not a member of a troupe. The thought was an encouraging one, and it gave Amelia confidence that she, too, could go about the streets of London undetected in her pursuit of George Davies's killer. For all purposes, people would see only a socialite. Not an agony answerer seeking the truth for a reader.

"I don't know what I'd do without your fashion sense, Lettie."

Amelia gave Lettie's soft shoulders a squeeze. "If it weren't for you, I'd still be dressed in country calico, putting off buying new dresses until my calendar cleared."

"Which would be never!" Lettie laughed.

"Exactly." Amelia tilted her head, watching the light reflect off the jewel. "But you take pains to make me look good. I don't know how to thank you."

Lettie's soft face turned serious, her almond-shaped eyes wiser than her years. "Enjoy yourself, my lady. You've earned it. Your happiness is thanks enough."

Amelia embraced her quickly before dashing out to meet Simon, who was waiting for her in the drawing room. He, too, was dressed in his finery, but whereas his ensemble was dark, all black and white with a cream-colored scarf, hers was bold. So bold that Simon's breath caught when she entered the room.

"I've been waiting to see you in red."

"And?" She tried not to fidget, forcing her arms to stay at her sides.

"And I'm not disappointed."

His voice was husky and sent a shiver up her spine. If she hadn't known better, she'd have thought he was closer than he was. Even from across the room, he could make her pulse race. "Where's Marielle?"

Simon lingered over the ruby in her hair. "She complained of a headache and stayed home. I hope she didn't catch a chill this afternoon in the rain."

"That does not sound like Marielle. Are you certain she is all right?"

He frowned, his focus off her outfit. "Her maid sent word, and I went around to her room. She sounded fine through the door, just worn out."

"Did she know of our real plan?" Amelia asked. "To find Miss Fairchild? To find out what she and Mr. Davies spoke of the night he was murdered?"

"Yes, of course . . ." His sentence trailed off. "Maybe I should have asked to see her myself. I didn't want to come off as demanding. You know what our relationship has been of late."

"I understand, but this is what Marielle has been waiting for. She must be more ill than she's letting on." Amelia pushed back a stray lock of hair swirling about her face. It took all her restraint not to tuck her tendrils behind her ears. "Tabitha will have something to say about our going alone."

"She was fine with our going before."

"We were with a group, and she thought I *was* the chaperone."

"You? A chaperone?" Simon laughed. "Lord help unmarried women everywhere."

Amelia tipped her chin, having to look up to give him a proper glare. "I'm a widow. I can be a chaperone, you know."

"You're also under thirty."

That's where things get tricky. But Amelia didn't give him the satisfaction of agreeing. She scratched her head, trying to come up with something. "Lettie. I'll bring Lettie, and she won't say a word. She never does."

"If Tabitha insists."

"Which she will."

And she did when Amelia told her.

Tabitha laid her book aside. "I understand you're a friend of the family, Simon, and it's completely unnecessary, but one can't be too careful with the Amesbury reputation. Especially at such a public venue without your sister."

"I understand," said Simon.

Lettie was confused by the decision until halfway to Bow Street, where they informed her that Miss Fairchild would be starring in *Macbeth*. Then she was elated. An admirer of the theatre, she hadn't had an opportunity to attend while Amelia was in mourning. She'd accompanied her to plenty of mundane events, but never an occasion such as this. She chatted the rest of the way there about the performance. "I heard Miss Fairchild sing at the garden party, of course, but to see her in a production!" She clasped her hands, and Simon smiled patiently. "I won't say a word, promise. I'll be as quiet as a church mouse."

Amelia smiled, too. Lettie was a lot of things but as quiet as a church mouse wasn't one of them. She loved scandal, celebrities, and gossip. A night of all three might be too much for her to bear silently. But Amelia was glad she finally had the chance to go. "We'll need privacy and discretion. I know I can count on you."

"Always," promised Lettie, who was good at disappearing at an opportune moment.

When they arrived at the theatre, well ahead of the evening's show, Lettie trailed them at a respectable distance. No doubt she was trying to sneak a peek at the red velvet curtain and royal coat of arms in the auditorium. When she came across a maid she knew, she straggled even farther behind, chatting excitedly with her friend. Amelia waited a few moments to inform her of their plans to speak to Miss Fairchild before the evening show.

As Simon pulled aside the theatre manager, asking to see Miss Fairchild, Lettie whispered, "I cannot believe Lady Marielle had lessons from Miss Fairchild. She's the best singer in all of England. Is she taking them up again? Is that why he needs to talk to her?"

"No, it's a . . . private matter," Amelia explained. "Stay here and catch up with your friend. We'll be back soon."

"I understand." Lettie didn't ask any more questions. "You know where I'll be if you need me, my lady."

The manager led Simon and Amelia down a narrow corridor to a small cluster of rooms, knocking on the last one. "Miss Fairchild. You have a visitor. Lord Bainbridge is here to see you."

"One moment," came a voice from behind the door. Seconds later, Miss Fairchild filled the doorway, looking more beautiful than Amelia remembered. Her skin was flawless, her high forehead unmarked by lines or blemishes of any kind. With her crown of red hair, Miss Fairchild might have been a porcelain doll, except for her smile, which was genuine and friendly.

She seemed pleased by Simon's company. "My lord. It's been a long time." Her blue eyes flicked to Amelia. "Lady Amesbury. I hope my performance was satisfactory. Lady Tabitha dismissed us when the rain started, and I never had a chance to inquire."

"Beyond satisfactory," Amelia assured her, checking the trill in her own voice. It was hard not to get caught up in the woman's beauty and talent. Suddenly, she felt a bit like Lettie—impressed and giddy.

"I'm sorry we didn't have the opportunity to talk earlier," continued Simon. "I hate to interrupt an already busy evening."

Miss Fairchild smiled, revealing two deep dimples. They were the only creases in her soft, fleshy face. "You're not interrupting, my lord. How can I be of service?" She stepped aside to allow them entrance into the small room. "I cannot imagine Lady Marielle wants to take up lessons again." She chuckled.

A long mirror and garment rack took up most of the area, and only one chair, which had a pair of shoes on it, sat in the corner. Cosmetics and combs and hairpins lay scattered on a nearby table.

Simon joined in the laughter. "No, never. I'm here about another matter—a man. Mr. George Davies. He used to be Marielle's groom before becoming interested in the races. He worked for us for many years."

"I remember." Her wispy brows knitted together intensely, making her face sharper for a second. "I always suspected he had an affinity for her, and it was confirmed when I spotted them together on Drury Lane."

Simon shot Amelia a look before continuing. "So you did see them."

"I did more than see them. I *spoke* to Mr. Davies." Noticing a minor flaw, Miss Fairchild leaned closer to the mirror and blended a spot of rouge on her cheek. "He was alone, and I warned him off Lady Marielle, promising I would go to the family if necessary." She returned her focus to Simon. "At the risk of being offensive, my lord, he was very close to her that evening. Too close, if you understand my meaning." Her crown of curls shook. "I didn't approve of the familiarity, and you wouldn't have, either."

Amelia could see by his face that he wouldn't. If George Davies were alive, Simon would've killed him again. She decided this was a good time to remind them that George was dead. "Mr. Davies was murdered the night in question. Perhaps you haven't heard."

Miss Fairchild's mouth formed a perfect O. "I had no idea. I haven't opened the paper in an age. I've been so busy with the production and spring concerts. One of the girls told me to be careful on my way home, that there'd been a murder, but I didn't know it was Mr. Davies."

"It's true," Simon confirmed. "He was stabbed right on this very street, and unfortunately, Marielle was the one to find him."

"Gracious!" Miss Fairchild exclaimed.

"Do you know what time you spoke with him?" Amelia asked. "We're trying to piece together his last hours for Lady Marielle. It might bring her peace of mind." Amelia watched Miss Fairchild carefully. She was a beauty, but she was also an actress with skills. Between her charm and voice, she might be able to make one believe anything, and she had been present at both Drury Lane and the garden party. Yet what reason would she have for killing George Davies? From all accounts, she was trying to protect Marielle. How far would she go to protect a young mentee whom she once tutored? Perhaps that was the real question.

Miss Fairchild's curled eyelashes lifted toward the ceiling as she considered her answer. "The theatre hadn't let out yet. He must have left early, because he was outside, alone. I pulled him aside for a private conversation. He said I was mad, but I told him I knew what I'd seen." She frowned and pulled her gaze off the ceiling, looking at Simon. "For a moment, I thought he might hurt me. He grabbed my arm and squeezed it tightly. There was a bruise . . . He never spared the whip with the horses, if you recall."

"The very reason Father so easily dismissed him." Simon's voice was gritty with anger.

"Then I left." Miss Fairchild's face cleared, and she looked at Amelia. "I've always been more singer than actress. But I know a performer when I spot one, and I spotted one in George Davies. He played the part of the gentleman, but he was no gentleman. He was a brute and a deviant. I'm sorry he's dead but also glad Lady Marielle will no longer be beguiled by his performances."

"Well said." Simon seemed relieved to hear the words said aloud. "I feel exactly the same."

Amelia silently agreed. She wished it were different, for Marielle's sake, but wishing didn't make it so. Indeed, if this investigation had taught her anything it was that George's falseness was completely true.

Chapter 30

Dear Lady Agony,

You seem like a woman who enjoys her fair share of excitement. How might I obtain some? My season has been dreadfully boring, and if I don't find adventure soon, I might curl up and die.

Devotedly,
Bored Stiff

....

Dear Bored Stiff,

I, too, once suffered the drawing room doldrums—and then I took up this column. My advice to you, then, must be the suggestion I took myself: don't be afraid to say yes to new things. Often, our first instinct is no. We can't, we shan't, we mustn't. Moving past the immovable no in your mind will open *a new door. An exciting door. I promise good things await on the other side.*

Yours in Secret,
Lady Agony

Though the theatre's production of *Macbeth* was first-rate, Amelia wasn't able to enjoy it. All she could focus on was that despite all they had found out about George Davies, they hadn't found his killer. The more loose threads they pulled on, the more that came undone. A man like George might have been killed for any number of reasons. But Marielle, who was as true as her word, deserved the right reason. Amelia needed to find it. Like a needle in a haystack, it evaded her. Search as she might, she came up with no answers, only more hay.

It was only when Lettie jumped out of her seat, cheering as if at the Derby, that Amelia realized the curtain had fallen and the show was over. She joined the applause halfheartedly, listening to Lettie praise the performance, which she did all the way to the carriage.

The night air felt like a wet coat, and Amelia shivered as Simon helped her into her carriage seat. Lettie immediately offered to find her a lap blanket, but Amelia refused, hoping the cold would awake new possibilities.

Nothing.

Simon leaned closer. "You haven't said a word all evening. What's on your mind?"

"George Davies." Amelia shook her head. "The more we investigate, the more I wish I had killed him myself. At least I'd know the murderer."

His mouth kicked up on one side.

"It's true," she said, even though it wasn't.

"Mr. Davies was the victim. No matter what he did, he didn't deserve to die."

Simon was right, of course. Despite his actions, Mr. Davies deserved justice. She was just upset it evaded them.

"And Marielle didn't deserve to find him in the street," he added, his eyes the gray-green color of smoke from a pipe. "Do you know how much it hurts me to see her brokenhearted?"

I do. It's why she'd agreed to everything. From the moment he'd shown her Marielle's letter, she understood how scared he was of losing her. Until the killer was caught, the angst would remain. "Of course I do." She smiled. "She's a very lucky sister."

He shook his head. "Sometimes."

"Most of the time." She feigned consternation. "Fifty percent at least."

He swatted at her hand, then his hand stayed there, covering hers. Even through the gloves, she felt the warmth. Their partnership. It was solid, and it gave her strength. Never in her life had she felt so uplifted by another. It gave her courage to do hard things: like find George's murderer. She recommitted to doing just that as the carriage pulled up to her house.

Amelia was surprised to see her footman Bailey toting a lantern. "What's he doing outside at this hour?"

"Probably looking for a piece of the silver," Lettie muttered. "Jones is always losing the silver."

"He's looking for something," agreed Simon.

Amelia squinted. "Let's find out what."

While Lettie dashed inside, excited to tell her mother, Patty Addington, about the play, Simon and Amelia approached Bailey.

His lantern clanked as he swung his head up, his warm complexion flushed in the lamplight. "My lady. Lord Bainbridge."

"Good evening, Bailey." Amelia tried to assure him with a calm voice, for she could see he was already under strain by the appearance of his pinched lips. "What brings you out of the house at this hour?"

"A horseshoe." His voice was tinged with irritation, perhaps at performing yet another task on top of his usual duties. "One of the others helping with today's event seems to have lost it, and now the set is incomplete. Jones just thought to tell me."

"We'll find it tomorrow." Amelia gave him what she hoped was a peppy smile. "No use losing sleep over it."

"It will be easier to locate in the daylight," added Simon. "It was probably tossed off course."

His words gave Amelia a different idea. Was the horseshoe thrown off course, or was it missing for another reason? "Bailey, did one of the footmen see the horseshoe in this area? Is that why you're searching here? It's far from the yard games."

"I'm afraid not, my lady." Bailey frowned. "After seeing some partygoers' attempts at the game today, I thought it might have been misplaced. Like his lordship said, thrown off the regular path."

"And how long have you been looking?" Amelia couldn't disguise the worry in her voice. As she recalled the incident in the maze, she realized one person and one person only was missing from the scene, and that person was in close proximity to Marielle. She might be in danger at this very moment.

"A quarter hour. I'll find it soon enough." Bailey's face was earnest, her worry perhaps mistaken for anger.

"No, you won't. You may stop looking and go inside. Lord Bainbridge and I must leave at once."

"My lady?" Bailey questioned.

"What is it?" asked Simon at the same time.

"Don't you see?" Amelia swallowed, trying to clear the shakiness from her voice. "Lord Cumberland was hit over the head with the horseshoe. That's why it's gone missing. It's the weapon that was used to hurt him in the maze."

Simon's eyes widened with awareness. "Of course."

"And that's not all," Amelia whispered. "His injury might have had something to do with Marielle. She could be in trouble."

Simon didn't wait for further explanation. Maybe he'd guessed at it already. "We have to go."

When they arrived at the Bainbridge house a few minutes later, Simon was out of the carriage before it fully stopped, leaving Amelia to lope behind with a very concerned footman at her heels. The front door was open, so she had no need for the butler, who, with another footman, stood staring at her from the entryway. She ignored them, her eyes following Simon's fleeting footsteps up the staircase. He was on the second floor, approaching the third, where the bedrooms were located. She took off behind him.

"Where do you think you're going?"

Amelia spun around and almost lost her balance. Still holding her skirts high above her ankles, she came face-to-face with the Duke of Bainbridge. "To check on Marielle."

"No, you're not." The duke's voice was insistent. "She's not feeling well, and it's very late."

"I understand, but she might be in trouble," she implored. "You have to believe me."

For a moment, Amelia wondered if the duke had anything to do with tonight's mysterious illness. If Simon thought him capable of his mother's death, couldn't he also be capable of keeping Marielle home? But the thought dissipated the next moment as he dropped the look and ran past her, taking the stairs two at a time.

She quickly followed.

They found Simon standing in the middle of an empty bedroom. "She's gone," he said, his voice full with disbelief.

The duke stalked by him, circling the room. "Marielle!"

"She's not here," repeated Simon.

"Miss Pimm!" the duke hollered. He stuck his head into the hallway and yelled again. "Miss Pimm!"

"Maybe you recall the last time you saw her this evening?" tried Amelia.

"*Saw* her?" He ran his hand over his wavy hair. "I didn't see her. Miss Pimm said she was ill and retiring early. Now I find her gone? With no maid or chaperone? What's going on?"

"Your Grace." Miss Pimm popped into the room, breathless. Her tidy bun was skewed to one side of her head. She wasn't accustomed to being summoned so late in the evening. "You called?"

"My daughter is missing from her bedroom." The duke's hand shook, and Amelia could see the crack in his composure spreading. "Where is she?"

Miss Pimm frowned. "That's impossible. She told me she was going to bed." Miss Pimm's skirt swished back and forth like a broom as she searched the same areas the duke had. "It doesn't make any sense. Where would she go?"

"It's your job to find out." The duke blinked rapidly. "Search the house."

"Your Grace," started Miss Pimm.

"Now!" commanded the duke. "There's no time to lose."

Miss Pimm hurried out, and Amelia shut the door behind her. "I wish there were a better time to bring this up, but as you said, time is of the essence." Between the two distraught men, Amelia felt like the calm one in the room. "We need to know what happened between you and George Davies the night of his murder, and we need to know now."

The duke began to protest, but Simon cut him off. "We know you spoke with him, Father. I found your horseshoe pin at the scene of the crime. We need to know what you said and did. Marielle's life might depend on it."

"What are you saying?" The duke choked back a cry. "She's in danger?"

"Lord Cumberland was injured at my garden party, quite seriously. I think someone was jealous of his affections toward Lady Marielle." As Amelia said the words aloud, the possibility cleared away all other possibilities. The notion was as obvious as the concern in both men's eyes. *How could I have been so blind?*

"Please, Father," pleaded Simon.

The duke must have detected the desperation in his son's eyes, because he answered without further dispute. "I gave Davies the pin the night of the opera. He threatened to continue courting Marielle, and I was naive enough to think the jewelry would placate him. I should have known it would only inspire future threats. I had no idea it'd be so soon."

"When?" Simon asked.

"That very night." The duke shook his head. "He sent word for me, and I met him at a gin palace near the theatre."

The duke was the toff at the bar! He fit the waitress's description. The duke had a distinctive mustache that would have easily revealed his hair color even if a hat disguised it.

"He needed money, and I gave it to him. That's all." Simon's father caught his eye. "You must believe me."

"How can I?" Simon asked.

"I give you my word." The duke held Simon's stare. "I can't have you blaming me for his death." A veil of moisture covered his steel blue eyes, and he blinked it away rapidly. "I know you blame me for what happened to your mother. You always have."

Simon shifted his gaze.

Amelia wished he and his father could have a private moment alone, but there was no time.

The duke went on despite Simon's indifference. His eyes took on a faraway look, like ocean-blue water. "I knew your mother was different the moment I met her. She laughed easily, cried easily. And the way she played pianoforte . . . The angels must have rejoiced to hear it." His eyes sparkled at the memory. "She was the most extraordinary woman I'd ever met, yet I regarded her as if she were any other well-bred lady, as my father regarded my mother. From a distance." He spat out the word. "Distance isn't what she craved. She craved warmth. Compassion. Love. Things she had to find in another man's arms." He took a breath. "I accept that. But I can't accept your blame for her death. The guilt I feel is punishment enough."

Simon's eyes snapped to his father's in disbelief. "You feel guilty for her death?"

"Of course I do." The duke's voice was incredulous. "I thought if I did as I was taught, our marriage would be safe. Little did I know it was the most dangerous thing I could do. I took her for granted. If I hadn't, she wouldn't have had to find solace elsewhere."

Which is exactly why he blamed Simon for Felicity's infidelity. The realization dawned on Amelia like the first spring day in March. The duke thought Simon neglected Felicity, but the situation couldn't have been more different. Simon loved Felicity ardently, and she ardently loved his title. Felicity was nothing like Simon's mother.

"I didn't know." Simon's voice sounded as young as a boy's.

"I didn't tell you. How could I? I wanted to be strong for you and your sister."

"We didn't need strong," said Simon. "We needed a father."

"I know that now. I'm here now."

A beat passed, and in that beat, Amelia felt their relationship take a step in the right direction. The gap was large, but with time and patience, she was certain they would be able to cross the void between father and son.

She hated to intrude, but she had to for Marielle's sake. "Your Grace, you stated that you gave Mr. Davies money, which explains the money we found on him. Why?"

The duke shoved his hands into his pockets. "I had no other choice. Mr. Davies threatened to take Marielle across the border, to Scotland, where they could pass the waiting period with his relative if I didn't give him the money."

"So he bribed you?" Simon let out a huff. "That little thief."

"He had a gambling debt he couldn't pay off and needed the money right away. That very evening."

Thaddeus King! He must have mentioned the debt during intermission and been unwilling to wait for payment. The only person George Davies knew who had that kind of money was the duke. He must have sent word right away. But another problem awaited George, a man he didn't see coming.

"You remember how fond Marielle was of George when he lived here," continued the duke. "I knew, with enough time, he might convince her to leave if I didn't do as he asked."

"He already had," Amelia confirmed. "Whether the money

would have made any difference, I do not know. What I *do* know is that you didn't harm him, which means someone else did, and I think I know who."

Simon pressed his palms together, bringing his fingertips to his lips. "For God's sake, who?"

Amelia walked over and pushed open the curtain. It was just as she suspected. Like Simon's, Marielle's balcony led to a veranda, which led to the grounds. The door was still ajar, and a breeze cooled her feet. "Mr. Hooper."

Chapter 31

Dear Lady Agony,

Matrons say it's easy to fend off unwanted attentions. Simply do not dance with, talk to, or look at the undesirable gentleman. I have tried all of these and brutal honesty, too, but this villain is not so easily swayed. I have done nothing to provoke affection, and still he seeks me out. What do I do?

Devotedly,
Fretful Francesca

. . . .

Dear Fretful Francesca,

It is his flaw, not yours, that has caused this problem. The villain has not been deterred by your blunt behavior, so you must take further action. Tell your mother, father, sister, brother—anyone who will listen. Involve them in the problem straightaway and do not meet with him alone. Please write back with your progress. I look forward to hearing of the villain's upset.

Yours in Secret,
Lady Agony

"Mr. Hooper," Simon repeated. "Captain Hooper's son?"

"How can that be?" the duke asked. "He's our friend and neighbor."

"And a man in love with your daughter." Amelia stepped aside, allowing them to see what she'd seen at first glance. An empty house, a lighted window, a weak son. Unsought this season, Mr. Hooper was alone most of the time, doing his father's bookwork. But one person did pay him attention: Marielle. Whereas other women wanted war heroes, Marielle wanted only kindness. He fell in love with her from a distance and closed that distance inch by inch, until he could no longer bear the thought of her being taken away from him by another man.

"I think you're mistaken." The duke walked to the curtain and peered out. Simon joined him. "His father's a decorated captain of Her Majesty's Royal Navy."

"I'm not mistaken," said Amelia. "He was the only one absent from the maze when we found Lord Cumberland. He must have become envious of Cumberland's attention to Marielle. Furthermore, he told us his father was hosting an event tonight, yet there is not a carriage in sight."

"By God, you're right," said Simon in a voice no louder than a whisper.

"We need to find where he's taken her." Amelia felt less composed than she sounded. Inside, she was frantic to find the girl. "If I'm right and he is in love with her, he might try to force her hand in marriage."

"Let's start with his house." Simon strode toward the door. "His staff might know his whereabouts." He turned around to make sure Amelia was following him, which she was. When he started again, he almost bumped into Miss Pimm.

"Oh, excuse me!" Miss Pimm apologized.

"Did you find her?" the duke asked.

"No, I'm afraid not." Miss Pimm fisted her hands on her hips. "I don't understand it at all."

Simon pointed a finger in her face. "You are the worst chaperone in all of London." Then he shot past her, out the door.

Amelia kept her head down, mostly to conceal the smile on her lips. Simon's comment was retribution for all the times Amelia had felt less than adequate in the woman's presence.

"Simon!" Amelia called. He was halfway down the staircase.

He waited for her at the bottom step. "I want to find him. I *need* to find him."

"I don't think he'll be at the house." Together, they walked out the front door and took a quick turn toward the Hooper townhome. "But as you said, the staff might know something."

When they arrived at the stone abode, Simon rapped loudly on the door.

A middle-aged man opened it, his eyes angry at the late caller until he realized the caller was Simon Bainbridge. His brow lifted in surprise. "My lord." He stepped aside. "Come in."

"Carter." Simon's eyes swept the entry for evidence of Marielle. "Is the younger Hooper here? I need to speak with him."

"I'm afraid not, my lord." His brown eyebrows knitted as if

he were piecing together the words used to explain the absence. "He had urgent business to attend to that could not wait until morning. He took his father's stallion."

"You're kidding." Simon's face turned ashen.

"No, I am not."

"Did he have anyone with him?" Amelia tried.

If his peaked eyebrows were any indication, the butler was confused by her question. "I don't believe so."

"I understand this is an unusual request, and I wouldn't ask it if we hadn't been neighbors for ages, but could we check young Hooper's room?" Simon took a step toward a staircase that swirled up three floors. "It's very important that we know where he went. He could be in trouble."

"I'm afraid that'd be most improper for me to say." The butler's voice faltered, and he cleared his throat. "Let me ask Captain Hooper. If you'll wait in the drawing room . . ."

Simon started to protest, but Amelia touched his elbow. "A splendid idea."

The butler led them to the second floor, where he deposited them in a room with plush carpets, gold frames, and a beautiful chandelier, albeit unlit. He lighted an oversized lamp on a side table that illuminated the room. "It'll be just a moment."

After he'd gone, Simon paced the room. "A *splendid* idea? The devil it is!"

Amelia put a finger to her lips. "It's one floor closer to the bedrooms, is it not?"

Simon caught her meaning. "Oh. Yes."

"Follow me," she whispered. "I've done this before."

The plush carpet continued up the second flight of stairs, and their steps were blissfully silent as they looked for Mr. Hooper's room. The house was not as large as Amelia's or Simon's, and the hallway was narrow, providing passage to probably eight or so rooms.

It was late, and most of the doors were shut. Only two stood ajar, and only one revealed a lighted room. It faced the courtyard of Bainbridge Hall. "Psst," Amelia hissed.

Simon peeked in. He waved her forward, shutting the door behind them. He crossed the area to the large window, pulling back the drape. "The little urchin could watch her every move from here."

"And probably did." She focused on Mr. Hooper's bureau. An open drawer caught her eye. Her stomach knotted as she opened it farther. A hairpin, a glove, a lock of ebony hair preserved under a piece of glass.

"What is it?" Simon asked over her shoulder.

She moved aside.

Simon's breath stuck in his throat. "Christ."

"They're Marielle's, aren't they?"

He nodded.

"Don't worry," Amelia said, continuing her search. "We'll find her."

Above the fireplace, a painting of Captain Hooper loomed as large as the real Captain Hooper did in his son's everyday life. The young Hooper couldn't follow in his father's footsteps, as his brothers had. He was too weak and perhaps not inclined anyway. Instead, he was left to add numbers and file receipts. He resented the tasks. And resented his father. Which was why he used the facon his father had plundered from a pirate ship to kill George Davies. Her breath doubled at the idea. "The facon. It was his father's knife."

Simon's jaw tightened. "Of course it was. I should have made the connection. As a navy man myself."

She lifted her eyes briefly. "Don't get me started on navy men." She froze. Below, the butler's voice grew louder. He was talking to another man. Captain Hooper? They didn't have much time.

She scanned the rest of the room. Everything was in its place. Nothing seemed out of order. The clothes in the closet were tidy. The small writing desk was clear of papers. The books were neatly aligned on the shelf. She bit her lip. There had to be something, some indication that he had abducted a young girl from her home.

Her eyes landed on two sheets of ivory paper on the nightstand. One possessed a large droplet of ink. She hurried to examine the papers, but both were void of writing.

Simon looked over her shoulder. "Blank."

"Not quite." Amelia bent over the cold fireplace, scooping up a fingerful of ash. She returned to the ivory sheets, lightly smearing the ash over the paper. An address appeared. Looking up at Simon, she smiled.

His green eyes searched her own. "Who are you, Amelia Amesbury?"

"Wouldn't you like to know?" She arched an eyebrow.

Approaching footsteps interrupted them.

Shoving the paper in his greatcoat pocket, Simon grabbed her hand and pulled her behind the heavy drapery. Her heart felt as if it might burst, and she had difficulty calming her breath. It wasn't the impending footsteps that had her rattled; it was Simon. He smelled like the ocean, and if real waves were crashing around her, she'd have a better chance at remaining standing than she did now. She reached for his arm out of necessity. Quickly determining the problem, he bolstered her against him, wrapping his arm around her. Unless she melted into a pool on the floor, slipping between his fingers, she was safe.

"They must've gone." A young man, most likely staff, entered the room. "You didn't move fast enough for 'em."

"I moved as quickly as I could." The butler's voice held reproach in it. "Captain Hooper is waiting. What am I to tell him?"

"Tell 'im they had no manners and left."

"And after waking him from a dead sleep." The butler tsked. "Shameful."

The door closed, and Amelia released a breath. *That was close.* But not as close as she and Simon. Their proximity became wildly apparent. Her exposed back was against his hard chest, and his warm hand was around her waist. Neither of them moved. They were waiting for the staff to leave the third floor. Weren't they?

That's what I'm doing, she told herself. She wasn't memorizing the lines of his muscles or the quickness of his breath or the pressure of his hand. She wasn't imagining what would happen if she turned around. She wasn't thinking of his dark hair brushing her forehead or his soft lips pressing against hers or his whiskered jawline brushing against her neck.

He released her. "They're gone."

"Yes." The word was shakier than she would have liked, and she remained silent for the next several minutes as she followed him out of the bedroom, down the dark servants' staircase, and through the empty kitchen.

Closing the back door quietly behind them, he headed straight for the Bainbridge stables. "I know that address. It's a coaching inn, in Basingstoke."

She hurried to keep up. "Why Basingstoke?"

"To rest his horse, presumably. Perhaps en route to the Southampton docks. You can get anywhere from there."

Southampton was a port town with which Simon would be

thoroughly familiar. Mr. Hooper might be planning to depart with Marielle by boat. *Heavens!* The idea struck fresh terror in her heart.

And Simon's, too. He summoned help immediately. Despite the late hour, a groom peered out from a window above. "A driver, if you please. Right away . . ."

A commotion followed, and a few minutes later the groom appeared with two sleepy-eyed men. "An emergency in Basingstoke, I'm afraid. Ready all six horses. We're leaving immediately."

"Certainly, my lord." The men hurried into the stables.

Simon followed. "If you want to leave, now is your chance. If we're seen . . ."

"We won't be." Amelia glanced at her dress. It was the worst time to be wearing red. "Do you have something to cover my gown?"

He scanned the area, taking a man's coat off a nearby hook. "Will this do?"

She nodded, shrugging into the jacket while the men hitched the horses. It was an old coachman's coat, complete with capelets and tall collar. *This will do nicely.*

"If Hooper's done anything to her, I'll kill him." Simon's jaw clenched. "I swear to God I will."

Amelia reassured him. "He hasn't and he won't. Otherwise, why make the trip?" She shook her head. "No, he loves her, or thinks he loves her. She's safe—at least for now."

Chapter 32

Dear Lady Agony,

Do you know how to use a knife? How about a gun? I imagine you're quite the bluestocking and carry one or both in your boot. Do you?

Devotedly,
Blue Looks Good on You

....

Dear Blue Looks Good on You,

I do indeed know how to use both. Do I carry one in my boot? I leave that up to your fine imagination, Dear Reader.

Yours in Secret,
Lady Agony

The evening at the theatre had wasted precious time, but the six horses made up for it. Their hooves pounded through the countryside like thunder, shaking the ground with force and might. Simon and Amelia arrived at the address, a coaching inn in Basingstoke, well after midnight. Despite the late hour, the establishment was abuzz with activity. In fact, another coach had stopped for the evening and was being unhitched as they descended the carriage.

Amelia quickly acclimated herself to her surroundings. Through the inn's front window, she saw a thirsty guest drinking a pint of ale. In front of him was an empty plate, a late-night snack to tide him over until morning. Their arrival wouldn't disrupt a sleeping innkeeper, which meant more freedom of movement.

Simon took a quick step toward the door, and she pulled him back. "Be careful. Mr. Hooper might be trying to force her hand in marriage. If they're found unchaperoned, it would do the trick. We must be discreet."

Simon took a raspy breath, straightening his stride. "Right."

"Bainbridge!" hollered a man near the other carriage. "Is that you?"

Amelia pulled her coat collar higher and stepped away from Simon. *I'd best heed my own advice.*

"Tayes," Simon greeted. "Good to see you." His voice relayed the opposite, however. He was anxious to begin looking for Marielle.

There was no reason Amelia couldn't get a head start.

"What brings you to Basingstoke this time of night?" asked Tayes. "Sail tomorrow?"

Amelia didn't wait to hear Simon's explanation. She took the opportunity to sneak through the front door unnoticed. Her investigations as Lady Agony had made her stealthy, even in a red dress. Understatement was key. So was the ability to look as if she knew where she was going, even if she didn't. Head down, steady footsteps. That's how she proceeded.

Amelia located the back stairwell, a towering, narrow passage that provided the help a way to come and go freely. Unlike the front room, however, it was pitch black, and she clung to the handrail as she navigated the unfamiliar climb.

She would start with the third floor and work her way down. One foot in front of the other, she crept up the stairs. Keeping her voluminous skirt from underfoot took concentration. So did keeping her petticoat quiet. The stiff fabric rustled in the noiseless dark despite her best efforts.

Amelia rounded the corner on the second floor, and a young girl with an armful of pillows squeaked in surprise. "Gracious! You gave me a scare."

Amelia held back her own exclamation, deciding to use the interruption to her advantage. She could pretend to be Mrs. Hooper's maid, for she was certain Mr. Hooper told the innkeeper they were married, the only acceptable explanation. She only hoped he'd used his real name. "I apologize. I didn't mean to startle you. I'm looking for Mrs. Hooper's room."

The young girl picked up a fallen pillow. "Storms always make me skittish."

"I heard one is headed our way." Noticing the girl's frown at her coat, Amelia continued. "The coachman lent me his overcoat while I fetched Mrs. Hooper's jewelry from the carriage." She pulled out her own ruby crown from the pocket, showing the girl. "He thought the rain might start soon."

The girl smiled at the hair jewelry, revealing a crooked set of teeth. "Any minute now. Sure as Victoria is the queen of England." She pointed up the next flight of stairs. "Room 5. You're one floor off."

"Thank you." On her way up the steps, Amelia paused at a small window. Simon was still outside with Tayes. *Drat.* Now that she knew Marielle's location, he needed to untangle himself, and fast.

Luckily, she was well on her way to apprehending Mr. Hooper. *But how?* She couldn't walk up to the door and knock, could she? What were her other options? She stood in the hall, waiting for another idea to come.

What came, however, was a whimper from Room 5.

Amelia froze. It had to be Marielle.

Amelia crept closer to the door, willing her heart to quit beating so loudly. If it kept up, Mr. Hooper would hear it through the thin wood. She held her breath and listened with her whole body.

Nothing.

Had she imagined the noise? No. It was Marielle. But where was Mr. Hooper?

For all she knew, he was gone. Marielle could be locked inside—alone—trying to break free. Maybe that was the noise Amelia heard. Either way, Amelia had to do something. It's why they'd come. Simon would be along any moment, and she *did* have that knife in her coat. Simon had given it to her for this very reason. In case they got separated, which they had. Albeit by her own doing.

She cracked the door. An oil lamp flickered in the corner, casting a low light over the room. She blinked, allowing her eyes to adjust. An empty bed, an empty chair. A footstool that had seen better days. All were unattended.

She stepped into the room. Silence. Feeling more confident, she took another step. The moan happened again, and she looked left and right. It was coming from the closet.

She took a step in that direction.

The door slammed behind her, and her heart fell to her stomach.

Blast it, she scolded herself. *I should've looked behind the door.* It was the place all bad men hid.

"You," hissed a voice. "I should have known you'd come."

The hairs on the back of her neck stood up like soldiers ready for battle. "Mr. Hooper." Determined to defend herself and Marielle, she calmly turned to face him. "We were looking for you. Thankfully, we've found you before you do something rash."

"Who's 'we'?" Mr. Hooper stared past her at the closed door.

"The marquis, of course." His light eyes were amber—wild, like a lion that's been caught in a trap. He'd been perspiring, and his hair was pasted to his forehead. The pulse in his neck revealed a rapid beat. "He's only a few steps behind me," she continued, hoping it was true.

"You're lying."

"Check the window," she suggested. "You'll see his carriage."

Not taking his eyes off her, he sidestepped to the window, pulling back a flimsy curtain. He scanned the area. "I see nothing."

She shrugged. "That doesn't surprise me. It's dark." Her eyes skimmed the room. "Where's Lady Marielle?" Another noise escaped the closed anteroom—a foot, perhaps, hitting the door. "In the closet? That's no way to treat the woman you love."

Mr. Hooper's brow puckered. He was confused by her comment, his conflicting emotions, or both. He looked from her to the window a few more times.

"I know you love her." Amelia smiled, hoping it came off as genuine. "It's why you've taken her. You want to be with her."

His head bobbed a little too vigorously. "I do. I've loved her for a long time."

"Why not do this the right way, then?" She tried a step toward the closet. "Let Lord Bainbridge and me help you make her your wife."

He didn't seem to notice her movement. "You would do that?"

"Of course we would." Her voice squeaked, and she swallowed. "Why wouldn't we? You've known each other forever, and the duke would like to see her married her first season out."

"She doesn't want to." He took a parting look out the window before dropping the curtain. "I asked her." He laughed bitterly. "She thinks of me as a friend, nothing more."

Amelia waved off the comment. "Girls at her age never know what they want."

His voice turned hard. "She knew she wanted George Davies."

"George Davies. Hmph. He wasn't half the catch you are." She hoped she wasn't laying it on too thick, but he seemed to believe her and even enjoy the attention. "She could never marry him. He was a horse trainer—her groom, for goodness' sake."

"That's what I said!"

"Which is why you took care of the situation." She arched an eyebrow at him. "Like a gentleman." His mouth opened in surprise, and she continued, cajoling him. "Don't misunderstand me. I'm glad you did it. I'm only sorry the association went on so long."

He rubbed his palms on his trousers, leaving sweat stains. "I couldn't allow her to be seen paying him attention in public. That wouldn't do at all. Especially if she was to be my wife. My brothers would have never let me hear the end of it." He swallowed, looking impossibly young for a moment. "When she rebuffed me, dismissing me for Davies and his friends, I knew I couldn't wait. I had to do it that night."

"Understandable." Her voice was steady, but a brief tremor of fear quaked her insides at the confirmation. She took another step toward the closet. "But how did you do it without being seen?"

Mr. Hooper's eyes opened wider. "I'm good at being invisible. I hid in plain sight. The area was occupied by people from all walks of life, from the very wealthy to the very poor. Lords. Ladies. Vagrants. Strumpets. Anyone might be on that street. Anyone at all."

"Even a murderer . . ." she said aloud. A murderer who wore a cloak, like any other theatre patron. The only difference was this patron was noticed by the watchful Miss Rainier.

"Yes, even a murderer."

"Why use your father's knife?" Amelia asked.

"Why indeed." His voice ground harshly on her ears. "It seems you're the only one who's discovered it's my father's. Scotland Yard couldn't uncover a clue if they were given a shovel. And yet anyone who's ever met my father would know the story of his heroic pirate plunder. How he'd fought off ten gauchos with one of their own knives aboard *La Gran Argentina*. It seems dear old Dad is not as famous as I thought he was."

"You did it to implicate him." Of course he had. Why else would one leave a knife of distinction at a crime scene? Amelia thought it was done in a moment of passion, perhaps by a woman, but if she'd thought it through, she would have realized it was left on purpose.

"Yes. If I could've rid myself of my father's overbearingness while gaining a bride, it would have been the perfect outcome." Noting Amelia's dumbfounded expression, he relaxed his face, the peevish lines around his eyes smoothing. "You cannot imagine what it's like growing up in a family of decorated military men, Lady Amesbury. My father constantly reminding me of my inadequacies. When I try to participate in family conversations, he dismisses me, reminding me of the bookwork I must attend to. I am nothing more than his second-rate accountant. A *bookworm*, he calls me." His hands clenched at his sides. "It's an insult."

"So you got back at him by killing George Davies with his infamous knife."

"The knife was entirely useful." His voice lifted. "I hid it in my cloak, which disguised my own appearance as well as any actor's. When Davies left the theatre early, I followed him, thanking my good luck. But a woman approached him before I could. He shrugged her off, disappearing into a gin house, and I had to wait."

"Very patient of you."

"Yes." He nodded. "I've always been patient, waiting and watching for my opportunity. When he came out, smelling like liquor, I took it. I knew there'd be no better time." An eerie smile spread across his face. "It wasn't as hard as I thought it'd be. Or as hard as my father claimed for all these years. The knife went right in. There was nothing to it."

Amelia felt sick but pressed her lips shut hard, forcing herself to keep up the charade. He was enjoying sharing the details. It was his first opportunity to boast of his exploits. She imagined he wished his brothers were there to hear. "And Lord Cumberland? Did you hurt him, too?"

He let out a breath that ruffled his hair. "*Lord* Cumberland. He's not fit for the title. The way he oozed affection for Marielle. It was revolting. When he went into the maze to retrieve Lady Jane's horseshoe, I followed him, and as he bent over, I hit him with my own horseshoe. But the stupid man bled like a pig, so I hid it in my overcoat."

That's why he wasn't in the maze. He was retrieving his coat from the house so he could hide the bloody horseshoe.

Amelia swallowed, reminding herself Marielle was counting on her. Unless Amelia wanted hand-to-hand combat, she needed to buy herself more time to free her. But how?

She didn't have time to ponder the question. A thud sounded against the closet door, and the door burst open, revealing an angry Marielle, sitting on the floor, gagged and tied. She, like Amelia, was dressed in her finery, her crinoline and petticoat intertwined.

Amelia knew it. Her clothes proved it. *She planned to attend the theatre.*

Marielle shouted something, but the words were lost in the cloth.

Amelia glanced at Mr. Hooper. His face was twisted into a scared snarl. The reality of the situation had hit him full force. He'd not only admitted to killing George Davies; he also had a duke's daughter tied up in the closet. He was trapped and afraid and, Amelia feared, desperate.

"Get back in there!" He kicked at Marielle and missed. He swung his foot again.

Instinctively, Amelia grabbed the knife out of her coat. It was heavier than she remembered. "Stop—before you regret it."

He spun around.

For the first time, she realized how tall he was. But his height was nothing compared to her anger. She couldn't bear seeing Marielle mistreated, and the emotion gave her superhuman strength. It radiated from her shoulder all the way down to her fingertips. She gripped the knife tighter.

He snickered a cruel laugh. "You foolish woman."

"You foolish man." She raised the weapon above her head. It

frightened her to know she would use it if he made one more move toward Marielle. "I won't let you treat my friend that way. I will take any means necessary to stop you."

He lunged at her. She stepped out of the way. She was next to the open closet now and pulled Marielle to her feet with one hand. The other she kept aimed at Mr. Hooper. Marielle might be tied and gagged, but two women were always better than one. Together, they would fight him as a team.

Mr. Hooper was beside the bed, where he pulled out a small gun from behind the pillow. He wagged it at her erratically. The situation had revealed the full extent of his condition, and perhaps the lengths he was willing to go to have Marielle for himself. "Didn't anyone teach you not to play with knives?"

His back was to the door. He didn't see what Amelia and Marielle saw: an enraged Simon entering the room. Simon put a finger to his lips, cautioning them not to react.

But the look of relief in their eyes must have been warning enough.

Mr. Hooper spun around to see the cause of the change.

Simon took Mr. Hooper down with a hard blow to the jaw, the gun flying out of Mr. Hooper's hand.

Amelia quickly picked up the firearm, pointing it at Mr. Hooper, who was sprawled out on the floor. "Didn't anyone teach *you* not to underestimate a lady?"

Epilogue

The next day, Amelia, Simon, and Marielle were recounting the previous evening's harrowing events over tea at Amesbury Manor, Tabitha listening with rapt attention. Amelia had no choice but to tell her the tale when Tabitha caught her sneaking into the house in the early-morning hours. She insisted on a brief summary before she allowed Amelia to fall into bed.

After the constable apprehended Mr. Hooper, the trio still had to get home, and that took time. If Amelia had her druthers, she'd have stayed in bed all day, but alas, parenthood waited for no man—or woman. Winifred had woken her up at noon with a not-so-subtle jump onto the bed, wondering what kept her from her morning walk. Amelia explained it had been a long night, and Winifred apologized and left. But Amelia couldn't fall back to sleep, especially after replaying last night's happenings, as Simon was doing now.

"And at that point, Lady Amesbury picked up the gun and turned it on Mr. Hooper." Simon finished the story and leaned back into the couch cushion. "He now awaits his fate in prison."

Tabitha turned to Amelia in astonishment. "Are you familiar with firearms?"

"I know enough to hold a gun steady and shoot straight."

"Goodness, Amelia." Tabitha blinked rapidly. "You might have been hurt."

Was Aunt Tabitha holding back tears? The possibility warmed Amelia's heart. Despite her scolding, Tabitha really did care about her. "I was in no real danger."

"That's debatable," grumbled Simon. "You would have been in less danger had you waited for me."

Marielle brushed a stray crumb from her dress. "Lady Amesbury had things under control the entire time. I can attest to that."

Amelia smiled smugly at Simon.

"It's a wonder Miss Pimm didn't comprehend the extent of Mr. Hooper's affection." Tabitha poured a second cup of tea through a pristine silver strainer. "She seems so . . . diligent."

Amelia jumped on the change of topics. "I'm afraid one can't replace a mother's intuition when it comes to relationships. I had a feeling something was not right from the get-go."

Simon reached for a tart. "If by get-go you mean final lap, then you're correct. Your motherly sensibilities were entirely useful." He popped the small treat in his mouth.

Amelia wrinkled her nose, resisting the urge to stick her tongue out at him.

Just then, Winifred made a timely entrance. Amelia hoped she might have the chance to demonstrate her motherly abilities, but it seemed unlikely, for obviously Winifred had something else in mind. Wearing a blue and white dress and matching bonnet, she was pulling behind her the oversized boat they'd purchased.

"Lord Bainbridge, Lady Marielle." Winifred gave them a quick curtsy and turned to Amelia. "Now that you've had your tea, are you ready for the regatta?"

Amelia sat up, plunking her cup in the saucer. "Is that today?"

"At four o'clock," Winifred prompted. "Remember? You said you were going to beat the pants off Lord Grey."

"Amelia Amesbury!" Tabitha reprimanded.

Simon and Marielle chuckled.

"Did I say that?" Amelia stood. "I'd better make good on my promise, then." She fisted her hands on her hips. "Who would care to join us?"

Simon and Marielle stood at the same time. Simon linked his arm through Marielle's. "We'd love to."

Amelia loved seeing them act like brother and sister again. Indeed, the entire Bainbridge clan was on better terms after the air was cleared yesterday. Finally, they might be able to move forward. "Aunt Tabitha?" Amelia reached out her hand.

Tabitha opted for her cane, using it to push herself up from the settee. "Do you honestly think I'm going to encourage you to challenge Lord Grey in a boat race?"

"Maybe?" Amelia tried.

A smile spread over Tabitha's face, lifting her already high cheekbones. "Then you'd be correct." She held out her walking stick like a solider. "Onward."

Amelia noticed it was new: solid navy with a gold compass in the handrest.

Tabitha flipped open the instrument. "Allow me to lead the way to victory."

ACKNOWLEDGMENTS

Writing this series has reminded me what is important and what is worth saving. Virginia Woolf once said, "History is too much about wars; biography too much about great men." Indeed, history is also penny weeklies and agony columns. So first I must thank editor Michelle Vega for giving this subject the space it deserves. Further thanks to editorial assistant Annie Odders for the constant support and advice. To copy editor Randie Lipkin for making my work so much better. To production editor Jennifer Lynes for producing another beautiful book. To publicists Stephanie Felty and Hillary Tacuri for helping my books reach readers and bookstores. You are magic! To cover designer Rita Frangie Batour for another stunning cover. To my agent, Amanda Jain, for being the calm person I need in my life. To Elena Hartwell Taylor for patiently answering all my equine questions in this book. I'm certain you'll never let me ride your horses now! To Amy Cecil Holm for being the friend and editor I can always count on. To librarian Jane Healy and museum manager Melissa Godber for championing my work locally. To all the generous book bloggers, book club organizers, Facebook group moderators, and Instagrammers for reading, reviewing, and sharing my work. To tea friends Diane Kellenburger, Bonnie Owen, Cindy Riddick, Susan Prouty Walsh, and the amazing Plum Deluxe community for being a spot of sunshine in my day. To the mystery authors who have reached out to support me and this series.

To my Honerman family for reading and sharing my books. To my sister Penny Dose, who continues to profess I'm a *New York Times* bestseller even though I'm not. It's wonderful to have someone believe in me as much as you do. To my niece Samantha Schroeder for absolutely everything. To my sister Sandy Robar and brother, James Engberg, for your love and encouragement. To my daughters, Madeline and Maisie, and my husband, Quintin, for loving me and my crazy brain. I'm so blessed to be on this journey with you.

Mary Winters is the author of the Lady of Letters historical mystery series. She also pens cozy mysteries under the name Mary Angela. A longtime reader and fan of historical fiction, Mary set her latest work in Victorian England after being inspired by a trip to London. Since then, she's been busily planning her next mystery—and another trip!

VISIT THE AUTHOR ONLINE

MaryWintersAuthor.com

Ready to find
your next great read?

Let us help.

Visit prh.com/nextread

Penguin
Random
House